ASPERGERS.

WHAT'S *YOUR* EXCUSE?

Adventures, Anomalies, and Achievements

in a World of Normals

By

Michael Cubbage

ISBN: 978-1-83663-389-1

Disclaimer: The events, places, and conversations in this book are the recollections of the author that have been recreated from memory and/or supplemented and/or condensed. Many names of individuals have been changed to maintain anonymity and to protect their privacy. It is acknowledged that some people may have memories of certain events that differ. The author makes no representations or warranties, express or implied, about the completeness, accuracy, reliability, suitability, or availability with respect to the information contained in this book for any purpose. The author of this book disclaims liability for any loss or damage of any kind suffered by any person as a result of the contents of this book.

For more information,

go to the author's website at: www.michaelcubbage.com

Contents

Dedication

My wife, Patricia E. Cubbage R.N., is a serial researcher. When I was diagnosed with Aspergers, the research commenced. The first day of research took her to a forum in response to her query, "What do I do, if my husband has Aspergers?"

The response was, "RUN!"

She didn't run. She has kept her intelligent, confident and beautiful self with me for forty plus years.

She's my muse. Without her, only God knows where I would have ended up.

Along with everything … I dedicate this book to Pat.

Acknowledgments

Kate Ward-Gaus, MS Ed., whom I've known as Kathy since we were five years old, was the first person I thought of to pre-read this book, to bring not just her years of experience as an educator and counselor to bear, but to fact check and provide perspective to my memories, as she's known me since childhood. She took the time to review the manuscript, providing valuable feedback, advice and intuition. Her help with this project was invaluable.

David M. Burns is a lifelong friend and confidant and was a given to pre-read the book and provide perspective. As an Enrolled Actuary, he took painstaking care in identifying many typos, which authors apparently cannot see in their own work. He also provided invaluable fact-checking and detail for many events in the book.

Jude T. McKenna, MACJ, was one of my first partners in the police department. He taught police science at the university level post law enforcement and also pre-read the book for me. He's the odd one out in this team, as he didn't know me before the department, and not having known me as a child, was able to provide yet another perspective on the content, readability, and my skill (if any) as a writer. He is on the hook to read the next installments, which start when our paths met on the first day in the academy.

Each of these friends provided not only input and feedback on the actual book, but encouragement to finally finish it. I would not have made it over the finish line without their help, and I acknowledge their contributions with humble appreciation.

Intro

Gathering arresting material for a book about my life required me to engage in police chases, gun fights, knife fights, rooftop pursuits, riots, and other less-than-normal activities. I also had to navigate encounters with celebrities, corporate America, politicians, teachers, exasperated doctors, exasperat*ing* doctors, fights with crazed dogs, cornered rats, peacock rustlers, Occupy Wall Street, and other malarkey.

I could have avoided much of this early on, if I had known about the condition—I would have known I wasn't capable of doing all those things, and avoided them altogether. But, since no one told me, I *didn't* know I couldn't do them - and, well, I did them…

Statistics indicate most people like me are single, unemployed, trapped in pedestrian jobs, or all of the above, so how did *I* find a wife and raise a family, rise to the rank of detective in a large metropolitan police force, work in corporate America on and off Wall Street, rub elbows with celebrities, and achieve a six-figure income?

I've tried to retrace my steps here in an effort to figure it out. Professionals find it incomprehensible.

Perhaps we can figure it out together.

I've written as myself, avoiding (as much as convention allows) masquerading as a normal person. I want you to get a feel for what this is like, and give you a view from the side of the lens through which I perceive the world.

In order to set the stage, I considered labelling normal people as *regular people,* like *regular gasoline, or regular cars* compared to Corvettes. I needed to get the point across, but hammering this in every chapter seemed extreme, so hopefully this prickly reference makes my point.

The point being: labels have an effect.

Having written that, however, I fully understand I am the odd one out in society: *not a normal person*. Within society, I'm an outsider. This was an important fact for me to reconcile, and I did early on.

I worked around the difference on my own for most of my life, while neither I nor anyone else understood the essence of the difference. And, as evidence, fate has a sense of humor; when I finally discovered what the difference was, I could find no one who really understood it.

The story of my life depicts several versions of me. There is the pre-assessment me, the post-assessment me, and the character who must often wear the mask of a normal person.

Operating in the world among normal people, knowing you are different, but not knowing the cause, is like looking for a black dog in the night - full of fleeting hazy glimpses. When I finally found the root cause, everything changed.

A butterfly cannot go back to being a caterpillar.

Perhaps it helps to explain; this is an account of someone who went through most of life with an undiagnosed condition described by one of the foremost experts on the subject as a *devastating handicap*.

During this time, not knowing the *source of my difference,* I lived my life a certain way. Once diagnosed, my life changed. During both stages, I often had to wear the mask of the normal person or at least stifle the real me to survive.

Survive is not too strong a word.

I asked folks if they would rather read a scientific study of the subject or an anecdotal account. The unanimous answer was anecdotal. And I agree; anecdotal stories are fun to read. But I wanted to make a point, and so I decided to intertwine actual anecdotes of my life with the current *science* around the condition. I wove the stories into the existing framework in an effort to alternately explain or dispel the current paradigm – to support or disprove stereotypes.

The stories come at you as life came at me, and I try to hint where anecdote meets science. I try to avoid getting unstuck in time but jump around a little to set the stage.

I do want the story to be enjoyable to read, but I have to get you into the right mindset and bring you, as much as possible, and as much as you can stand, into my world. The next passage is designed to give you a taste of what the condition is like. The rest of the book, though, is story-like and anecdotal, so if you survive this, you're good to go.

Try reading straight through the next passage!

I'm told it's hard for normal people to write a book; that they struggle with new ideas and are frightened of the blank page. With me, it was hard to take the constantly emerging and evolving ideas from an eidetic memory and weave them into a comprehensively easy-to-follow narrative for *someone else to follow.* A blank page is, to me, like a white wall would be to a two-year-old with finger-paints while mom and dad are busy making dinner. As I write this and try to deal with the mistakes this word processor makes with spelling, grammar, word usage, juxtaposition, and nuance, I want to write a separate book, or at least include a chapter on how aggravating *that* is. This idea suggests a spin-off to another topic on how non-English speaking computer techs have trashed the messages coming from computer devices, which have been passed on to the computer generation, and have them at a point where they no longer know or follow the rules of English grammar. Allow me to paint a picture. I get into my car. My phone connects to the internal PC. The message displayed is, ***"Your phone has been connected."*** BAD ENGLISH! I know it *has been connected*. I need to know, if it is *connected* _now_!

That is just a tiny example of what happens inside my head, all day, every day. I promise not to do it again, and I also promise that what I write is grammatically correct and logically sound, but I will skate to the edge of correctness!

I do, do that sometimes.

I will avoid run-ons, but I never liked the American English rule which suggests repeating the same word in the same paragraph is frowned upon and absolutely to be avoided in the same sentence. I do do this when it is the best way to deliver my point!

I won't nitpick. To paraphrase Sir Winston Churchill, "*Pedantry is something up with which I will not put!*"

I will, therefore, allow myself a modicum of poetic license.

A stereotype suggests folks like me have no sense of humor. That's confusing someone who doesn't laugh at something not funny, for someone with no sense of humor.

We can take ideas normal people spout and wring some excruciatingly funny things from them. Our sense of humor is on a parallel plane with different points of reference and a different level of intensity, like the difference between checkers and chess.

This book will *test* your sense of humor.

This book is a hybrid, so it's environmentally friendly as well as being a catch-all, do-all, be-all on the subject. In it, I attempt to illustrate that this subject is everything people think it is and none of what they think it is. I wanted it to be practical, but I also wanted it to be balanced, so you can use it as kindling for a campfire, but I've purposely made it too thick to level a table.

I've heard we do not understand sarcasm. Anyone who believes this obviously never visited our house when I was growing up, where sarcasm was raised to a high art form!

Those who point this out probably mean pedestrian sarcasm.

When I worked in Manhattan for one of the *too-big-to-fail* Wall Street monoliths, my duties included re-writing the architectural plans drawn up by the non-native English-speaking IT contractors, who were all Hindu.

The men were engaged in a constant macho duel with one another. There was only one woman, who was very gentle.

You see, women, being able to shatter with a sigh and melt with a look, don't have to be macho.

Her contract was about to expire, and as part of her farewell, she said, "Mike, you are a very humble person."

I can still relive the glow I felt with this level of compliment. Knowing Hindus hold humility in high regard enriched my enjoyment of the compliment.

But, humility should not degrade into a self-abasing and negative narrative. I see writing on this subject in an apologetic mode.

Don't look for it here.

My disability presented huge barriers within the existing society, and it definitely slowed me down, but it never stopped me. And, don't confuse this for self-righteous indignation or self-promoting. It's just a simple truth. There is a test for this.

Another part of my job in Manhattan was to write technical training manuals. A frequent request was, "Can you write a procedure for this, in that way you do, that makes it easy to understand?"

They wanted me to translate the social babel in the stream of consciousness they wrote into something everyone could understand. In other words, take out all the crap and just tell me how to make this machine do what I want it to do. This was a technical equivalent of High German - a common and consistent language.

Eventually, I became the source for all written communication in the department. I created the manuals, training materials, bulletins, communications, and emails. All management had to do was add their by-line.

Documenting procedures involved distilling all the noise normal people make into something precise that worked for everyone, which I had to do for myself to navigate within their world. I was highly practiced in this, because I needed it to *blend* into normal society.

I had to reverse engineer what people said, render it into something resembling fact and objectivity, then try to reply in a manner to make myself understood without engendering too much umbrage or confusion.

Doing this with technical subjects was easy.

This book is a test to see, if I can do it with *this* convoluted and misunderstood subject. A subject that reveals a mostly unknown and highly misunderstood human variation to normal humans. I can put humans and computers in the same room and have them interact. I've rendered my human variation in the hope you can relate to me at some level.

Hopefully, not the same as you do to the computer.

It's a rule in books like this to describe how I came to know about myself. If I didn't, you would not be properly grounded in the coming stories, but I'll make it as painless as possible.

You'll need some terms defined, so you're in synch with what's going on. I'll put it in the next section, so you can skip it, if you want.

Don't!

If you do, you're only going to have to come back to it and read it anyway.

"If you don't have time to do it right the first time; when will you have time to do it over?"

– The Author

In my experience, the view from the *other* side of the glass is, in many ways, and in many instances, at best highly misunderstood – at worst categorically wrong. I write this in the interest of those with the condition, those who care for those with the condition, and my own personal satisfaction.

Another reason for my renderings being anecdotal, is so experts can't come back and say, "*What do you know about it?*"

Well, *I'm living it*, and these are the anecdotes.

After a lifetime of the frequent and familiar question, *"What's Wrong with You?!"* usually and lovingly coming from my wife, I've *earned* the right to respond:

"Aspergers – What's *your* Excuse*?"*

Terms – My Definitions

Establishing a natural flow for something this unfamiliar is facilitated by definitions. These are my definitions and are what I mean, as I tell my story. I'm fully aware they appear in other tomes with different meanings, but in the context of this book, this is what they mean:

Asperger syndrome – A social disorder caused by a brain variation limiting the ability to auto-process and apply social norms within the larger society. This is the standard I use in the book.

AS – Acronym for Asperger syndrome. This is used differently elsewhere, but in this book it means Asperger syndrome.

Asperger – This is what German-speaking people call a person identified with Asperger syndrome. The area around Vienna is the epicenter of AS, where the meaning is understood to be one of *Asperger's Kinder*, or *Asperger's Children*, the original reference to the boys in Dr. Hans Asperger's papers. Hence the title of the article, "*Hans Asperger, selbst ein Asperger?*" (*Was Hans Asperger himself an Asperger?*)

Aspie – This is what some of us call ourselves informally. It's our term. Only we may use it. It's like *cop*. Only cops may use the word cop.

Note to the Reader

I really did all those things in the first paragraph. As I wrote this book and the stories flowed, I found myself with such an abundance, I had to decide where one book ended and another began. In this book, I will take you from year one to the doors of the police academy. Once I walked through those doors, book two of my life began.

I've changed the names of the characters for privacy reasons, but the stories are as I remember them. I played around with some time-lines for the same reasons.

I have to get this out of the way early, and judging by what I've read recently, it might not go over well with some folks. In case you haven't caught on yet, *let me be clear*: the stories here are about someone with Asperger syndrome.

I'm not on a spectrum, and I'm not autistic, so those terms won't appear in this text connected to Asperger syndrome. Other authors use the terms interchangeably. My belief is: Asperger syndrome is a distinct human *variation*.

I've christened it Variation-A.

Autism is something altogether different.

Utilizing the word spectrum as an analogy or visual aid is problematic, because it would have to include everyone, rendering the word spectrum useless.

I limit references in this book to salient stereotypes and diagnostic criteria where I feel the story reflects either an affirmation or refutation. This is an effort to point out the unique interaction of AS with the anecdote without weighing the story down with technical detail.

This is not a treatise on Asperger syndrome, but anecdotes of my life with just enough info sprinkled in to show where one element affected the other.

The treatise on Asperger syndrome is the subject of a subsequent piece.

I've dispensed with buzz-words such as neurodiverse and neurotypical, because I frankly haven't been able to find as many as two consistent definitions of any of these terms. In this book, anyone who is not an Asperger is referred to as a normal person. Anything else becomes too convoluted.

Society seems preoccupied with the words *normal* and *not-normal*. I know I'm not-normal, and based on what I've seen in my lifetime, I really don't want to be.

Don't expect this book to be.

Chapter 1

Opening

We live our lives upside down and backwards.

– The Author

Life on planet Earth nearly ended the morning I was born.

I'm being literal here.

Get used to that!

I don't know that my being born had anything to do with it, but everything nearly came to a halt in a blinding flash that day. And, not in a good way - more like a, *"Honey why is the house shaking and, what's that bright light?!"* kind of way.

While my mother and I were involved in what she would later describe to me as her easiest of six deliveries, some *rocket scientists* on the other side of the world, *real* rocket scientists, were playing with something they clearly did not understand.

My mom told me this not later that day, of course, but years later—the part about the delivery, not the rocket scientists.

Picture a bunch of boys who just found a large firecracker in a sock drawer. Having nothing better to do, they decide to put it in a mailbox.

Just to see what happens!

They light the fuse!

They run to a safe distance, and watch the mailbox transform into a fog of sawdust! Along with the elimination of the gas bill; the term *junk mail* takes on a whole new meaning.

Amid the self-congratulatory cooings of "Wow!" and a general feeling of a job well done, a bit of apprehension begins to creep in, as doors begin to open, and adult voices shout, "What was that?!"

They also begin to ponder how they are going to explain the wood screw embedded in Johnny's leg.

With the same general mindset, as I was busy being born, the rocket scientists decided to take a new toy they had found, lithium deuteride, out to the middle of the Pacific Ocean and blow it up.

Just to see what happens!

I guess Uranium and Plutonium were just too 1940s.

Lithium deuteride is derived from natural lithium, so at least they didn't use anything artificial - concern for the environment being central to their thinking.

This firecracker was called Runt TX-15. It was slightly larger. Weighing in at 40,000 pounds, it dwarfed a city trash truck.

Not being able to find a big enough mailbox, they stuck Runt on a barge in the middle of the Pacific Ocean and tied it to a group of islands called Bikini Atoll. These islands were riddled with tropical plants, tropical fish, and about 184 Bikinians.

They called this little exercise *Castle Romeo*.

Castle Romeo became a popular 1970s poster. If you search for images or videos of thermonuclear explosions, the ones you'll see the most, the really scary red ones, are Castle Romeo!

They were considerate enough to relocate the inhabitants of the island, before they reduced their homes and the place where their church used to stand, to permanently glowing molten glass.

That is, the parts still above water.

The rest of the island became the Earth's newest crater.

They expected Runt to produce four megatons of destruction; I'm sorry, to *yield* four megatons of *energy*. They *calculated* the margin of error within a range of 1.5 to 7 megatons.

Would you like some perspective? Hiroshima was reduced to ash with a device 1/1,000th the size of Runt.

They lit the fuse!

When it got to eight megatons, it was designated a run-away, and they started to get concerned. Think - *run-away-train*!

When it reached nine megatons, they really got nervous.

At ten megatons, I can't imagine what they thought. Interviews of witnesses reveal that they began to seriously consider the gut-wrenching possibility of an *absolute-run-away*, because *regular-run-aways* are not sufficiently bad.

I have this mental picture of them in their observation bunker, processing the idea of where to hide.

Another popular poster from the 1970s outlined the steps to prepare oneself for a nuclear attack. It began with, ***Move away from open windows, Remove sharp objects from your pockets***, and progressed through several more steps, culminating with, ***Place your head firmly between your knees*** **and** ***Kiss your ass goodbye.***

Sailors on observation vessels reported that as the explosion continued to grow, they covered their faces with their hands, and they could see their bones! They were 20 miles away.

The rocket scientists began to consider; since the air contains Hydrogen, and air is everywhere, this particular explosion, the third largest the U.S. ever detonated, might not stop!

This is the Ice-Nine nightmare. Had Castle Romeo decided to keep going, and keep fusing Hydrogen atoms, it might well envelop the entire globe in a blinding flash of light, in all the places where there is air.

Or, stated differently, "Where every living creature – lives".

Just in case you're thinking, "What about the fish?" Guess what the *H* stands for in H_2O.

The blast grew from the center at about 2,200 meters in 10 seconds, and unabated, it would consume the entire globe in 15 minutes.

The first A-Bomb called *Gadget* was tested in New Mexico in the 1940s. Albert Einstein and other scientists cautioned, *"It might not stop!"*

Castle Romeo finally stopped at what is officially recorded as 11 megatons, but other sources cite closer to 15 - almost 1,000 times more powerful than Gadget!

So, was this the cause for my brain being different? Did one of the largest-ever EMPs do something to my brain as I was navigating the transition?

After having read the *science* on the subject of Asperger syndrome; this fits in as well as any other theory. It fits right in with DES, vaccines, refrigerator-moms and mercury tooth amalgams.

But, none of those help explain why I can trace it all the way back to my grandparents. Not unless they were exposed, radioactively, to Castle Romeo. Or, maybe an EMP can time travel.

There were no vaccines back then, so maybe they caught it from me!

(Did you get the *radioactively* pun?)

Or, maybe, just maybe, Asperger syndrome is hereditary. Is this too simple?

What did Occam say? The simpler explanation to a problem is preferred. I get the part about hoof beats, but if it looks like a duck, and walks like a duck and quacks like a duck; it's not a horse!

In the case of AS; the simplest answer has simply not been the *right* answer.

Chapter 2

The Realization

No book on Asperger syndrome is complete without the foundational discovery chapter. It's a rule. You need a starting point for the rest of the book, or nothing would make sense.

By age eight, I had formalized the belief I was different from the other children. As the only boy being invited to all-girls birthday parties, I somehow knew things would not change any time soon. I clung to the hope that somehow, people would change to be like me, and everything would work out.

I wasn't preoccupied with being different and alone, as I see in other books on the subject. I expected the *other* kids to change. It doesn't align with what I experienced with myself and what I see with other Aspies I know. We expect *you* to change. We have a life-long expectation - at some point, everyone will evolve and become life-long learners.

Normal boys were rude, crude, and socially unacceptable. The girls were soft, standoffish, and unaccepting. There were exceptions, but I figured out how to ruin it fast, and things evolved into my version of normal.

I was alone much of the time when I wasn't in school, but I wasn't lonely. I was neither sad nor happy. I just settled into my routine and went about life as it came.

I read a lot. I was able to put more distance between myself and the other kids by joining the library's summer reading club - one of my mom's best ideas - seriously!

I took long walks and observed everything along the concrete, brick, and asphalt confines of my neighborhood – leaving only on store-runs for Mom. I found it odd that everyone knew me. Not just the neighbors but those from outside the neighborhood.

"Hey, Reds!" came from milk trucks, police cars, and down from telephone linesmen. Apparently, Asperger syndrome was not enough of a challenge – it was topped off with red hair.

Corner stores full of canned goods too high to reach and impatient adults were exhausting. The lunchmeat store, four blocks distant, required navigating the crush of adults to the glass display cases of sausages.

The pungent smells of someone else's favorite meat, the din of shouted orders, slamming doors, bothered workers, hands wiped on soiled white aprons, and gritty sawdust floors tested my endurance.

Mom would caution, "Make sure to count the change!" which I found strange. I knew if the change was correct by the look and feel of it. It went directly into my pocket.

If it was light, I could feel it. Incorrect change set off immediate alarm bells, because breaks in patterns are physical events for me. Correct change was as it should be; incorrect change had a jarring effect.

My problem was: not knowing this was unusual.

As I wrote earlier, I read a lot. Although I read almost anything, my favorite books were about travel and adventure, like Marco Polo and Tom Sawyer. Through these books, I could leave the grey inner-city and travel to Cathay or float down the Mississippi.

I was also drawn to books about biology and chemistry, because they seemed to have the tools I needed to figure out what was going on with me, or more correctly, what was wrong with everyone else.

I was genuinely concerned for them and wondered how they would survive.

I was drawn to Gregor Mendel, Charles Darwin, and Mr. Wizard. I quickly devoured anything that helped explain genetics, biology, and chemistry.

And, I read anything by Dickens!

I struggled every day to manage every social situation. It was that basic! I could do anything academic thrown at me, fix any machine and solve any puzzle. Humans were the problem. They were a confusing mess, resisting any form or level of engineering.

I had to find a formula to follow - one to facilitate relationships, maybe a family. I pushed and shoved my way through life, until I finally settled on the formula of: find a job with a pension, and everything else will fall into place.

When I did this, I was able to better navigate life among these aliens. I was able to find a place for myself, settle down, and do what was required of me. Routine was my friend.

Until, I found my Rosetta Stone.

The decades went flying by, and I had finally come to a place in my life when I could slow down and relax. The kids were grown and gone. The dog had just died. I was taking jobs that were fun instead of ones you have to take to get the kids through college and such. I liked where I was living. Life was good.

Most importantly I liked myself – probably a good thing – not many others seemed to.

After many years of working within organizations, I took contractor gigs, because contractors don't have to subscribe to nonsense such as evaluations and mandatory-fun social events. I was in my third year working on Wall Street in NYC, and it was too much fun!

There really are, actually were, lots of really unique things about NYC you won't find anywhere else, but there is a price to be paid.

Mary Schmich's 1997 column turned commencement address, which became the song *Everybody's Free (To Wear Sunscreen),* cautions:

"Live in New York City once but leave before it makes you hard, Live in northern California once but leave before it makes you soft."[1]

---

[1] OPINION - Advice, like youth, probably just wasted on the young - By MARY SCHMICH PUBLISHED: June 1, 1997 at 3:00 a.m. | UPDATED: May 23, 2019 at 8:24 a.m. https://www.chicagotribune.com/1997/06/01/advice-like-youth-probably-just-wasted-on-the-young-2/, retrieved June 15, 2024.

I learned the California lesson after two weeks in L.A., but although I fought becoming a casualty of NYC, I was getting testy.

The work had become mundane. I had asked for a raise and been turned down. I had survived Occupy Wall Street – on one occasion getting trapped in a post office when they took over entire streets - and had endured the protests on Broadway.

Then one day, I was late for work and, in my haste, accidentally stepped on a tourist's foot. A nine-year-old tourist in town with her family.

I felt horrible.

It was time to go.

My friend Nancy said, "Get transferred to New Jersey!" Gotta love Nancy! Her imperative solved multiple problems. By transferring to the N.J. office, I was able to cut my commute by almost an hour, get out of the Wall Street rat race, and since the taxes in N.J. were 6% lower, I gave *myself* a raise!

Perspective is an interesting word. Whether it was better to be in NJ with a view of NYC or be in NYC with a view of NJ invites debate. The view was fantastic *from* NJ, showcasing Brooklyn, the Atlantic, and the entire New York City skyline! But, it was *in* NJ.

The debate was settled when I realized the bus from PA stopped ten feet from the door to our building – essentially a tunnel directly from PA to work.

I had more time and still enough energy to devote to finally finding out what was up with me. I could finally figure out why I did not fit in.

At the time I considered my red hair largely responsible for people treating me differently.

I also considered amalgams, and the possibility they had been put in purposely to slow me down, but since so many others had those, I crossed them off the list.

After I considered every other theory, I targeted the red hair as the main cause for the odd treatment, but still couldn't reconcile why I felt something else was amiss.

I figured if I retraced all my steps, I could find what I missed.

For instance, since I hadn't finished kindergarten, perhaps I missed what I needed there. Or, maybe I was out sick from school the day they gave out the secret to how algebra works.

I created a plan to go to every bookstore on the web, visit the NYC library, and find every book from kindergarten through high school. I would retrace my steps and find the missing link.

It sounds silly, but at least it was systematic!

I already had an outline for research because I still had my report cards from school with the course names. I figured it would take me a year or so to get through K – 12, and I settled in one morning on the bus to dig in. I spent most of the ride working the plan and searching for the books I needed.

As we pulled within sight of the city, my phone pinged. I had recently added the BBC newsfeed to my mailing list. A new article popped into my inbox, *Lesser-known things about Asperger's syndrome* by Robyn Steward.[2]

It was my Rosetta Stone.

I had heard the term Asperger before, but never paid much attention to it. For some reason, this had not previously piqued my attention, so I had no real knowledge of what it was.

Did you ever see a movie with a robot processing information on a screen with the data going by? I have to think an Aspie created those characters with an image of how eidetic memory works.

When I saw the term Asperger, a reference popped up. I recalled hearing it mentioned behind my back on several occasions. I didn't research it then, but now I read the article.

I began to realize I knew someone like this. It's ironic I missed the pattern. The further I read, the more I realized I really did know someone like this.

---

[2] Lesser-known things about Asperger's syndrome By Robyn Steward accessed August 16, 2014 https://www.bbc.com/news/blogs-ouch-28746359

Then the hair on the back of my neck stood up! A rush like I've never felt before came at me! it I'm in the moment now, and I can feel it.

Time stopped.

It hit me in an instant—I had finally found the key! The description, the symptoms, the behavior - all of this. This article was about me! I read further, and I realized I finally had my answer. It was a eureka moment, if there ever was one!

I finished the article and dropped my phone. It hit the floor, but I couldn't move to pick it up. Something strange was happening.

Everything around me froze - I froze.

External sensory input stopped, as I relived my entire life. I was seeing all those moments of confusion, and all those times when I felt hazy coming into focus. As the final piece dropped into the puzzle, I watched the events of a lifetime - replay on a heads-up display.

I knew in that instant why Kay was at the front door of my house at fifteen. I knew why Joyce was clutching me so strongly on the dance floor at twenty-three.

I knew why people gave me strange looks, and why I didn't know why they were doing it.

I knew why I had had so many first dates. And why few people wanted to be my friend.

I knew why I could talk to certain special individuals when no one else could, and why I was the only one for whom certain special people would bend their routine.

I understood why most teachers hated me, and those few special ones treasured me. I knew why I could listen to my wife for hours on end without feeling the need to interrupt her.

I knew why others ran from danger while I stayed put, and why I didn't understand their jokes.

I felt feelings I never felt before and probably never will again.

I knew why I could hear not just the motor running but the bad bearing inside it, why I could hear conversations that were *out of earshot*, and why the conversationalists *thought* they were *out of earshot*.

I knew I really could see stars in the daytime (I still can), and why I instantly knew how many birds were in the flock flying past.

I saw all the opportunities I missed, because I just couldn't process them at the time, and had I been aware of this then, I could have done much more and been much further along.

Most importantly, however, now that I knew what was wrong, I could figure it out and accelerate things. I could find the manual. I could get past what had been holding me back, and do things I was told I couldn't do before.

I realized I had to write it all down – chronologically, so I didn't miss anything.

I started in the crib.

Chapter 3

Refrigerator Moms and Other Myths

There are three big indicators of success. IQ, conscientiousness, and industry, or the ability to work hard. Mom had all three. My mom always worked. I never saw her asleep. Even if you crept into her bedroom in the middle of the night, her sapphire blue eyes pierced the dark!

An AS stereotype is - in the early years, we are overly attached to our mothers. I suppose if we need a generalization this is as good as any. But, if this is true – the refrigerator mothers theory is false.

It was rare to have a mom who worked outside the home in the early twentieth century. She was 19 when she and my dad were married. She worked in the jewelry and appliance store they owned in Southwest Philadelphia daily from 1939, until I was born in 1954.

Mom performed most of the customer facing work behind the counter.

She had a true entrepreneurial spirit, so when the store closed, she started a business in the house, making dresses for special occasions, mostly wedding parties. She made dresses for the maid of honor, the bridesmaids, and the mother of the bride—everything except the bride's gown.

She also ran the house, doing all the cleaning, washing, and cooking, but running the house also included plunging toilets, fixing cabinets, and hanging wallpaper!

Many assume my mechanical skills came from Dad. It was a 50/50 proposition.

The dress-making business included a constant parade of young women aged 18 – 22 flowing through the house in the early afternoon and evening. Awaiting their turn in the dressing room, on the landing behind the door to the basement, they put *Bandstand* on the T.V. and used me as their dancing partner.

Almost all of my interaction before starting school was with adults. I found it hard to relate to children. I spoke to adults as an adult, and saw no difference but size. Many adults spoke to me as an adult, often disregarding lines, inappropriate given my age.

My parents kept the dialogue to a level appropriate to what I could and would accept as a suitable answer, but it was pushed much further with me than with other children. This would blow up on me when I hit a certain age; when I failed to appropriately recognize the authority represented by an adult's age or title.

I wouldn't challenge a police officer, because the officer's authority was obvious. I would, however, overlook the authority of a person who was simply older or who held a title, such as teacher, whom I was accustomed to addressing as an equal.

Mom patiently taught me to sew, how the machine worked, how all the accessories functioned, how to replace the belt when it broke, thread the needle, and fill the spools of thread.

A mom who had worked outside the home, spoke to everyone as an equal, fixed things, worked machines, managed the household *and* her business made for a unique female role model.

My perception of girls and women was that they were equal partners who smelled better and were easier to look at. They were, aside from obvious internal plumbing – no different – a perception immune to *non-tangible-and-non-observable* social norms read, contradictions.

If I couldn't see social norms manifest in reality for myself, I just ignored them.

At some point, Mom had taught me what she could, but with the constant interruptions for questions about how this worked and why is this the way it is, she finally realized she should teach me to read. This became necessary with the welcoming of child number five.

Mom figured teaching me to read would keep me occupied, so she could do the other things she needed to do. I read everything in the house. If I came to her and asked, "How do you spell this?" or "What does this word mean?" She would always give the same answer, "Look it up in the dictionary."

This, naturally, prompted the question, "How can I look it up, if I don't know how it's spelled?" Which she consistently ignored, until I got the message to go figure it out. After a few such incidents, and after having finished the latest reading material, it came to me to simply read the dictionary.

Starting with Aardvark, I read the dictionary cover to cover. I carried my stale, old, yellowed Webster's pocket dictionary like a teddy bear.

Reading it was interesting, but I needed the missing context. In those early days, it took a while to get through heavy reading material. When I read, the dictionary was always next to me for the frequent stops to look up newly discovered words.

When I ran out of books or magazines, I read the labels on the soup cans. When I finished those, I read the labels on the contents of the medicine cabinet.

I would wait for the evening newspaper, so I could read that. The beginning of each month was anxiously anticipated, as *Look* magazine was due.

My older siblings had to watch their textbooks, because they would disappear. I got interested in history and German. Any unattended textbook, magazine, or novel was mine.

I feel the stretch in the back of my neck as I remember the day I first started to stare at the *Encyclopedia Britannica* high on a shelf behind glass in the basement. The shelves Dad built to hold them were at his eye level, so I had no real chance to get at them without help.

Mom often said, "You could talk the birds down out of the trees."

It took all I had to get those encyclopedias. I fell into those books and remained there, until kindergarten started. Kindergarten lasted two weeks for me, so it was back to the encyclopedia!

My older sister introduced me as *"My Brother – the Encyclopedia of Useless Knowledge"* because I wouldn't hesitate to wade into a conversation to demonstrate my understanding of a subject.

This type of behavior led Hans Asperger to call us *Little Professors*.

That *Useless Knowledge*, which I've added to since, kept me alive, and still prompts the oft-asked question, "How do you know that?!"

Everything Mom taught me was useful, but I have to point out some pivotal elements.

I would have learned to read in school and probably would have survived without knowing how to run a sewing machine, but I would not have made it to adulthood without manners and her favorite catchphrase, *"Can't means won't."*

Mom saturated me with good manners. I should say really good manners. *Teenagers* would say things like, "You are the most polite person I've ever met."

Manners took much of the edge off the extremely cold affect we project to normal people. It's absolutely essential that an Aspie is saturated with good manners, or life will be a hard-slogging way.

The politeness and good manners are what got me invited to the all-girl birthday parties – a good reason in itself to be polite!

Can't means won't is a motto - turned Credo that carried me past the hurdles the condition presents. If someone believes that there is no such thing as *can't;* anything is possible.

If she had not done this, I would never have made it out.

Chapter 4

Examining Stereotypes

This is the chapter the professionals weren't expecting.

One of the most pushed theories about AS is: we are fixated on our mothers. At the same time, they also push the refrigerator mother theory. I haven't figured out, why they haven't figured out; these two theories clash rather badly.

The brother to these theories is abusive or neglectful fathers.

I have photos of Mom going back to when she was six years old. Her facial expression never changed—one of those AS variances I like to think of among *Asper Girls* as a *Mona Lisa smile.*

She was, despite the frozen countenance, one of the warmest human beings I've ever known.

My dad's face was along the line of the flat affect, unless something happened, rating a different look.

Hans Asperger described this as the *Princely Countenance.*

This is a long way around to say that the countenance did not necessarily depict their mood as a normal person's would. Under the flat affect of each of my parents was a warm and nurturing person.

My dad was a product of the tough environment of the inner city during WWI, the Great Depression, WWII, and other mind-numbing events in the early half of the 20th Century. And, although his father had apparently been something of an abusive brute, as were some of his siblings, he remained a calm, patient, and nurturing gentleman.

Dad was also creative and could draw; he was trained as a cabinet maker and teased creations from wood; he was a watchmaker, so he could fix just about anything, and he could also dance, sing, and play the trumpet.

As he had relinquished his retail jewelry and appliance store the year I was born, he was now engaged in the conversion of thousands of row house carriage garage doors into the newest and latest, overhead garage doors.

He would also replace the old double-hung wood windows in people's homes with the newest aluminum innovation, and he installed front doors and storm doors.

Every night, after a day of physical exertion and unloading the station wagon of old doors, tools, and wood, he would come to my room to read children's books and sing songs from the '20s, '30s, and '40s.

He created games like the humming game, where he would hum a tune and you had to guess the name of the song, or he would sing a line from a song, and you had to sing the next line.

I still remember the words to many songs by Irving Berlin, Bing Crosby, and Dad's favorite, Al Jolson.

Dad would also tell stories of his childhood when he would accompany his father to the stables to rent a horse and wagon to haul away the trees his father cut as a tree surgeon. He told stories of the days before refrigerators when they would deliver ice to homes in his dad's Model A Ford truck.

There were stories of his experiences in grade school, as a teen attending cabinet-making classes in lieu of high school and later earning his diploma as a watchmaker in the John Wanamaker's School of Watchmaking.

He spoke of the depression, the tension and build-up to WWII, the rationing, and being one of those thousands injured in the blackouts.

He taught me to sing, work with tools, create with wood, and fix just about anything. He taught me a work ethic where one should be proud of what they did and an indefatigable attitude of never giving up.

And, all through my life, right up until he died at 97, whenever I had a problem with which I needed advice, he was always there with the right solution.

So, we've dispensed with an *unhealthy* attachment to moms, refrigerator moms, and abusive dads. More stereotype busting to come.

Chapter 5

Two Dimensional World

My world was extremely small. Mom chose where we lived carefully. It had to be within walking distance of the school, have a trolly line close by, so the older ones could get to high school; it had to be safe and quiet, and have a corner store.

There had to be a doctor, and our house had to be on a one-way street. The one-way street ensured a level of safety for children, because aside from the safety feature of cars coming in one direction, there was a law—cars could only park on one side of a one-way street.

School had to be close, because there was always a child at home. You had to be able to let your first grader go to school on their own without worry, so we lived a block away.

The trolly stopped on the corner by the drug store, also a block away, and directly across from there sat Dr. Kotloff's office.

There was a *corner-store-slash-butcher* on our street as well.

The neighborhood was safe, because everyone knew everyone else, and there was always someone watching out a window. Almost everyone in the neighborhood went to the same school and church.

The quiet came from the parkway - the next street over.

Once I started grammar school, I was allowed to go, without permission, anywhere on our street, which was two blocks long and included sixty row houses.

I was allowed in the driveway behind the house, which included the parallel driveway behind Cobbs Creek Parkway on the opposite side of a small wall. I could also venture into the driveway that adjoined ours behind 65th Street.

Mom had an eagle's eye view of both driveways from our back porch.

Red hair was a mixed blessing.

I needed permission to cross the two streets perpendicular to ours, both of which were two-way, go to the next street over or to the park on the other side of the row behind us, as well as to the playground two blocks away within sight of the school.

So, my world consisted of a two-block long, two-row deep rectangle, demarcated by the places named above. Outside that world, nothing existed. If one of my classmates lived outside that perimeter, I had to wait until the next school day to see them, unless they came into the box to visit someone.

No one came in but Kathy.

This had the effect on me of seeing everyone, even those I knew from school, as somewhat of a foreigner. I knew little about them. When they left school, they literally disappeared, until the next day when they walked back out of the fog into the schoolyard.

I met a girl at a party two blocks from my home when I was 15. I went to introduce myself, and she said, "I know who you are." I don't remember ever having seen her before, either in the neighborhood or in school. She lived a block away, but on the other side of 67th Street.

It was like the Indians when Columbus arrived. They couldn't see his ship, because, to them, nothing existed past a certain distance from shore. Murkiness existed on the other side of 67th Street. Viewed from my side of the street, it resembled an out-of-focus photograph. It had no depth, little movement, and no discernable detail.

There were actually four girls on my street who were the same age as I and who would have been in my classes. One was Eileen. I have a photo of us at four years old, standing on the pavement in front of the row houses in our Easter outfits. She in her white Easter bonnet, bright dress, and patent leather shoes, and me in my shirt and tie.

I spent as much time as I could with her, until suddenly she was gone. Apparently, her parents moved her out of the neighborhood – never to return.

Another of the four was born in Ireland, making her a kind of novelty in the neighborhood of second and third generation Irish - most of the folks in the neighborhood being a generation removed by then.

She gave me a penny from Ireland which was as big as a U.S. half dollar, both of which would be considered fossils today. I spent as much time as I could with her, until I was told she and her family were moving back to Ireland.

I began to think if I really applied myself, I could drive the next one completely off the planet.

The remaining two girls had the same first name, were friends, and must have spent their time inside one another's houses, because I rarely saw them outside. I saw them in class each day, but never saw them going to or from, and didn't speak to them.

Maybe they took a different route home or feared being driven into outer space; either way, I only saw them in class.

Chapter 6

Not Much Kindergarten

I expected wonderful things from Kindergarten, and anticipated all the new things to learn and everyone in one place for the purpose of sharing and obtaining knowledge. Having read everything in my house; just imagine how much I was going to be exposed to at school.

The first day was a numbing shock to all those senses decried among Aspergers. It was full of screaming, crying children, many of whom were hanging onto their mother's skirts, having to be pulled away into the class. The class itself was chaos: kids crying, dripping from the nose, and wetting their pants!

I was totally confused by *nap time*. I didn't even want to sleep at night; why would anyone sleep during the day?

There were a lot of scary kids I didn't know. I expected it was going to be all my friends from my street!

I lasted a week and a half, before I announced to Mom - I wasn't going back. I would just stay at home, move on in the encyclopedia, and wait for the real school to begin in first grade. Besides, who wants to go to school with publics?!

This experience set the stage for formal education for the next twenty-five years.

Chapter 7

So, Grade School

"Eidetic memory is good news – bad news. The good news is you remember pretty much everything - the bad news is you remember pretty much everything."

– The Author

Ok, grade school. Now we're talking. The testing was over. I was being received with great acclaim, because I apparently performed well on the standardized testing. The nuns already knew me by my first name. I was good to go. Now I was at the place where they would lay the foundation for me to be a doctor and rule the world.

Let the learning begin!

Picture walking into a place where all of your special senses are assaulted at once by stimuli to which you've never before been exposed. The sights, smells, sounds, textures, colors, all coming at you at once. A strong chemical smell - some mélange of turpentine, varnish, slate cleaner and paint, strange soap, chalk dust, felt, and dank cloth.

And, since one of the new students felt this wasn't comprehensive enough, he added the piquant smell of vomit.

The stereotype about heightened senses is accurate, although I dislike the characterization of sensitive. Sensitive has too much negative nuance. I'll show later in the book objective evidence my senses are *enhanced*. I prefer this label much more, and they're my senses, so I get to choose the label!

If I'm distracted when I'm thinking, it has a physical effect. There is a direct relationship between distraction and the ability to do other things. This is often confused by professionals as innate clumsiness. It almost shuts down the receipt of input. It can cause tunnel vision. In order to be able to tolerate all of the stimuli; I have to compensate.

Now, don't get me wrong. This place was neat and clean and somewhat sterile. Almost immediately after the student launched the vomit, a man named Mr. Sullivan showed up with additional smells. He had a clanking galvanized pail of sawdust he applied in good measure to the vomit, which he then scooped up.

It was a sort of vomit cat litter.

The sawdust, of which he seemed to have an unlimited supply, had its own peculiar smell. It was a lumberyard potpourri of pine, mahogany, ash, and maple. Perhaps that's where he got such a large supply, at the lumber yard.

Mr. Sullivan was a mystery. He would appear and disappear like a wizard. You would go a whole week without seeing him anywhere in the school, and suddenly when someone would vomit, or a doorknob would fall off; there he was. It was a form of magic - conjuring thoughts of secret passageways known only to him.

There were rows of desks all attached by big flat-head slotted screws to shiny foot-polished planks of wood. Each one of these pairs of planks was long enough to attach five desks, so they could be slid as a unit on the polished, rubbery brown floor. The rings in the planks wore slower than the softer grain between them, imitating wind-blown sand.

The desk frames were decorative cast iron cousins of Bourbon Street balconies who could trace their heritage to the same Philadelphia foundry. We stowed our books under the wood writing surface, drilled for ink wells, and mottled with fossilized India ink preserved in fresh varnish.

The wall of windows on the left faced the public school across Chester Avenue, where the *publics* went. The publics were those unfamiliar people I encountered in kindergarten. Catholic schools didn't have a kindergarten.

The front of the room and the right side were covered with blackboards made from heavy Pennsylvania slate running from three feet off the floor to a height of six feet.

Some teachers had to stretch to write at the top.

At the bottom was a chalk ledge protruding three inches from the wall and on which the chalk and erasers were kept.

Above the blackboards at the front of the room was a continuous horizontal frame displaying an advertisement for The Palmer Method Cursive alphabet in bright white letters on green card stock. I lost myself in figuring out which letters represented the printed ones I knew from the books at home. Learning to write them was just a matter of practice.

I discovered later in life, that most schools teach children to *print* before allowing them to learn cursive. We were not taught to print, but went directly to cursive.

Writing fluidly with AS was a challenge. Each stroke could be interrupted by a cough, dropped pencil, squeaky shoe, or dust particle twinkling in the sunlight.

There were ten rows of desks, each with ten desks. They were full!

There were two doors in each class, so the boys could flow to their seats in the front while the girls came in the back. We were separated 50/50.

My seat was just to the right of the center of the room in the fourth row from the right wall. I could see everything happening in the room, because I was tall for my age. Much of what I saw was terrifying.

The teacher was a sister. She was new to teaching, and it wasn't long before the pressure got to her.

We are often referred to as Baby Boomers, but there were actually two Baby Booms. What I like to call the minor boom in 1946 and the real BOOM in 1954 with the largest surge in births in the history of the U.S.

That's why there were so many of us in the first grade.

The usual number of students in a class was 60, but we swelled it to 100. Our classes remained at 100 until third grade, because we were physically too big by then to fit. The remaining grades consisted of 60 per grade.

The BOOM changed many things, and supported Gregor Mendel's theory concerning number of replication - the more replication, the more anomalies. It was soon apparent that we had distorted the IQ curve just enough to push it off the normal distribution.

When the curve swelled with the increased number of samples, it pushed in all directions. When the curve rose, it contained more normal IQs of 100.

When it swelled from side to side, it pushed the standard deviation and numbers of outliers just enough, so there was a higher-than-average number of high-IQ children and a higher-than-average number of low-IQ children in our class.

A bizarre and confusing atmosphere resulted. Some of the children couldn't follow even the most elementary direction. One boy ran around the room screaming and had to be physically restrained. When the mischievous boys realized this, they would aggravate the mayhem, goading him to "Stand on your seat!" or "Pull down your pants! or "Shout at the nun!"

When conventional methods failed to re-establish the required control, the boy was roughly imprisoned under sister's desk, so she could multi-task. Multi-tasking involved teaching us from her desk while preventing his escape with those black nun issue boots, different from army combat boots only by noticeably thicker stacked leather heels.

It was still being talked about in the 50th-year reunion. Everyone remembered it, but couldn't remember the boy's name.

I remember his name. I can still see his face.

Someone remarked we could still remember this after 50 years, and to accentuate her point; I noted it was actually 58 years.

Years later, a colleague at work asked me how I could remember so many different things.

I told her, "I have an eidetic memory."

"That's not fair!" she protested, "That's not fair!"

She and others have said it must be quite a gift.

I'm not sure.

I'm not sure I want to remember that boy's name, see his face, or hear his screams - to be able to replay the video.

The desk treatment was practiced on several other students. One was a girl of a similar nature who had no control, couldn't sit still, and shouted and cursed vulgarly, emitting the screams of horror movies.

The other was a boy who, although quite handsome, had no light behind his eyes.

He asked early on in the first week of school if he could be excused to go to the bathroom. After about 15 minutes the nun asked me to go and *check on his whereabouts*.

I reported back; I had checked the bathroom and he wasn't there. I checked the 2nd and 3rd floor bathrooms, as well as the halls and office, and could find him nowhere.

The nun reported it to the office, who called his home. Apparently, he wasn't aware there were bathrooms in the school.

His paradigm was: bathrooms were at home.

The next day, he asked to go to the bathroom, and the nun told him no, apparently fearing a repeat of the previous day. So, he just sat in his desk and quietly wet his pants.

Enter Mr. Sullivan with his pail.

After a stint under the nun's desk, dodging leather heels, he got to go home anyway.

With the realization that wetting your pants was a ticket home, pants wetting became a daily problem. Only when the nun made someone sit all day in wet pants, did it stop.

I was lucky to have been seated with children on the East end of the continuum. We were left pretty much alone because we easily did all the work, had nice handwriting, sat pretty still, kept our mouths shut, and were mostly compliant.

I experimented with trying not to go back to first grade, as I had done in kindergarten, but only halfheartedly. Mom was not going for it this time.

I did my work, responded when called upon, absorbed everything on the first go around, and *tried* to keep my mouth shut. I went into my own place during most of the day in class, just waiting for it to be over.

Kathy was always quick to point out that I wasn't always successful at the *keeping-my-mouth-shut* part.

The fact that everyone was kept in line by the nuns and were expected, for the most part, to be nice to each other made things easier for the first five grades or so. All the subjects were easy and required little work to understand and memorize.

I spent most days in my own place. This *going-into-my-own-place* is one of those things that results in AS being mistaken for autism – the simple, *hoofbeat* assumption.

The difference being: I was aware of what was going on around me, and I was deciding when I would come out of it.

The autistic kids can't do this.

Although it may have looked like I was zoned out, I was fully aware of my surroundings. If I was called upon for any subject, I would surface, answer, and resubmerge.

Chapter 8

Then there was Religion

I can easily understand, memorize, and regurgitate anything that makes sense, can be related to something else, or has a logic about it. Religion in the '60s was nothing like that.

The difference between mortal and venial sin, heaven, hell, purgatory, and limbo, the fact God always was, always will be, and always remains the same, while studying the transformation and the death and resurrection, was not an easy learn.

These rules, remember, were made up by what can best be described as *wizards*!

Normal adults had less flattering labels.

Adding the infallibility of the pope, the fact the nuns were ill-treating children and the priests were drinking and touching you in a non-Kosher way, created ambivalence.

It became a challenge to sit frozen in your seat for the time you had to be in class, find a way to do acceptable work, and generally keep everyone off you. This required the skill to out-think them, because they were all much bigger and stronger.

An Aspie acquaintance once told me that his doctor said, "You hide behind your intelligence. You wield it like a weapon."

We have to work with what we've got. You see, without the battery of automagic social tools, intelligence is our main armament.

Attempts to participate in a more fulfilling grade school experience was a waste of time. I asked the nun in charge of the altar boys, if I could participate.

She looked at me sideways and said, "No, your red hair would be too much of a distraction for the priest and everyone else!"

Nice, huh?!

I tried to join the choir, but I didn't have a dime. Apparently, you needed a dime each time you showed up for choir practice. Maybe the organ ran on coins.

I was allowed to run errands, however, and any excuse to get out of your seat for even a short period of time was a godsend.

A sister in second grade sent me into the cloakroom one day to retrieve penny candy for sale in class. Among penny candy choices were small anise-flavored jellies in the shape of a doll. These were black jelly with a coating of granular sugar.

Of course, everything had a nickname back then.

Sister said, "Michael, go into the cloakroom and bring me a box of n-word babies."

See why I was a little confused? You see, we didn't have the word *n-word* back then. And the real word was strictly forbidden at home, heightening my confusion.

This was a time when the lack of ability to read faces and expressions may have been a benefit - a shield against PTSD - I have an inkling we are somewhat immune to it.

Third grade was the first time we had a layperson teaching us. It was taught by a teacher, which is how we differentiated between nuns and lay-teachers. Lay-teachers were civilians.

Mrs. Soyka was in her '50s and was married with children. She smelled heavily of cigarettes, but that was not uncommon. Having a family made her much more accepting of children in general and definitely more mature. Her methods of discipline were firm but instructive.

I can't remember an instance of her hitting anyone.

I met David in this class, who became my only lifelong friend.

The nun in fourth grade was from Ireland and still spoke with a brogue. She had me talk Dad into making her a bookcase for the classroom. This was a mixed blessing, because every other teacher also wanted one, and Dad's limit was one.

He made hers because he said, "Her brogue reminds me of my mom."

So, no Irish brogue, no bookcase.

Chapter 9

The Cop Personality

Weekends were a welcome break, both in the temporary reprieve from school and the sometimes-interesting events they brought with them. One Saturday, at age nine, I attended a wedding for my cousin.

Families were much larger then, and weddings had hundreds of people in attendance. This particular venue was hosting at least two weddings; one on each side of the building, so there were lots of people.

And, lots of alcohol.

As we were leaving, a sudden squeal from the direction of the other wedding froze me in my tracks. I was next to my dad, and when I stopped, he stopped.

On my left was a man holding a woman, presumably his wife, by her wrist, and they were involved in a heated discussion. His face was bright red and malevolent; she was leaning back, trying to pull away, and her face was contorted by fear.

Suddenly, with his free hand, he slapped her in the face!

I bolted in his direction! I didn't know what I was going to do when I got there, but I was on my way! My mission - to *prevent* additional slaps.

My dad, who was extremely quick, came after me and grabbed me by the shoulders. I stopped and looked up at him.

He said, "That's not our business."

I was confused on several levels. I felt once the man did this in public, it was everyone's business. I *felt* the slap, and it rippled over everyone!

I also felt when someone was attacking someone weaker, regardless of who they were; it was everyone's duty to intervene. I couldn't process that I was the only one who reacted to the situation and was disappointed that my dad, of all people, saw it the way he did.

That instinct, the intense instinct to run to someone's aid and apply just the requisite and appropriate intervention techniques, is absent in most humans. If it wasn't, we wouldn't need cops.

This is also my first recollection of a situation demonstrating my lack of the *fight or flight* response; an observation of Aspergers that is accurate in my case. The fight or flight response should not be confused with the *startle response or startle reflex.*

If a gun goes off near me, I'll flinch like most folks, perhaps sooner, given the enhanced senses. If I didn't have this; it would have been picked up in the initial Apgar test at birth, identifying an anomaly and perhaps saving us all a lot of trouble.

The fight or flight response is an automatic physiological reaction to a situation perceived as stressful or frightening. The short story is: I don't have one.

In such scenes, when there is a shooter, and everyone is running away, I'm running toward the shooter. If I decide to retreat, it's a cerebral response, not an automatic reaction. The wisdom of running toward the shooter is open for discussion, but it remains a cerebral decision.

Die-hard professional first responders feel that emergencies require one of the three elements: fire, flood, or blood. The first to arrive on the scene of such emergencies is the police, followed closely by firefighters. In Philly, they're housed in the same building.

There's a running joke, pun intended, that a firefighter will say, "You cops are crazy; you run toward gunfire."

To which we reply, "We're crazy?! You run into burning buildings!"

I've observed on many occasions involving either gunfire or a burning building, cops and firefighters running past each other in opposite directions.

But, even without the fight or flight response and notwithstanding running toward gunfire, I'm not ashamed to say I have and would not hesitate again to run from a burning building!

At this particular point in time, however, *cop* information was just incidental and was placed in storage. The strong inclination to join the police department would not emerge until later.

Chapter 10

I Witness

Fifth grade was a new low, full of contradictions, awakening new levels of awareness. The teacher was one who all the girls loved and all the boys crushed on. She presented a petite portrait of purity, beauty, and innocence.

This image had already been shattered for me earlier in the year when I was sent to the teacher's lounge to deliver a note. I knocked on the door, and as it opened, I saw her at the end of a table, mid-drag on a cigarette.

She turned toward me, screaming, "*Get the hell out of here*!"

Behavior like this, common in the '60s, was simply passed off as *a bad temper*.

One Monday, there was an unusual buzz at school. There was always weekend news being discussed, and to me, it *was* literally a buzz, but this day was different in its intensity and its unusual and perceptible effect on the other students - they were visibly upset.

It was a break in a pattern.

As usual they weren't including me, but the atmosphere was palpable and bad. I asked what was going on.

Apparently, over the weekend, several of the special kids got together and ganged up on one of the others. The object of the exercise, Alan, was a quiet soul who had an emaciated appearance and was awkward and slow.

He apparently had done something that irked his droogs, so they chased him down, cornered him, and beat him up. Home with two black eyes and other injuries, he represented a pathetic figure, so this event provoked immediate remedial action.

There was an instigator, Lucy.

Lucy was not only mentally challenged but physically as well. She was morbidly obese and walked with a swaying cadence, like a Halloween blow-up fat suit. She alternately barked and muttered obscenities that made us cringe, so we kept our distance.

She spoke forcefully - launching little *spit-parachutes* - another reason to maintain safe distance.

Another member of the special group was Carl, the boy who went home in first grade to use the bathroom. Carl came to me after our eighth-grade graduation ceremony and wanted to know, as he handed it to me, why his diploma was blank, as a testament to his academic limitations and the attitudes of the administration.

Finneas, the third member of the group, was big for his age. He was tall and proportionately built, and he hunched his considerable shoulders when he walked. He never made eye contact; I never heard him speak, and he hung with the special kids. He did, however, go on to graduate high school, so when he got out from under the thumb of the nuns, he was better able to function.

Now, please remember as you read this passage that I was not a signatory of the social contract. I wasn't even aware of a social contract at this point. I felt for Alan, but it seemed to me to be something that was all in the family.

The intrinsic evil I saw in this event was the numbers. Three-on-one is never good, but as far as the other issue, he was one of their own.

He was not singled out as different or special and victimized as such. He was part of the special klatch who fell out with mutual members. It was an issue for the families to handle - not something directly concerning the school.

The teacher, having a different slant on relativity, thought otherwise.

What unfolded next was surreal. Time would stop, and my brain would race to process what I was seeing. Scenes would unfold with no place of attachment or link to context. I would experience this again in the police department as witness to other acts. This was just the first - a new pattern.

A captured audience, we watched as a show trial in the theatre of the absurd unfolded. The front of our classroom served as a stage, and prelude prescribed strict attention and focus on the lesson. It would be hard to watch, and impossible to look away.

The actors were assembled, and we, an audience of 60 fifth-graders, observed apprehensively.

Act I was the trial. It was a speedy trial, lasting a few minutes. The drafters of the Sixth Amendment would be proud.

The teacher served as prosecutor and judge and, after detailing Alan's injuries, interviewed some witnesses, one of whom I suspected was a co-conspirator.

I had seen the same guilty look on him in first grade when he instigated bad behavior among the same special kids.

I couldn't picture Finneas and Carl hurting anyone. Seeing this *witness's* reaction to the questions told me he had played an active part, but safe behind tacit immunity, he told his side of the story.

The teacher fast-tracked the process, moving straight from investigation to punishment. The trial and sentencing apparently occurred inside her head, and I sat watching what I thought was going to be just another typical display of absurdity when she whipped around and faced the class!

She snarled, "Someone give me their belt!" - in the same breath - "Boys stand up!"

Walking downstage she created a participative theatre among the audience, as she inspected each boy's waist like a general reviewing troops. Belts were immediately proffered, and years of institutional conditioning found me reaching for mine. It hadn't hit me what was about to happen. I don't think it had yet hit anyone.

Had we known, would anyone have cooperated?

She slapped each belt against her hand, testing weight and thickness. Belts were all leather then, synthetics not yet in vogue. Flimsy belts were rejected.

After requisitioning one boy's belt, she returned to the stage.

I wonder what after-effects this had on him.

The punitive part of the proceedings began, lasting longer than the trial.

I was concerned about the normal kids exposed to the emotional barrage about to hit. As if from the wings, I watched the events on stage and in the audience.

Young eyes riveted to the stage revealed confusion. Apprehension spoiled innocent faces. I saw fear and wanted to fix it, but became numb as the blood rushed to my brain to find a remedy.

The lesson about to be taught would affect even the most salty and disaffected among us, and the meaning of trust would falter. It would still be a topic of discussion in the 50th year high school reunion 57 years in the future.

Act II began with the four actors center stage and some boys standing to get a better view. The teacher let slip the discordant cry, "This was a horrible thing to do!" as the belt whipped through the air.

Physical effects of the belt would heal, but the emotional impact did not.

She moved toward Carl, her intent now obvious. He realized what was about to happen and shielded his face, earning the warning, "Put your hands down. Don't try to avoid this, or it will be worse!"

Carl moved like a boxer - like someone who had been hit before, and was savvy to deftly disguise attempts at avoidance. He moved his head around the belt and took blows at a glancing angle or shrugged his shoulder as a guard. When it came directly at his face, he would wait until the last second to use his forearm, so it was not as obvious as using his hands would have been.

His performance was apparently enough to satisfy the teacher, because she finished with him and took a breath. He slunk off to a corner, with the affect of a dog in a rescue commercial.

It was Finneas' turn. He was big, so she had to reach up to hit him, and he instinctively raised his arms. This she took as a threat, as it appeared he might hit her back! She renewed the cry of, "Put your hands down, or it will be worse!"

Unfortunately, he did.

The belt made an odious arch to Finneas' head. I don't know what was worse: watching the beating itself, or watching him stoically take it without a sound. Empathetic moans and whimpers in the class were drowned out by the sound of the belt buzzing the air and landing on Finneas.

Silence swept over the class when she focused on his face!

Academics were not completely missing from the lesson, as context was provided for a new word. I was not familiar with the word *welt*, because it represented something I had never seen: the raised stripes whippings leave behind.

Also, there was a history component. I recalled my grandfather telling me that as a boy in the 1800s, he witnessed public whippings in Philadelphia. I think this is what it was like.

Petrified, the class watched while she beat him in the face with the leather belt as she told Finneas what a beast *he* was! As she raised welt after welt, Finneas just stood there; he made no sound and barely flinched, as she striped his head and face.

When she finished, Finneas looked like he had run into an airplane propeller, as he slunk off toward Carl.

We were ten years old!

While this was going on, I sensed activity outside the front door of the classroom. Faces of teachers and nuns appeared then quickly disappeared from the window, as the action continued. The coming act would be even harder to watch.

While the boys were being attended to, Lucy, simple in every sense of the term, watched, detached from a safe distance. She was between the teacher and the door, and I wished she would run out.

Maybe someone heard the voice in my head, because a whisper observed, "She doesn't know she's next."

The teacher spun and focused on Lucy. "And you!" she shouted, pointing with the belt. "You are the one who encouraged the others to hit Alan. You are in for the worst of it!"

Lucy instinctively took a half step back, and the teacher shouted, "Don't you run away!"

As the teacher assumed her stance, Lucy finally realized what was about to happen. The look on her face of extreme surprise combined with horror made even my hair stand on end.

Finneas' unsettling muteness was replaced with a series of sounds that intensified the communal revulsion. Lucy wound into a scream like the first notes of an air-raid siren. Not words at first, but a from-the-diaphragm, building, frightening scream of horror movies.

The room drew a collective breath.

The belt whipped around and landed on Lucy. Her screams tore the air as she tried in vain to ward off the blows. It was sickening to watch - impossible not to.

Lucy tried to run but hit the wall. Her parabolic midline hit the chalk ledge, and she winced. Trapped there, she continued to shriek horrifically, intermittently cursing and screaming obscenities, which instantly justified intensifying the beating!

She was hurting herself, rolling to and fro against the chalk ledge, trying in vain to avoid the belt - trying to get through the wall!

The teacher realized this was not efficient and paused to adjust the belt. Morbid relief replaced the horrible thought, she was going to use the buckle, when she instead doubled the leather.

She caught one of Lucy's wrists and held her so she couldn't run, and bore down, whipping her around the forearms as Lucy tried to shield her head. The leather propellor spun around, alternately hitting and missing, as Lucy ducked, dodged, and ran around to avoid being hit.

The door was right behind her, but she couldn't hear the voice inside my head shouting, "Run out the door!"

Her screaming like an animal and trying to avoid being hit, as much as it terrified us, further enraged the teacher - appalled Lucy would not *stand still and take it*!

"Put your hands down, or it will be worse!" had become her war cry! It was getting to the point where it was starting to physically affect me, when Lucy slipped around her and ran toward where Carl and Finneas licked their wounds.

All three started to get hit again.

I guess Lucy thought, *I don't have to outrun the bear, just outrun you.*

Although Lucy was still the object of the exercise at this point, Finneas and Carl were in the line of fire, so they got added licks.

The teacher got ahold of Lucy's arm, but Lucy wriggled away, so she grabbed a handful of hair! Back on center stage, where there was plenty of room to swing, it started up again. Some grisly algorithm prescribing the requisite number of licks had not been satisfied, so the clock was reset.

"Put your hands down!" she warned. The belt hissed through the air again! It hit Lucy square in the face. The class had a physical reaction, as her screams went through us.

She screamed like she was being murdered.

And yes, I *have* heard that scream.

Whack! it hit her in the upper arm, *whoosh* and slap it hit her in the head. *Woosh* again in the other arm. Lucy was now completely feral, and I began to think she was going to go postal on the teacher; she outweighed her by at least 30 pounds, but she had nothing left and collapsed on the floor.

Fate, and the fact she was a smoker, intervened, and the teacher finally got winded and had to take a break. Breathing heavily, blouse half-untucked, hair disheveled, crimson-faced, and sweating, she crouched and glared at the three children.

Lucy was cowering on the floor, whimpering and covering her face with her arms like a Praying Mantis.

Catching her breath, the teacher was winding up for the finale, when I noticed Mother's marble face filling the window in the door.

Mother Superior was both the head of the convent and the principal of the school. She was not a warm and fuzzy person by any means, but this affected even *her* sensibilities.

Act III - Mother opened the door and entered the scene, ordering the teacher to stop. The teacher whipped around, exclaiming, "I'm not finished!"

Mother told her she *was* finished and again told her to stop. She mouthed off to Mother one last time and then got a hold of herself. When she had finally exhausted her rage, she stopped, heaving to catch her breath – her face twisted in an angry mask.

Mother marched her out of the room and had another teacher come in to watch the class and establish order.

Lucy was still screaming and rolling around on the floor, and since she couldn't be calmed, she was taken to the nurse.

Carl was cowering in a corner; Finneas stood catatonic. They were ordered to take their seats, and they did.

Tension cramps my shoulders as I write this.

We sat the rest of the day in silence. I'm surprised no one vomited. I guess we were just jaded enough at that point - this was just an incremental iniquity. The next level up from those who were under the first-grade nun's desk with her combat boots.

That was bad, but at least *she* wasn't *aiming* at their faces.

I was about to decide there was no justice. Until, I would soon discover; there was a Final Act.

Justice was waiting in the wings.

Chapter 11

A Measure of Justice

The climax came the next morning, as a quiet riot of 1,200 alto voices echoed between the school buildings, awaiting the bell signaling dispersal into classrooms.

I was just a little surprised to see the teacher with a knot of girls clustered around. I could hear their unique voices amid the cacophony.

I was enjoying the word song - ignoring the content.

Waiting is mindless, so I was miles away inside my head when I became aware of a presence beside me with a mass so large, it couldn't be a classmate or teacher.

It altered the morning light - I felt it, before I saw it.

I can feel it now.

I slid my attention from the klatch of girls to the pressing figure, and found myself eye-level with pockets of long navy-blue trousers. My eyes traced the royal blue stripe down the leg to highly shined patent leather shoes.

Very large patent leather shoes.

My head swiveled upward and upward, until I was doing something I rarely needed to do. Look up to find someone's head!—a huge shoulder obscured part of it - being only inches away magnified the effect.

My brain raced to process the input. This was a police uniform. This is a policeman. He is wearing only a white t-shirt, so he is off duty. It was just after 8:00 AM, so he was probably coming home from the midnight tour.

He was the biggest man I had ever seen! He was 6'6" and 240 lbs. of solid muscle, with shoulders so broad, I found it hard to picture him in a police car. My memory was gathering data fast.

I did not interact with people in school much, but I caught all the undertones and stashed them away, and thoughts dovetailed inside my head, fitting police officer into the current setting.

Who was this mountain-of-a-man standing next to me? Why was he looking so intently at the teacher? Suddenly, it hit me! I remembered someone saying Finneas' dad was a cop.

This was Finneas' dad!

He did not slouch like Finneas but stood ramrod like a soldier, and when he stepped forward, his shadow fell over the teacher. The girls, who were facing her, bugged, and conversation stopped, and as they craned their necks up, the teacher turned around.

Finneas' dad's voice was substantial and commanding, piercing the clamor as it boomed, “Are you Finneas' teacher?!”

She started and looked up, folding backwards, straining to look into his face. She was riveted to the ground, balancing to avoid falling.

She replied in her familiar, confident voice, “Yes I am.”

She was almost two feet short for a nose-to-nose confrontation. All she could do was peer up from the hole created by his shadow.

He bent his towering presence slightly at the waist and glared at her - just a second.

Then his voice, the voice of a police officer, of a soldier, boomed, “I'm Finneas' father. If you ever put your hands on my son again, I'll break your fucking legs!”

A ring of silence grew from where we stood and spread across the yard. The crescendo of sound that normally built as the bell approached evaporated, and quiet rushed the void.

The sudden change hurt my ears when the pressure of sound waves instantly stopped!

With the message delivered, he turned with a military bearing and disappeared behind my periphery. I did not follow him, but intently watched the teacher. I felt the pulses of sensation, contradiction, and pressure rebounding in my head, but I needed closure. I needed to witness her reaction.

She, momentarily frozen, began to wither - his Herculean words echoing in her head.

Her defiance, her confidence and self-righteous indignation, fled and left her standing alone.

She broke into violent sobs, doubled up as though overcome with agonizing cramps and running, disappeared into the school.

We didn't see the teacher for the rest of the day. I don't remember exactly when she came back into the class, but when she finally did, she was visibly changed - humbled slightly.

This event would have effects on our class through eighth grade. Someone finally waded straight into that nest and stood up for us, driving the first wedge into their system of abuse.

We would meet these abuses head-on from now, and we would do it ourselves, since no one else's dad was a cop with the minerals to do it for us.

Chapter 12

A Note about Classmates

There was a pretty girl in my class: one I saw only in school. As stereotype dictates, she had an entourage in constant orbit.

I never had a conversation with her, but I must have, in some unconscious AS moment, articulated I liked her. I found out later one had to be careful with the remark, "I like her." It had nuance I didn't understand. All I meant was, that she was pretty and I liked her. There was no hidden meaning.

Someone apparently heard me say it and passed it on, probably to one of her satellites, who passed it to the girl, precipitating the episode.

One bright sunny day, she and her team approached me in the schoolyard. Standing in the vanguard, in front of God and everyone, she regally proclaimed, "I'd rather be dead, than red in the head!"

She and her team gave me a collective stink-eye, and they all marched off.

I'm told I can have a negative effect on people, but since I never even talked to this girl before this incident, I have to conclude it was a manifestation of something else.

But, there are always positives!

I never got the old Irish expression – *gobsmacked!* Kathy was kind enough to provide a lively pantomime and bring it to life. I turned to the sudden movement of her hand as it flashed to her involuntarily gaping mouth. I couldn't hear her eyes bug, but her open hand hit her face with an audible slap.

I also appreciated, as she watched the drama among the other spectators; this honest expression let me know she enjoyed the girl's performance – *not at all*!

I stood there pondering the ginger bashing poem, the reason for it, the collective dirty looks and failing any understanding of what had just happened, made the girl the first entry on what remains a short list – *people to avoid* – forever.

Our paths crossed many times in the remaining years of school, but she had the substance of vapor.

I tell this story to highlight several things: The obvious one is the effect something this insensitive, albeit juvenile, can have on any young person.

More importantly, I tell it to highlight - it is the *only* time in the entire 12 years of school any of my classmates exhibited this type of behavior toward me, and with the exception of the story of the special kids, the only example of classmates exhibiting this type of behavior within our class at all.

I mentioned earlier the predictable effects on the Gaussian curve, but another interesting enigma emerged. A later chapter on austerity contains details about the numbers associated with the baby boom. The timeframe we were born produced the largest spike in U.S. births - 40% higher than average.

As expected, the outward pressure of our group produced increased behaviors of bullying, anger and violence, but the enigma was not within our group. It came only from the outside.

An increased number of people in any venue normally increases social pressure and heightens these behaviors. It should have resulted in bullying and other negative behaviors among our classmates, but it had the opposite effect.

Except for instances where I can, in 20/15 hindsight, see were clearly provoked, our class was extremely patient, tolerant, and kind.

My best guess is with the increased pressure from the outside; we had turned to one another for safety and comfort. I don't mean we stood outside one another's homes with pitchforks to ward off evil, but we certainly had a better appreciation of each other than I saw from the other age groups.

I also want to make it clear, for whatever reason, unlike other AS stories I read, that I was not bullied or picked on systematically in school. The social system at large is set up for an atmosphere of bullying for anyone different, but among my classmates, it simply didn't exist.

When you read among the stories, instances where I note, "I was not included." the causes were mostly my fault, and when I made conscious efforts to join, I was given fair and equal chances and access. In short, they knew I was different, but they went out of their way to be tolerant where the outside groups were having none of it.

I consider myself to have been extremely lucky in life in general and with my classmates in particular.

Chapter 13

Kathy

By now, you've got to be wondering, "Did I miss something? - Who is Kathy?"

By the time I finished high school, I had accumulated two friends. The irony is they were both popular. Among the bevy of Aspies I know personally, none have any friends.

I was 200% better off at this point!

Kathy was the only one of my classmates who braved entering the small box where I lived, and since her cousins lived two doors from me, she was one of the few I saw outside of school hours. Two doors from me was less distance than the frontage of most suburban homes - a stone's throw away.

In row houses, news literally travelled through walls. If Kathy came to visit, I knew within a few minutes, because whenever something newsworthy occurred, our next-door neighbor tapped on the adjoining wall with a soup spoon.

I don't know how she would react to being compared to Ben Franklin, but Kathy had a similar position at our school. She was the effervescence of the place, the spark who kept it interesting. Everyone knew and loved her. She was ambassador, cheerleader, scholar, planner, and friend to everyone. Without her, the place would have been flat, stale and monotonous.

She was frequently at her cousins for birthdays, holidays or casual visits. The best of these events was the yearly 4th of July Barbeque, where the entire neighborhood would block off the driveway behind the houses to automobile traffic and roll out the charcoal grills.

At these events, we could converse without the specter of some teacher threatening sanctions for the *crime of talking.* Whereas most girls would run from the red hair alone, Kathy would patiently and openly converse and offer valuable observations, advice and always a compliment.

She was rarely cross, even when disciplining me to "Try not to talk so much in class!"

In class, it was just enough to hear *"Michael!"* whispered behind me, to short-circuit something I was doing or about to do and keep me from *stepping on my poncho*. She even had seconds trained who would jump in to chide me, if she wasn't there.

Aspergers need someone they can trust, even if it is only one. Someone who tells the truth and doesn't equivocate. Someone to keep you from *sticking your fingers in the social fan*. In grade school, it was Kathy.

Chapter 14

In the Cloakroom

In the flood of information, when I read the AS story in the BBC article, this hit like a solid object, and it hit hard!

There was an extremely attractive girl in our seventh-grade class. I'm not sure what other classes we had together, because close proximity was often necessary to evoke significance. In seventh grade, we were close to coming of age, and many of us were in an adolescent hormonal haze.

The close proximity came when the nun decided to seat us one seat apart. I was on a diagonal directly in front and to her right for at least one semester.

She had a movie star's air and aching good looks - Joan Crawford's unsmiling beauty and the melancholic look of Greta Garbo. But, on those rare occasions when she did smile, she was Vivian Leigh at her provocative best.

An aloofness came with her age. She was two years older. I never learned why she was in our class. Maybe I misread the aloofness. Perhaps she was just frustrated being stuck with younger kids. I can see how that might sour someone.

She didn't talk much. I didn't spend much time wondering why she was there, but I did think about her a lot! A certain bad girl vibe enhanced the allure.

That morning on the bus after reading the BBC article, I was back in seventh grade, hanging my coat in the cloakroom:

At the rear of the class, there was a wall running from floor to ceiling with a doorless opening at each end. There were rows of hooks on the facing interior walls.

When the cloakroom was empty, it was five feet wide, but when full, in those spots where heavy winter coats didn't touch, was a long *five-inch-wide-damp-wool-coat-moth-ball-smelling-tunnel.*

When I entered, I turned sideways and squeezed in to find a hook.

I thought I was in there alone, and was hanging my coat when I sensed her to my left. She gave me a playful look and squeezed behind me.

I could feel her breath as her chin slid around my neck, hesitating with each sidestep to press past me.

I can almost swear I felt the buttons on her blouse; I'm sure I felt everything else.

She emerged on my right and teased a smile.

She left a cloud, my head spinning, and intoxicated, but no idea what had just happened. My back felt like it was humming.

The experience was one of the first puzzle pieces to surface 47 years later. This one didn't so much fall like a domino as hit like a brick - a solid object in the haze.

My kingdom for a mirror neuron![3]

[3] A mirror neuron is a neuron that fires both when an action is performed and when you see someone do the same action. This allows babies to imitate other humans they see, practicing and learning new skills. It also causes us to feel emotions when we see other people experiencing them.
National Library of Medicine – National Center for Biotechnology Information
https://www.ncbi.nlm.nih.gov/pmc/articles/PMC3898692/#:~:text=Mirror%20neurons%20are%20a%20class,act%20performed%20by%20another%20individual., retrieved June 15, 2024.

Chapter 15

Rose

Rose was also a year or so older. My best guess as to why she was there was: they spoke no English at home. She had come into the school either as a first or second-generation European and started at a disadvantage, learning English as she went.

I don't know this to be a fact, but I've pieced it together over the years, and this is the conclusion to which I've come.

Rose was also in full bloom, presenting a figure further developed by her parents' skill as tailors. Instead of the mass-produced jumper or *blue bag* the other girls had to wear, she wore uniquely hand-tailored uniforms and blouses - clothes that fit!

Rose was wearing the equivalent of Saville Row; the rest of us couldn't even afford John Wanamaker's.

Rose resembled a refined Sophia Loren. Yes, she was that beautiful! She was a refined Sophia with delicate features, chestnut brown hair, and soft, beautiful almond-shaped sparkling blue eyes - Sophia without the sharp edges and excess.

She was quiet, behaved, did what she was asked and created no problem in any class I had ever seen, and I remember Rose over several years.

In seventh and eighth grade, the nuns experimented with moving people around, abandoning the usual, year-long static arrangement. I was sitting directly in front of Rose in the last row nearest the window.

I'll leave the exploration of why nuns did anything to someone with government grants, lots of time and several more degrees.

The nun was the living embodiment of the wicked witch. Anyone who looked at her sideways got hit. Depending on her mood, you could be hit with a ruler, yardstick, pointer, open hand or fist. I had seen her pull girls' hair so hard, I thought it would come out in bunches!

I saw her almost pull a boy's ears off on one occasion.

Another time, a boy came in to deliver a message and got her angry; she slapped him five or six times, alternating hands, so she didn't miss a beat. He was smart enough to retreat back into the hall.

She broke an oak pointer over a boy sitting in front of me one afternoon, looked at me, and laughed.

I had had several run-ins with her. On one occasion, I was standing in line when someone slapped me in the back of the head. I got hit hard! I dropped my books, turned and confronted the boy directly behind me!

When things quieted down, I was approached by someone who said, "He didn't hit you. It was the nun."

Apparently, she came up behind me, and I was doing something she didn't like, so she slapped me. She snuck up and, after she hit me, stepped into my periphery. I thought the boy hit me. When I play back the tape, I can see her skulking off to the side.

I apologized to the boy at lunchtime.

In another incident, on the way to class, I felt something hit my bookbag from behind, and when I turned, she was standing there nursing her wrist. Apparently, she had come up behind me with the intent of punching me in the kidney, but I turned unexpectedly, and she hit the bag full of heavy textbooks instead. She hit them on the edge, so she hurt her knuckles and twisted her wrist in the bargain.

She didn't bother me much after that.

But, on this day, she had a wild hair about Rose. I was daydreaming as usual, when I heard her shout at Rose. I looked at her; she was looking in my direction because Rose was right behind me.

She said, "What did I tell you about your tie?"

Apparently, this nonsense had been brewing for some time, and I tended to ignore nonsense, but I was paying attention now!

I looked at Rose and noticed the clip-on tie the girls were required to wear with their white blouse hanging by one side of her collar.

Rose quickly fixed the tie, and in one of the few times I can remember hearing her speak in class, she explained, that unlike the cotton blouses worn by the other girls, hers were silk, so the tie wouldn't stay.

I see facial expressions, but lacking the mirror neurons don't get an autonouncement of their meaning. The term theatrical describes an *über-expression* used on stage, so the distance to the audience doesn't dilute the message.

The theatrical expressions of the nun told me she was not happy with youth, beauty and tailored silk blouses. The only thing missing in the scene was the green theatrical makeup.

I started to watch the nun. Every once in a while, she would shoot a dirty look over her shoulder - waiting for an opportunity.

Suddenly, she stopped what she was doing, threw the chalk at the ledge, and turned, screaming, "I told you about that tie! It's that Italian silk!"

The TMI said it all!

As she ran across the front of the room toward the aisle leading to our seats, I spun to look at Rose. She had a bewildered and frightened look on her face. Her tie was hanging by one side of her collar - she looked at me imploringly.

The nun was halfway to us, almost running. I foresaw carnage.

Something came over me. I just could not bear the idea of this creature putting a hand on Rose. Rose was like a delicate work of art, and the idea of someone even touching her without gloves on, well, I could see the potential damage.

The nun turned the corner and entered our aisle under a full head of steam. Her rosaries were flying! She had passed the first few desks in front of mine enroute to Rose.

I decided: she wasn't going to touch Rose!

She wasn't going to touch her even if I had to take the beating for her.

I prepared for the beating of my life as I found myself standing in the aisle between her and Rose!

Almost at eye level, I could see the pupils of her eyes contract. I stood still. She came closer. I leaned toward her. She stopped!

For what seemed like forever, the room contained nothing but silence as we stood and eyeballed each other.

She balled her fists; I balled mine.

She leaned a little closer; I mimed her.

I started out a buffer, but suddenly, something inside sent me to battle stations. I was not going to let her hit me - I was ready to fight, and she knew it!

She got religion!

She feigned composure and stood up straight. She looked me in the eye one last time, tossed her head, turned on her heels and returned to the front of the room.

There's an interesting dynamic among bullies. When the scenario includes sharing in the physical pain, they reevaluate. She went back to whatever she had been teaching before the incident started, like it never happened, like she had no conscience.

I can deescalate fast and go back to daydreaming. This stereotype is pretty accurate - quick flares followed by a rapid return to normal.

As I replay it, I can see other kids in the class looking at me with wide eyes and open mouths. I gave it no thought at the time.

The salient AS issue here is: I had no idea what I had just done. I was doing the right thing in my mind, but I had just fractured many norms and rules. I completely disregarded the authority figure.

I compounded it by actually challenging her!

About a minute or so after the nun returned to the front of the class, I could feel Rose's closeness, preceded by her scented soap.

She leaned up to my ear and, in her soft voice, whispered, "Thank You."

I turned and looked as she sat back, a serene smile on her face.

"You're welcome," I said. And went back to daydreaming.

This flashed by 47 years later when I read that article.

I last saw Rose when we were about 23 years old. I ran into her near her parent's tailor shop. She was expecting a baby - appeared to be happy and was still as beautiful as ever.

The thought of someone hitting that face - not on my watch!

Chapter 16

Basketball Game Fallout

When my kids were in school, they came home with permission slips for a field trip about once a month. They went to zoos, theatres, national parks, aquariums, Marine World, museums, planetariums; you name it, they went.

They even took senior trips to France and Hawaii. The closest I'll ever get to Hawaii is a pineapple in the supermarket.

Here's a list of the places we went on field trips in the entire 12 years of school:

- Nowhere

So, when someone decided to pile us all onto chartered city buses to attend the first time our basketball team made the playoffs, it is no surprise we didn't know how to act.

During the ride back from the game, pumped with adrenaline by the overall excitement of the experience, some kids got frisky and started to remove the cardboard ads from their frames above the windows and alternately throw them at each other or fashion them into large paper planes to launch out the open windows.

The bus company was apparently not pleased by this and reported it to the school.

The next day saw the tipping point for me and many others. Having received news of this heinous act of vandalism on a city bus, Mother superior initiated her quest for the perpetrators.

A favorite tactic was to bring in a group of people and threaten the entire group with some punitive action, unless the guilty party stepped out. This behavior produces one of two results: a false confession or a hardened resolve among the group.

Mother elicited the latter.

Lining the hallway walls with the entire class, she gave the all-too-familiar speech. "If the guilty party does not step out, the entire class will be punished."

I didn't believe she would do it.

I was wrong.

What she had threatened to do was punish the innocent along with the guilty. This is wrong in any case, and most of us saw it as just standard operating procedure, until she crossed a line. A line that became the last straw.

Among the class were brownies. Brownies were exceptionally good children who were personal favorites of the teachers. Brownies had a special standing in the school and were untouchable by everyone: nuns, teachers, and the rest of the class. This was respected by everyone.

The time elapsed, and no one stepped out; I mean, why would you step out, not knowing what the punishment was. Her whole plan was flawed. As we stood against the wall, and mother paced up and down, she went to one end of the queue and started slapping children in the face. She would slap one person, move to the next, slap that person and so on down the line.

I saw what she was doing and thought, "If this is the punishment, let it come."

A slap in the face in this place was just an attention-getter.

But, as she moved down the line, slapping each student, I suddenly thought, *Will she bypass the brownies, or hit them as well?*

My anticipation heightened as she neared me, and I watched the anxiety on the faces of girls who had never been hit in school. They had probably never been hit in their lives, especially in the face.

The first one she reached was Dolores. The best way to describe Dolores is *one of those people who just made the world a better place*. She's in just about every picture I recall from grammar school.

Never cross, always in a good humor, kind and empathetic.

Two very salient memories are:

She had the most beautiful handwriting I've ever seen. There were other girls who had handwriting that mimicked the examples on display in the front of the room, but Dolores' handwriting included the quality of her own particular artistic expression. Her handwriting was better than the suggested examples. It was like viewing a work of art.

The other was her sense of humor.

Dolores was one of the girls the teachers considered trustworthy enough to sit in the front of the class at the teacher's desk when they took a break. Her duty was to make a list of anyone who talked or otherwise misbehaved while the teacher was out of the room.

She would put on her serious face and pretend that she was noting and recording anyone who got out of line, making it a point to point at them with the pen as she recorded their names on the bad list.

This got everyone thinking that she was actually recording their misbehavior, which had the effect of making everyone keep quiet, which actually kept them out of trouble.

What she was doing was doodling on the paper, and when the teacher would enter the room, she would wad up the paper, secret it in her pocket and tell the teacher that everyone was well behaved while she was out.

Everyone would exhale as she returned to her seat with a tricksy smile on her face.

Dolores had a face like a Hümmel figurine.

On this particular morning, as Mother prepared her gauntlet, I watched Dolores' face.

I still really thought she would just pass Dolores, but she stepped up and slapped her squarely in the face. The entire class shuddered!

Dolores' world was shattered. The look on her face was horrific. I watched as she tried to recover from the shock and put her hand to her newly crimsoned cheek.

I saw a change come over her.

It got worse.

She got to Kay, whom the other girls referred to as "That pretty girl." (not the one in the red-head story) Kay was the smartest person in the school – surely, she would skip Kay.

Kay took it stoically with only the slightest involuntary blink. She did not wince or move to deflect the assault. She stood motionless even after the blow.

Hiking up her sleeve, Mother continued, as a wave of transformation swept over us.

The final blow came when she reached Kathy.

As Mother approached her, my body began to involuntarily react. Kathy's face was searching everywhere for the answer to the question, "What is happening?!"

Then she was hit!

It reverberated through the entire class.

Her face showed shock, disappointment and a confused shame she hadn't earned. The die was cast. Anyone who was on the border crossed over. The group was galvanized into a Battle-of-Brittan-like resolve.

On the sixth child in round two of the slapping, Mother became exasperated and simply walked off. As expected, the exercise produced nothing, except the new paradigm among us.

The faculty had created us enemies.

Chapter 17

Summer of '66

I began working in the neighborhood drug store in sixth grade. No one called them pharmacies in the '60s. At this time, they were corner drug stores which were sentimental landmarks sporting soda counters, varnished wood shelves, and colored apothecary show globes.

They served as a nucleus for the neighborhood. Picture the store where George worked in the film *It's a Wonderful Life*, and you have a pretty good idea.

It had been owned by Ed Pearlstein forever. Ed would arrive to open the store each morning, driving his 1939 Plymouth. He would park this museum piece in the garage of the house he also owned, next to the drug store.

I would wave to him as I passed on my way to school. Ed told me he bought that car new. It's the only car I ever saw him drive.

When Ed retired, the store transitioned to a young pharmacist named Irv. With the change in ownership, the soda counter moved across the street to another Philadelphia institution, the hoagie shop, making this a popular corner.

Many romances began or ended between these two spots.

Irv was a nice guy, and I delivered prescriptions for him. I would get a dime or so tip from the customers at the other end, and he was happy I could make change without making a mistake. He offered me a job, and I started working there in the sixth grade.

I would get supplies from the basement, cough syrup bottles and bags and such, stock the magazine racks with the comics and periodicals, sweep the floor, make deliveries and eventually run the cash register.

It was here in '66 that I met Sean, who would become a pivotal person in my life. Sean was ahead of me in school, and when I met him for the first time, I remembered my mom mentioning Sean's dad was the coach of the rowing team for the high school. She knew I had an interest in the sport.

I was fascinated by the idea of rowing. This originated in conversations with my mom about her younger brother, Dick.

Dick served as an airman in a B-24 bomber during WW II. His plane was shot down over Yap Island in the Pacific near the end of the war, so his body was never recovered, engendering a vague and haunting hope he may have survived - a topic of conversation every holiday when the family was together.

There were few pictures of Dick, mostly in his uniform, but there was one with him wearing his high school sweater with his varsity rowing letter. He had won a national championship, and my mom gave me both the letter and the national medal.

I still have them.

When I heard Sean's dad was the coach of the high school team, I let Sean know I wanted to try my hand at it. He took me down to the river the following Saturday.

Boathouse Row on the Schuylkill River in Philadelphia is a well-known landmark. It sits just above the dam, separating the upper and lower parts of the river.

The dam creates a waterfall with a four-story drop, but it also creates a great platform for the graceful wood racing boats that would become my focus for the next six years.

Chapter 18

Rowing 101

The boathouses, all over a century old, sat like small castles built from stone with spires and large porches overlooking the river. Our boathouse, Vesper, midway in the row with the University of Pennsylvania's house to the right and Malta Boat Club to the left, occupied center stage, both literally and figuratively among the houses.

The clubs occupying these houses make up the Schuylkill Navy which coordinated and officiated races and posted the results. It is situated at the end of East River Drive, later renamed Kelly Drive for Jack Kelly, who at that time was the president of Vesper.

John B. Kelly Jr., known to us as Jack, was a prominent oarsman in Philadelphia, a Philadelphia City Councilman, the owner of Kelly Brickworks and big brother to Princess Grace. He was a frequent and familiar face in the boathouse and at the races.

The boathouses held the racing shells and skulls used by their teams. College and high school teams rowed and competed out of the boathouses under the school's name during the school year, and then under the club's name during the summer season.

When you launched a boat from the boathouse, you had no choice but to go up river, because the dam was only a few yards to the left or down river. A safety cable ran across the river just above the dam for you to grab if, for some reason, you lost an oar or couldn't get back to the bank.

Several boats went over the dam in the time I was a member of Vesper. I gave it a wide berth.

The dam created a predictable current and surface, providing almost ideal conditions for rowing. Only after a storm would the current be somewhat fast and the river dotted with debris. Most of the time, however, conditions were mild - the river flat.

The river was marked with milestones. You would row to a particular milestone, for instance, the Girard Avenue Bridge, which grew out of the beautiful raised granite stone bank corralling the river as it flowed through Philly.

The bridge was one-half mile from the boathouse, so returning to the boathouse, you would enter one mile in the log book, recording your row - one-half mile to Girard Avenue and one-half mile back to the boathouse.

Further up the river were additional milestones, with the official racing course finish line at the Columbia Railroad bridge, the three-mile mark, one and one-half miles from the boathouse.

Races started just above the Strawberry Mansion Bridge, approximately two and one-quarter miles from the boathouse. The racing course ran under the Strawberry Mansion Bridge and ended at the grandstands just above the Colombia Railroad bridge.

The course was one mile long for high school races and 2,000 meters – approximately 1.25 miles for college races.

I was 12 the first time I entered the boathouse. Sean took me on a tour starting in the locker room with its huge mahogany fireplace mantle and brightly painted wooden lockers. There was a circular meeting room within the spire of this castle-like structure.

A kitchen adjoined the meeting room.

There were large porches front and back and a third-floor dormitory. I never did figure out who the people were who were living there.

Of course, there was a trophy room.

The trophy room was a large room with 20-foot ceilings and mahogany walls. The walls were festooned with plaques and glass cases literally stuffed with silver trophies and what we called *loving cups*. There were photographs documenting the 100 years of winning Vesper teams.

Prominently displayed over the mantle was a large photo of a group of oarsmen on the slip celebrating some event. There were eight oarsmen, a coxswain and a coach, all proudly smiling at the camera.

I remember Sean mentioning the Olympic eight, but I was overwhelmed by this time.

Then to the best part, as far as I was concerned—the boathouse itself.

The boats were in racks along the walls leading out to the river. Each boat had a name, most beginning with the letter V. Some privately owned boats had other names, such as the Manning, named for its owner.

At the end of each row of racks were slots where the long oars were hung. The oars were painted with Vesper's colors - maroon and gray. This was so you could identify the club's boat from the grandstands during a race.

Large overhead doors lead out onto the slip. The slip was a boat dock which started at the edge of the stone bank running the entire width of the boathouse. The slip slanted downward at an angle dictated by the height of the river.

When the river rose, the angle flattened, because the large flat part of the slip, which actually floated on the river, had risen. Since the two parts were attached to each other via hinges and the upper part to the wall in the same way, they would change position as the river rose and fell.

Usually, you would walk out of the boathouse, down the ramp-like part of the upper slip, onto the lower slip to launch your boat. The slips were made from wooden planks and were large floating boardwalks.

At the side of our slip was a cut-out for the motor launches used by the coaches to follow the crews and give them coaching advice.

There was also a private boat belonging to the treasurer of the boat club. I never saw him use it. It sank within the first year I was there; I think from a combination of too much rain and too little use.

Next to the cut-out was the rowing box. This was a fake boat purposely built onto the slip. It had two sets of seats, riggers and oarlocks.

The idea was, that while still on the slip, you sat in this box, which simulated the inside of a boat. It had a seat on rollers that moved back and forth. It had what resembled shoes at one end, called foot stretchers. On the side of the box, there was an oar lock. The box was situated on the edge of the slip, so when you sat in it and put an oar in the oarlock, the oar could be set in the water, simulating rowing.

Except, you couldn't fall out.

The special oars for the rowing box had large holes in the end, so you could pull and not snap the oar.

In this way, you were able to teach a novice to row without the danger of upsetting a boat and drowning. It worked well. There were two seats. One facing North and the other South simulating port and starboard.

Sean spent some time teaching me to row in the box and then assigned me a practice routine. After he felt I had the hang of it, he took me out on the river in a double-oared skull. In this way, he could watch what I was doing in an actual boat and coach me on the water.

Skulls are boats in which each oarsman has two oars. In a shell, by contrast, each oarsman has only one oar. The big boats, the fours and eights, are shells with longer oars called sweep-oars.

After he felt I had the hang of that, he put me in a large single-seat boat called a gig. Gig was the Philly name for what New Englanders and New Yorkers called a weary or dory. It was a fat single-seat boat almost as wide as a canoe. It was hard to tip this over, so it was a beginner's boat.

The gig was meant to prepare you for a *single skull*, the most prestigious and difficult boat to master. It was different from the gig. It was longer, sleeker and narrower.

Gunwales were built around the seat, because the single skull itself was narrower than your bottom. You sat *in* a gig; you sat *on* a single skull. Getting into a single was my passion.

During the summer, I was to row this gig back and forth up and down the river. It was exhausting. I was in shape, so I thought. I was on the track team, but this was really hard!

I could only go about ten strokes, and I had to stop. Then ten more, and stop again. It took me an hour to go a mile to the Girard Avenue bridge and back. I was spent and drenched with sweat.

While this was going on, Sean was being coached by his dad and older brothers to get him ready for high school. He would start next year, while I would remain to finish grade school.

Sean was training in a single skull. I wasn't ready for that yet; I could barely get the gig moving. I even had to have someone help me carry it back and forth from the boathouse to the river. And, even though you weren't supposed to flip a gig, I managed to do it one day, so I definitely wasn't ready for the single, but that's where I wanted to be.

When school started, until the river froze, I spent every Saturday at the boathouse. I would row the gig as much as I could. I was getting to where I could go almost a mile without stopping, and I would spend the rest of the day poking around the boathouse or teasing the sunfish at the end of the slip.

Now, there were some notable people in the boathouse, although this didn't really have the expected impact on me. There were important businessmen, politicians, and champions whose gold cups and plaques festooned the trophy room. To me, it all had the feel of some old black-and-white movie.

I mentioned earlier, Grace Kelly's brother, John B. Kelly Jr., was also often in attendance at the boathouse. I saw him often, especially on race day.

Chapter 19

The New Eight

One Saturday, there was inexplicable activity at the boathouse - lots of people - and something occurred with a lasting effect. Since I was immune to celebrity, I didn't realize the impact until years later.

A *bigger-than-life* person in the boathouse was Walter. Walter was the senior rowing coach - the head and most visible person in the day-to-day. Walter was from Berlin and still retained his accent.

I would sneak peeks at him from time to time, but pretty much kept my distance.

He was tall, muscular and powerful. He didn't talk as much as he give commands. He was not what one would consider shy. I was to learn shortly, why.

The boathouse had recently purchased a new eight-oared shell. It wasn't the usual American-built boat comprising almost all of the larger shells. It was of German design and manufacture - quite sleek. It also had the novel feature of having the coxswain positioned in the bow of the boat.

This coxswain's seat was a chaise lounge affair where the coxswain would recline facing the bow with a forward-facing tiller versus the conventional setup of sitting upright in the stern steering with two wooden handles attached to ropes.

This new set-up gave a much-improved view of the river ahead, unobstructed over the bow. Normally, the cox would sit face to face with the oarsman in the eight seat, or stroke seat. In the traditional set-up, the cox had to lean left and right to look around the entire crew to view what was ahead and steer the boat.

The *stroke-man* or *stroke* set the pace for the boat. The rest of the crew kept in time by following the rhythm of his oar. Behind the stroke was the seven-seat, then six, and so on up the boat, until the bow was reached. The oarsman in the bow seat was called simply *bow*.

I had watched them bring the boat in and assemble it. It was kept on the next to the bottom rack, and since boats were stored keel up; I had to stick my head under to look at the interior. It was nice.

Everything was done in a lighter-colored wood with laminated seats with eye pleasing grain. One of the most innovative features were the foot stretchers. Usually a plain wood and leather affair with nasty black laces, the new boat eclipsed them with built-in Adidas sneakers - a real innovation at the time!

The boat was kept isolated, and no one was allowed to touch it. It was complemented by an equally slick set of matching sweep oars, freshly painted with Vesper's colors. It was like a museum piece, and I would sneak past the ribbons meant to keep everyone at arm's length and inspect it whenever there was no one around.

This Saturday, I was poking around the slip, waiting for everyone to finish their routines. As I mentioned earlier, for some reason there was a full house, so I kept to myself and out of the way.

All of a sudden, I heard Walter's booming German accent. "Hey, you!" "Waat are you doink there?"

I spun my head around to see who he was hollering at, a pretty frequent event, to realize, he was looking at and calling to ME!

I just froze and looked at him. I rechecked my surroundings, as one instinctively does in these situations, which was silly, because there was no one else around, and I was at the edge of the slip with my back to the river.

I responded with the predictable, "Me?"

"Yes!" he boomed. "Waat are you doink?"

"Nothing!" I replied.

He said, "Komm here."

Walking not being an acceptable response; I ran straight at him.

He asked me if I had ever coxswained a boat before. I told him I had not. He looked at me from head to toe and then said, "Komm wit me." He turned and went into the boathouse with me in tow.

Inside the boathouse, there were seven monsters whom I had never before seen. The smallest of them was 6'2" and 210 lbs. They got incrementally larger from there. Their arms were bigger than my legs! My mind was racing - what was going on?

Walter looked at me and said, "You come wit us. I will tell you wat to do."

Bug-eyed, I nodded an affirmation.

Walter became the eighth man and barked commands to the crew. "Line up at the boat!" They all snapped into line from bow to stern at one side of the long gleaming eight.

"Take hold!" As they seized the boat with huge hands, it began to hover.

"Lift!" Walter commanded. And this unbelievably heavy shell leapt from the rack.

"Valk it back!" And the shell moved from the shelf to the middle of the aisle of the boathouse. With the next command, "Port side under the boat!" four men ducked under the boat and took a handhold on the other side.

Now, there were four men holding each side of the boat.

"Valk it out," came the next command, and with me scurrying to keep close but out of the way, they walked the eight out of the boathouse like it was a long feather.

When they were halfway to the edge of the slip came the command, "Lift!" and the boat went over their heads; by now, we were at the edge of the slip, and the command came, "Roll it over!" and the boat was now upright with the bow facing up river and the seats and riggers in the proper upright position to go into the water.

"Set her down!" was the final command, and the new eight was sitting proudly in the river, ready to go.

Walter looked at me and said, "Holt her!"

This I knew, because much of my time was spent helping other oarsmen get their boats in and out of the water. I immediately went to the middle of the boat and took hold of a rigger. I squatted down while holding the boat snug against the side of the slip.

Walter looked pleased, nodded and walked off to follow the other seven oarsmen into the boathouse. I knew they were picking out a set of oars. Soon they came out, each equipped with a brand-new Pierce sweep oar.

They were obviously familiar with one another and were talking and joking and jostling each other. I was still at the edge of the slip, watching them, thinking, *I'll just hold this until they're ready to go and push them off. In the meantime, I'll keep my distance so as not to get squashed.*

Although I was approaching six feet tall at this point, I weighed under 125 lbs. and was like a pencil next to this crew.

I held the boat and watched, as Walter gave commands and assigned seats. When all but he were in the boat, he came to me and said, "Ok, here's wat wee're goink to do."

It hit me now they had no coxswain. I almost panicked. *Me, the cox, in the new boat! What happens if I screw up. What happens if I hit the bridge. They'll throw me in the river!*

Walter said, "Ok, we're going to test out this new boat. You're the coxswain."

I started to remind him; I'd never done it before, but he cut me off and said, "We'll tell you wat to do. All you really have to be sure of is we don't hit anything. You listen to him!" and, he pointed to the bowman, whom I would come to know as Hugh, "He'll tell you wat to do."

"Ok," he said. "Now get in."

Chapter 20

One and Only Stint as a Coxswain

I gingerly, no pun intended, got into the coxswain's seat. It was a little too short, but since I was so thin, it wasn't bad. Walter told Hugh to tell me what to do, and Hugh nodded.

I looked over my shoulder, and Hugh said, "You'll be ok. We'll do all the work, and you just keep us straight and watch for debris in the river, Ok?"

"Ok," I replied.

I sat for a few seconds, getting used to the seat. I tried the tiller line to make sure the rudder was moving and the tiller was operating freely.

I knew most basics, like—only steer when the oars are in the water. And I knew at this point what all the commands were and what they meant. I had been paying attention during my time at the boathouse, absorbing everything.

Walter occupied the *seven-seat* of the boat and gave the command for everyone to check their oars and stretchers.

He said, "Sit ready, push off!" And with that, we were far enough to allow the oars on the starboard side to easily clear the slip.

The back of their blades slapped the surface of the water.

Walter gave the command for the bow pair to "Pull us out!" and Hugh and the number two quickly set up and took several strokes to get us clear of the slip and out into the main stream of the river. There, they lightly paddled so we wouldn't drift back into the slip.

They held us about 30 yards from the slip, until the command came to, "Let her run!"

Then came the command, "All eight, sit ready."

There was a jolt as all eight of these giant human machines took a position at the bottom of their slides, and those 12-foot-long sweep oars poised in unison alongside the boat.

"Row!" came the command.

I had been in almost every kind of boat on the river to this point—either filling a seat, or being taught to row. Still, I wasn't ready for what came next.

This boat felt like it was going to leave the water and stand up on those oars!

The power coming from those men instantly sent us slashing through the water at a speed I thought impossible by a man-powered boat! With each stroke, they moved ten times the distance I could move a gig with the same effort.

We were absolutely zooming through the water. It was at once frightening and exhilarating! Walter was taking the boat through its paces. He was barking commands for Power-Two, Power-Five and Power-Ten, indicating for that many stokes they should give it all they had.

What an experience!

Who were these people?!

In the time it usually took me to go a quarter mile, we were approaching the half-mile marker, which was scary, because it was a bridge we had to go under, and not hit, and it was coming fast.

A few minutes and the marker was history, and we were in a part of the river I had never seen before. That's because I couldn't make it more than three miles in any one go, so I never went past the three-mile bridge.

We were miles from the boat house and had already passed the grandstands and Peter's Island. We were coming up to the next mile mark, the Strawberry Mansion Bridge. Several minutes later, with some power commands from Walter, we were under and past the bridge.

I was getting into my groove now - listening to Walter, feeling the oars hit the water, steering at the right times and watching ahead.

The Schuylkill River is an inner-city river and you are likely to find pretty much anything in it at any time. I've seen it all: logs, trees, overturned boats and even floating bodies.

Knowing this, I was keenly aware that, at any time, there could be something in the water capable of damaging our boat.

It was then I saw it, and just in time!

Thirty yards directly ahead, bobbing just below the surface, was a slimy, rusty 55-gallon steel drum! It was like an iceberg with just the tip sticking up out of the water. I knew the 4 inches I saw was just the visible part. 99% of this thing was just below the surface, waiting to tear the side out of this thin-skinned racing boat!

Until now I had been completely silent, except to say "Ok" to what Hugh was telling me.

Something came over me!

Without hesitation, I slapped both sides of the boat with my open hands and tucked my head so my voice would be conducted down the length of the boat.

I shouted, "Weigh 'nuf!" - the command to immediately stop rowing! The forward movement was instantly checked as the oarsmen's power stopped.

I shouted, "All eight, hold water!"

Immediately, all eight oar blades dug into the water and held firm at a 90-degree angle, checking the movement of the boat and slowing it down.

The drum was about ten feet from the bow.

I shouted, "All eight, prepare to backpaddle - backpaddle HO!"

The boat lurched - the forward movement was completely checked, and the boat came to a stop.

"Let her run!" I called out.

"Sit ready to row, starboard side back paddle port side row, ready all... row!"

The boat pinwheeled to the starboard.

When I felt it was in the right direction, I called out, "Let her run!"

At this point, Hugh called to me, "What's going on?"

I shouted, "Debris in the water!"

Then I called out, "All eight, sit ready, hard on the starboard, ready all … row!"

As we made a wide forward moving turn to get back into the running lane, the 55-gallon drum could be clearly seen passing about five feet off the blades of the port side oars.

Someone said, "Whew, nice job!"

I got the boat around the drum, pointed back, straight up the river and called, "Let her run!"

I turned to Hugh and said, "Did you see that?"

He said, "No, but it's a good thing you did, nice job!"

I said, "Ok, you can take over again."

He told Walter we were clear, and Walter took over the boat again, giving commands.

The rest of the workout went without incident. Within an hour, we were back at the slip.

When we pulled alongside the slip, there were people everywhere. They were standing by the boathouse, on Penn's slip, on the grass between the boathouses and on the second-story porch of Vesper, Penn and Malta. All open areas were crowded with people!

Walter gave the command to stop rowing, and the boat slid in. Sean was waiting and grabbed one of the oars to help glide the boat in safely.

I couldn't understand why there were so many people watching us test the new boat.

I got out and grabbed the riggers to hold the boat while the oarsmen got out and removed their oars, put them in the boathouse and returned to get the boat out of the water. One by one, they came to me, patting me on the head and slapping me on the back. Each of them asked my name.

"Nice to meet you, Mike!" came the chorus.

Then Walter barked the commands to remove the boat from the water and put it back in the boathouse. Sean's dad was standing at the top of the slip, motioning to him. He said something to him, who came to ask me what was going on.

I told him that Walter told me to come with him to test the new boat, and about the workout and avoiding the drum. Sean ran back to report to his dad, who looked in my direction and nodded his head in approval.

I followed the eight into the boat house to wipe it down. This is the duty of the coxswain after a row, so I picked up a large towel and started toward the boat. The crew saw me coming and laughed, remarking I really had the routine now!

I was met with handshakes and pats on the back. They told me I did a great job and even picked up towels themselves to help me wipe down the boat, a show of respect to a coxswain.

At this point, the crew shared a few comments with Walter about the boat's performance and began to walk off one by one toward the locker room. I was still aware there was a huge throng of people in the place but couldn't put it together.

Walter thanked me for coxing the boat and for avoiding the drum, adding I did a great job taking command to avoid a collision.

He patted me on the shoulder and said, "See you later Mike!"

He walked off; I turned around and found everyone looking at me! I looked back, still wondering what was going on.

Sean said, "Do you know who they were?!"

"No," I replied

"That's the 1964 gold medal Olympic Eight. This is the first time they've been together as a boat since winning the Olympic gold in Tokyo."

Now I understood the crowd.

The word had gotten out; the Olympic eight was there to try out the new eight. And I had gotten a ride on the maiden voyage. I ran up to the trophy room, and sure enough, there they were in that picture above the mantle! The 1964 gold medal Olympic Eight!

I went from being some red-headed kid hanging around the slip to an instant celebrity. I was on a first-name basis with the Olympic Eight, the most celebrated crew, not just in our boathouse, but among the entire rowing community!

You see, the eight was the *big boat*, and the bigger the boat, the greater the notoriety.

Suddenly, everyone in the boathouse not only knew my name, but wanted to talk to me.

"What was it like?"

"What did they say?"

"How far did you go?"

"What happened?"

I also suddenly had gold medal coaches. Everyone wanted to give me advice. And everyone wanted to be part of coaching me every time I hit the water.

I was in big demand. Sean would always take me in the double when he went out. I was now allowed to use equipment I previously couldn't even look at or touch. And my rowing skills greatly improved because of the attention.

Hugh took a particular interest in me and made it a point to watch everything I did, from running, to lifting weights, to pulling the oar. He was a great coach too. He not only had the creds; he had a humble and nurturing way.

Walter was also attentive. He had helped coach the boat to Olympic gold in 1964. His style was different but equally valuable – including racing strategies with personal coaching.

All but one of the crew and the coxswain had shown up to try out the new boat. Since they were short an oarsman, Walter took his seat and made me the coxswain.

Sean's dad and older brothers, who were all national champs, never missed an opportunity to point out some detail or help me polish up my style.

In this environment, my skills improved exponentially!

Chapter 21

Summer of '67

I was learning not just how to row but also how to pick up tidbits peripheral to the sport. I would watch, as a fly-on-the-wall, the gamesmanship among the crews and individuals in the boat house, paying close attention to the cut-fights and name-calling.

Gamesmanship was something new to me. I could see it happening, but I wasn't good at it - Yet!

I was often exposed to the banter of a group much older, among Sean's other brothers on trips with their crew on their university's crew bus and as a fly on the wall of the discussions in the car among the coaches during the commutes between home and the boathouse.

One member of the boat house, Ken, was brusque and vocal, and I avoided him as much as possible. His idea of gamesmanship was unsophisticated and consisted largely of verbally diminishing everyone around him.

One race day, I was at the grandstands, and Sean said, "Ken is going to give us a ride back to the boathouse."

'Ugh,' I thought, but it was better than walking. I followed Sean to where Ken was waiting in his brand new sports car - a graduation present from his parents or grandparents - the whole idea of which was mind-blowing to me.

As I got in, I congratulated him on the car. He spent the trip to the boathouse alternatively complaining about the car, wasn't the right color, wasn't what he really wanted, or some other nonsense.

He shifted gears to complaining; he was peeved by not having been part of any winning crew to date, and he was anxious for the summer season to prove himself.

These things were good to know. I filed it all away, adding intel farmed from others revealing their assessment of him as an oarsman.

I compiled intel on other potential competitors by visiting the Schuylkill Navy boathouse bulletin board, where they posted upcoming races with the competitors' names and affiliations. I made use of this by attending all the races I could to put names with faces and see for myself the individual oarsmen's styles and capabilities.

And, I was always standing ready to take any vacant seat in a boat either for a practice run or actual completion.

I began to be drafted for empty seats in some of the quads and got my first racing experience in what were called *match races* - informal races run by the Schuylkill Navy to give novices experience and pit them against others their age and skill level.

Chapter 22

Noel Harrison

I think it was this summer I was approached by Walter with a new ask. He told me there were some folks coming to the boathouse to do a TV show, which included celebrities taking a boat out onto the river. I was asked to familiarize them with the equipment and do some training to get them ready for the shoot.

I took this on the same as I would have if Walter had asked me to get something out of the trunk of his car. What I mean is: celebrities making a TV show impressed me about the same as the other task.

I just did not relate to these folks any differently. I didn't know they deserved special treatment.

When they showed up the next day, I recognized one of them as Mike Douglas. Mike Douglas had a daytime TV talk show popular in Philadelphia in the 1960s. I assumed he would be the same in person, as he was on the show, congenial and pleasant. In person, however, he was different! Once I realized this, I kept my distance.

The other was someone with whom I was not familiar. I was told he was from England. I expected him to be the stereotype of stuffy and aloof.

I was completely wrong.

This gentleman was just that, a perfect gentleman. He was soft-spoken, approachable, and congenial. We immediately hit it off.

He was introduced as Noel Harrison.

I was unfamiliar with his work, but he mentioned his dad, Rex Harrison, was also an actor. His name I knew and was familiar with a number of his movies.

Noel and I got to know each other. He let me know he had rowed in England but needed a refresher. He also needed to become familiar with the equipment we used, as there were some subtle differences between the American and English boats.

I took him out on the river in a double, a boat where each oarsman has two oars. I took him up a few miles, until he had the feel for the boat, and it was obvious; this was all he needed.

During the trip, he told me that the show was being filmed for broadcast later in the week, and the idea was that he and Mike Douglas would row in a double together, and this would be captured on film for discussion during the show.

After he felt comfortable with the boat, we returned to the boathouse, where other folks were dealing with Mike Douglas. They were trying to familiarize him with rowing so he could get in the boat with Noel and row long enough for them to shoot a short scene.

I was glad I had Noel. I had the easy part.

Noel thanked me and returned to the klatch, which included the producer and the film crew. The interaction there was interesting with this cultured, articulate Englishman among the rest.

I accompanied the film crew in the motor launch as they shot the scene for the show. It took about a half hour of shooting to get about 30 seconds of airable film.

After they left the boathouse, I was asked by a number of folks about the event. I told them in my usual succinct manner that I showed them how to use a double and watched as they filmed the show.

This was not what they really wanted. They wanted *juicy details*.

The best I could do was to say, "Noel Harrison was nice. I stayed away from everyone else."

This is where the devastating handicap surfaces. Are you keeping up with all the connections I'm squandering?

Imagine if I had known the value of these types of relationships: Olympic gold medal winners, city council members, T.V. and Hollywood celebrities, not to mention rich folks, which these folks also happen to be.

Imagine, if I had leveraged all this.

Keep reading; it gets worse.

Chapter 23

Detention – Girls to the Rescue

"Everything was going fine, until you hit me back!"

– *Ann Azzole*

After the summer of '67, it was back to grade school for the final year.

Detention in grade school was like punishment in the army. It could be for any reason or for no reason. It could be for not having your homework, or talking in line. It could be for turning your head in Sunday mass during the sermon, or not having your rosaries in class.

It could also be for the enforcement of some unknown rule as a pretense to conscript enough *volunteers* to clean the classroom at the end of the day.

So, the fact that I don't remember the exact reason for us being in this particular detention is not surprising. I do remember that it was a blanket detention, because there were brownies in there who had never seen detention.

Some of the usual suspects were there. Dolores and Kathy were in there as well, indicating they had been at the wrong place at the wrong time.

Kathy told me we were both there because I couldn't keep my mouth shut in class, but I think she made that up. (This is sarcasm - just in case you missed it.)

I was doing whatever punitive task had been assigned, writing some mindless crap. Dolores was in the front of the room wiping down the board. Dolores may have been there as an actual volunteer to help with the cleaning, but considering the prior slapping event, maybe not.

Some additional infractions developed, and Richard was now in front of the room with the nun administering the appropriate lecture, when suddenly she noticed his face displaying some *disgraceful* expression. Disgraceful was one of many all-purpose nun-words for something violating the nun-code.

We were 14 at this point; it was close to the end of the school year, and grade school was anticlimactic. The windows were open; Spring was in the air, and we were officially sick of the whole business.

I was half paying attention when the volume in front of the room suddenly increased. Richard, like the rest of us, had had enough of this whole thing, and was not appropriately responding to the important lesson being proffered by the nun.

Since her verbal admonitions were not sinking in, in her mind, she had no alternative way to go. She hit him a few times, which he took, but she still didn't like the look on his face and told him so.

He hardened the look.

Dolores, who had been wiping the board, stepped back out of the way and into a ringside seat. I watched the other heads in the class turn toward the action; some stood.

The nun grabbed him by both ears. She was a head taller and outweighed him by at least 30 lbs.

Now, I've seen this type of torture many times, and I've pulled my own ears to get an idea of what it's like. I didn't pull them hard. It hurts!

She was dragging Richard around the front of the room by his ears, throwing his entire body weight from side to side using his ears as handles.

In an effort to keep his ears attached to his head, he grabbed her by the wrists, infuriating her, because only she was allowed to touch. She became angry, pulling him from side to side, unloading broadsides of invective at him.

Finally, Richard had had enough and shouted, "Get off of me!" and broke away and straight-armed her!

She sounded the alarm, and almost immediately, she was joined by several other nuns who subdued Richard by beating him to the floor. They took him out of the room.

The next day came the inquest. Each of us was taken one by one into a room and interrogated by Mother with the nun at her side. We all returned similar answers.

"I was looking out the window."

"I was looking at my paper – doing my assignment." And other nebulous, useless responses.

Questions like, "Did you see Richard hit sister?" or, "What did he do?" were similarly answered. We were consistent and said, "We did not see Richard hit the nun."

However, remember the brownies?

Dolores said, "I was standing right there. Richard never hit her."

Kathy gave a similar answer. We were galvanized not to implicate Richard, but they went even further. They not only would not validate the claim he hit her, they vindicated him.

They stated unequivocally that he did *not* hit her!

Since then, I've been through riots, gun fights, knife fights, fights with multiple attackers, serial killers, and vicious heinous felons, but nothing I've ever done is as brave as what those girls did that day!

They not only pulled Richard out of the fire, they ensured an end to the whole behavior.

By contradicting the nun's story, they did several things: They got Richard off the hook, and they introduced doubt. The entire faculty crew was bemused.

Was the nun a liar?

The girls they asked had always been upright and reliable; would they actually lie?

If they were telling the truth, the nun was in the wrong, but if they were lying, that was intimidating. We were showing a powerful solidarity - displaying a loyalty to the group instead of the faculty.

It got them thinking. They were afraid to touch us now. What if the entire class wolf-packed them the next time they hit someone? They knew we wouldn't back them up; that was for sure!

They were gridlocked. They could do nothing but wait 'til we were gone. We were now a force to be reckoned with, and they slinked off. They never regained their former strength, and the idea of beating us became a thing of the past.

Those girls were then, are now, and will always be my heroes!

Chapter 24

Independence Day

"(He is)...only himself. And is not an active member of a greater organism which he is influenced by and which he influences constantly."

– Hans Asperger

The *ability to recognize patterns*, *attention to detail* and *legendary focus*, thought of by us as positives, consistently appear among the long list of negatives associated with AS. When these positives combine, the amalgam is powerful. It leads to comments from normal people like, "The worse things are, the better you get." and "How do you solve puzzles so easily?"

Normal people separate enigma into categories. Everyday problems, puzzles, and mysteries are seen as different. I see them all the same; I solve them the same, and I'm often castigated for not emoting appropriately.

As something of an enigma myself, I've made a good living out of solving other people's problems. Opportunities are enigmas turned inside out, and when they appear, I see them as clearly as I see stars in the daytime.

I returned to the boat house for the summer season as grade school disappeared rapidly in my wake. Among my distinguished rowing coaches and mentors, I flourished, and I stood on the slip, waiting for opportunities to surface.

No one does the 4th of July like Philadelphia, and the Independence Day Regatta is a big part of the festivities. The boat houses are sporting new flags, and red white and blue bunting decorates the grandstands.

We dye the river red white and blue ... just kidding!

The regatta is much anticipated in the national rowing community, because winners are awarded engraved gold wristwatches. And, it's one of the few national regattas held each year in which an oarsman can ascend the ranks from Junior to Intermediate to Senior Oarsman.

I was educated early about the importance of this race, but the idea of actually competing in the 4th of July Regatta was something I saw as far in the future for me - maybe. Everyone wanted to be part of it, so a newbie like me had no chance. It was not part of the schoolboy rowing schedule, so I set it aside as a wish-list item.

At the North end of Boathouse Row is the Philadelphia Girls Rowing Club. I saw the girls on the river often, but never saw them race. Apparently, they had been politicking, and the Schuylkill Navy announced they would add the first-ever *mixed-race* to the 1968 regatta.

I was a fly-on-the-wall in the locker room when it was announced.

The manly men in the locker room were compiling a:

List of *Bad* Things about the Race: (In order of bad to worst.)

- Since it was an added event, there would be no time to order watches, so the winners would receive regular medals, not watches.
- It was a shortened 1,000-meter race, so their pride would be adversely affected.
- There were girls in the race.

Most stated emphatically that they would *not* enter, which to me *screamed* opportunity!

I compiled *my*:

List of *Good* Things about the Race: (In order of good – better – best.)

- It was an opportunity to be an owner of a rare 4th of July medal, not a watch.
- It was a shortened 1,000-meter race, so it was shorter.
- There were girls in the race.

This was a rare opportunity, if I could wrangle a way into it. They had already formed two boats and were looking for a third, the minimum number needed to add the race. Some folks on the periphery of the issue (some other odd ducks) approached me to join a boat they were putting together. I readily agreed.

We threw our hat into the ring, or water, or whatever - we volunteered.

The idea gave the locker room a good laugh - a good sign their guard was down.

We approached Walter with our boat, two men (actually one man and a boy – me) and two women. A wry smile crept across his face, and he looked over my head at the two other crews laughing in the locker room.

He pulled out his clipboard and wrote us in!

It was justifiably expected - we would come in dead last.

Gamesmanship and speculation rose to a crescendo as race day approached. The two other boats purposely ignored us during their gamesmanship sessions.

The message was, "You have absolutely no chance of winning, so we're not even wasting time trying to game you!" They weren't alone in this belief.

Much of the Gamesmanship was initiated by Ken, who was in one of the two other crews scheduled to race.

You remember Ken – *Mr. Sports-car*.

The line ran: One of the other boats would win, because they were all seasoned, were older and carried 30 to 40 pounds more muscle per crew member.

Everyone agreed this would be a classic *two-boat race*. They really did have everything going for them. They spent weeks circling each other posturing.

I climbed a tree and watched, and our crew brainstormed a plan.

Having spent the past year among the other crews, I was familiar with their usual race plans. I suggested that since we were all skinny, we had one advantage: skinny oarsmen are able to maintain a higher stroke count. And as luck would have it, the highest stroke count can be maintained in a quad, the type of skull in which we were racing.

We decided we had one chance: come off the starting line at a high-power stroke and maintain as long as we could. The other crews were too heavy to be able to maintain a high stroke, and would execute a familiar plan, powering off the start and holding back something for the end.

If we took the lead, the race was too short for them to be able to catch us. All we had to do was take the lead and sit off their bows until we crossed the finish line.

We agreed it was our one chance.

Race organizers had the idea that all the strokes should be girls. I think their narrow logic was that if men set the stroke, the girls wouldn't be able to keep up.

They got it all backasswards.

They didn't consider that girls were capable of a much higher stroke count. Ours hit a count that was the highest I ever experienced. I thought she was going to row my arms off!

I heard after the race that she hit over 36 strokes per minute. My normal stroke was 24 – prior to this race, my highest was 28.

When the race started, the other boats came off the line executing what they were accustomed to: *a 2,000-meter race plan*. They did a Power-Ten off the line and eased up.

Once they did, they fell behind our Power-1,000 meters.

They panicked when they realized we were in the lead, but it was too late.

Maybe it's mean, but I really enjoyed the looks on their faces as we pulled away. Remember, when you're rowing, you're going backwards, so the losers are where you can watch them.

So, in the end, it *was* a *two-boat race*. We watched the other boats compete for second place, from our vantage point, in first place.

Chapter 25

The Debrief

Ken was especially mortified by being beaten by us.

Gamesmanship is appropriate before a race, but anything afterwards comes across as sour grapes. True to form, shortly after the race, he delivered his trainwreck.

Waiting until he had a full audience in the locker room, he confronted me loudly, exclaiming, "Well, you really screwed yourself now!"

"Excuse me?" I said.

I still didn't know; I was supposed to have lost.

"Now you're an *intermediate oarsman*," Ken replied. "You won't win any races for a long time now, because all of your competition will be bigger and more experienced than you!"

All eyes turned to me.

I checked the faces of the crowd, turned to Ken and said, "You mean like this race?"

I thought he would lose his mind! Everyone laughed, and he stormed off.

I could never understand this line of thinking. I should hold back and not win, so I might win later? That's like people who say you shouldn't make more money, because you'll have to pay more taxes!

And he was wrong. It wasn't *a long time* until my next win.

Lessons from this encounter? Bias caused the other boats to be beaten!

Quads were considered undesirable boats and often disparaged as *girl boats*. The girls' races were 1,000 meters long.

Remember the idea of looking for any and all advantages to win?

I remembered the advice my dad gave me years earlier. He was known as a great dancer. When I asked him why all the women liked to dance with him, he said, "If a woman wants me to lead, I lead. If they want to lead, I follow. So, they all like the way I dance."

I felt, if this was a girls' race, in a girls' boat, and the strokes were all girls, we should probably row like girls. All we had to do was follow them.

The men in the other boats were trying to make the girls row their race plan. I rowed the plan our stroke designed. She was accustomed to a 1000-meter race at a high stroke count in a quad. Why would I try to change her style?

Normal people, not just men, find it difficult to let someone else lead. I don't have that paradigm to overcome. As I pointed out earlier, with a female role model capable of doing anything, I could easily follow the stroke set by a girl.

The other boats fought it, so we beat them.

Aspies are born immune to bias. When adults, or peers for that matter, try to attach bias to a group or person, we have to see it ourselves. We won't take the word of the crowd over our own experiences.

Hans Asperger observed about his boys, *"(He is)...only himself. And is not an active member of a greater organism which he is influenced by and which he influences constantly."*[4]

Common sense prevails. It made only sense to follow the girls' lead in a girl's boat in a race in which they normally competed.

---

[4] *Die "Autistischen Psychopathen" im Kindesalter* - Hans Asperger, Tranlated and annotated by Uta Frith – *"Autism and Asperger syndrome"* edited by Uta Frith – Cambridge University Press 1991 Pp. 37 - 92

Chapter 26

David

I met David in Mrs. Soyka's third-grade class. I liked him immediately for many of the same reasons I liked Kathy. He was to become the most popular boy in school, was easily the best-looking, and attracted girls like gravity.

He was easy to talk to, was always in a good mood, had an even temper, and, like Kathy, was, and still is, one of the smartest people I know.

We were casual friends in grade school. In high school, we were inseparable. He got me through that mess, as Kathy had gotten me through grade school.

I introduced him to rowing; which brings me to his athletic ability. Yeah, he had that too. He could play any sport: baseball, football, basketball – his favorite, and, of course, rowing.

I brought him to the boathouse after I had been rowing a year, and a year later, he eclipsed my ability by winning the nationals.

It's not an exaggeration to say I would not have made it through high school without his constant companionship, advice and help!

His sense of humor alone was worth knowing him.

He would drop a remark with just the right timing to make people lose their minds – in a good way. I would see this look coming over him and think, "Ruh ro." Then he would deliver. He could make my older sister cry laughing.

I never got tired of this: If we went to a dance, I would find a vantage point at the edge of the dance floor. A girl would come straight at him and say, "Wanna dance?"

They would get on the floor, and while they were dancing, another girl would come up to him and tuck a folded piece of paper in his pocket with her phone number on it. The first girl would always get an attitude, and sometimes confront the other girl. An argument would ensue.

He would turn away, but before he was able to leave the floor, a third girl would jump in to dance with him, leaving the other two arguing on the dance floor. He would get home, throw two or three folded pieces of paper in the trash and go to bed.

Funniest thing ever!

He was an artist, and participated in the high school talent show performing Simon and Garfunkel. One day, my father showed him his trumpet. Within a few minutes, he was in the driveway, belting notes from the horn! He had a tune going within a few more.

He also drew and painted. He painted the entire solar system on the ceiling of his room and painted a portrait of Joni Mitchell, which he presented to her backstage after a performance.

I don't have any regrets in life, but emotional empathy would have been nice. Not for my sake but to know when to do something nice for someone else. He picks up on these things and does something nice and unexpected, but I don't get the cues.

I was one of six kids and my family would routinely forget my birthday - like every year. Every year, regardless of where I was, or how long I'd been out of touch (another of my faults), my phone would ring, and David would wish me happy birthday.

My wife and kids have picked up where my family left off and routinely forget, but not David. He always remembers.

He threw me my only birthday party for my fifteenth birthday, and after I whined, they forgot again. He had a nice group of folks from school attend. It was one of the most pleasant surprises of my entire lifetime.

Chapter 27

High School – Day One

The first day of high school, I got Kathy mad at me on the trolley before we even left the neighborhood. I have no idea what I said, but I filed the event.

Years later, when I played back the video, I could see the anxiety on her face that first day. She was the person who lit up a room with her energy, but this morning, the idea of leaving the neighborhood, going into the unknown, and becoming a fish in a larger pond was having an obvious effect.

When I saw this happen in other instances in later years, I was able to apply the lesson.

As this was just another trolly ride for me, I was just as flat as ever when I said something that pushed her over the edge. She blasted me! My response was some remark that made her feel worse, and she moved away.

This is a clear example of this condition earning its reputation as a *devastating handicap.*

I had absolutely no emotional empathy for Kathy. I could see her face was not its usual happy image, but I could not translate it. Instead of saying something comforting, I said something inappropriate and got nailed for it on the spot!

At the time, my confusion was off the chart, though, because in the same instant, we approached a new and larger neighborhood where many new faces got on the trolly.

By faces, I mean girls.

As they boarded the trolly, a fellow student was making what I felt to be incredibly obnoxious remarks to the new girls. He was introducing himself as "a part-time student, full-time *skin-man.*"

But Kathy had no reaction to his behavior at all.

I filled in the blanks on this piece later as well. He was a known clown. Kathy had no expectation; he would not act the clown. It was his persona.

I, however, was expected to be an ally and be supportive. This difference made his behavior, which I think was intrinsically worse, acceptable, and mine unacceptable to the point where I had to be severely remonstrated.

I get it now.

Chapter 28

Trolly Primer

After 60th Street, as the trolly left our parish and pierced the next, we were treated to something new. The girls from beyond 60th Street!

Neighborhoods in Philadelphia are defined by location and position, so there was South Philly, SW Philly, etc., narrowed for us by parish.

Much in the way New Orleans evolved from the overwhelmingly Catholic influence into political parishes, Philadelphia was divided into religious parishes. We were in the SW Philadelphia in Good Shepherd parish; the folks along the # 13 Trolly route closer to Center City were in West Phila, in Most Blessed Sacrament or MBS parish.

We also skirted Saint Francis de Sales parish, but MBS contributed the most. MBS was the largest parish in the Archdiocese.

Good Shepherd contributed 1,200 kids to the archdiocese; MBS contributed over 5,000.

After the initial greetings, additional bonding occurred in the back of the trolleys with the sharing of ciggies – ironically referred to by the participants as *nails* – short for *coffin nails*. The pall of smoke contributed to the already overwhelming stench of new uniforms, sweat, BO and mildew.

I dreaded this part of the day. Being stuck in a closed space with cigarette smoke made me sick. The driver was supposed to stop this, but I guess he felt the responsibility of piloting a 28,000-pound rusting, clanking pile of iron with 50 souls on board was responsibility enough.

The ride to school was not complicated. Board the # 13 trolly at 65th Street, make sure you get a transfer-stub, get off at 49th Street. Then get on the 49 bus, which goes directly to school.

Here was the rub. The schedules for trollies in Philadelphia were nebulous. I'm sure the drivers would differ, because that was their bread and butter, but to the rest of us, you waited, the trolley came, and you got on.

The question, "When does the trolly come?" would be answered with a quizzical look, and the response, "How do I know?! Just wait for it!"

If you ran up as one was leaving and said, "I missed it!", someone would shrug and say, "So, wait for the next one."

If the next one was full, the driver would say, over the shoulders of passengers packing the doorway, "Wait for the next one!"

Trains can be operated on tight schedules because they are the only vehicles on the tracks. Trolleys and buses have to contend with cars, trucks, and people along their route. On a Saturday morning, you might get a trolley adhering to a schedule, but on weekdays, you waited for the trolley, and when one came, you got on.

But there really *was* a schedule. And, in the AM, along the routes we traveled there were just enough trollies and busses to get us to 49th and Chestnut Streets, the terminus for us, and the location of West Philadelphia Catholic HS for Boys.

There was always a crush at 49th St., where we had to transfer from the trolly to the bus, which ran north on 49th Street to Chestnut Street.

The Philadelphia Transportation Company (PTC), dedicated just enough 49 busses to accommodate the crush of students to this location. If you missed one of those, you could be in a bad way, so we packed those busses like blivets.

I can still hear and smell the Diesels straining as the busses, packed to the doors, lumbered off, teetering from side to side, because they were so overcrowded.

The dedicated busses created a safe passage to and from school, and took us out of a relatively safe enclave into one of the worst neighborhoods of West Philly. All other busses were hit or miss, meaning, if you missed the window of time in which the 49 busses packed with your droogs were traveling, you had to wait for the next one.

The next one could be hit or miss regarding safe passage.

I met Dexter Bean on one of these; *I missed the 49* occasions. If I can fit Dexter Bean into this book, I'll do that.

If not, you'll have to *wait for the next one.*

Chapter 29

Sly's Dad

When you grow up in Philly, you rely a lot on public transportation. I think this is actually a big advantage to intercity kids. They can get anywhere they want, hopping from trolly, to bus, to elevated train.

You had to know the rules: avoid certain lines - know where to sit - and not travel after dark.

Every once in a while, especially in the winter, when it got dark early, I got caught on the trolly or bus just as the undesirables were coming out. On just such an occasion, while coming home on a Saturday, having stayed too long at the boat house, I was seated just past the center door on the trolly, bouncing along, engaged in typical Aspie behavior, zoning out - reading the walls.

Want an eidetic memory demo? I was reading a poem posted among the advertisements along the wall over the windows. Remember the ads the kids threw out the windows in a previous story?

Apparently, there had been a poetry contest among middle-high school students, and several of the winners were on display in the trolly. Here's the poem I read:

The Wise Old Owl

There was an owl, lived in an oak;

The more he heard, the less he spoke;

The less he spoke, the more he heard;

If, only more were like that wise old bird!

I read that poem once, fifty years ago. Ok, that's your parlor trick for this chapter.

At the next stop, a drunk got on. You could immediately tell when a drunk got on, because everyone on the trolly got their antennae up.

He staggered down the aisle, made worse by the fact the trolly was now in forward motion and was bumping from side to side, trying to hold on and stay vertical. Well, as was inevitable, he bumped into someone, and they told him to watch where he was going.

The drunk took umbrage to this and started to tell the man off. The man told him to shut up and sit down.

The drunk announced, "I'm Sly father."

To which the man said, "What?!"

The drunk repeated, "I'm Sly father – Sly and the Family Stone father."

The other man, who was still seated, said, "I don't care who you are. Go sit down, or I'll throw you out the trolly!"

The drunk didn't listen.

The other man said, "Listen, old man. If you don't get out of my face and sit down, I'm going to throw you off this mother!"

And, because he was drunk and was important, being Sly's Father, he said, "I'd like to see you throw me off!"

When the man who had been seated stood up, I thought his head would hit the ceiling of the trolly! He must have been 6'6". He wasn't thin either. His shoulders spanned the width of the aisle.

With no further ado, he grabbed the drunk and spun him around. Walking to the center doors of the trolly, he shouted to the driver, "Open the door!"

The trolly had, by this time, come to the next corner.

As the doors opened, he took hold of the drunk's belt in the back and, in a scene from some action movie, snatched him completely off his feet.

He flung the drunk head-first, through the open door, into the street. After adding the ever-popular two-word *sendoff-expression* - and I don't mean *Bon Voyage* - he returned to his seat.

In the winter in the big city, there are often piles of snow at the sides of the street, which are assembled there by snow plows and people digging their cars out, often rising to waist level and higher. I've seen them stories high in Anchorage, Alaska, but that's another story.

At this time on that twilight Saturday in Philadelphia, they were about four feet high at this intersection. When my man threw Sly's Father *out the door*, he landed head-first into a traffic-darkened grimy mound of snow with his body sticking out from the shoulders down. When the trolly pulled away, he passed by my window and quickly disappeared from my view with his legs and arms flapping in the air!

Not much respect for Sly's Father!

Chapter 30

Soup Sandwich

"One man's heaven is another man's hell."

– Olde English Proverb

I like precision, so I have mixed feelings about cliché. I like cliché in the proper context, because it adds color to a conversation. I especially like clichés when I can see them in real life because they provide the bridge I need to fully understand the richer meaning.

The subject of high school came up the other day at breakfast, and my wife said, "I loved high school. It was the best time of my life."

Her experience was heaven.

If I had to characterize high school today in as few words as possible, I would have to go with *soup sandwich.* I consulted several thesauruses (if that's even a word) and couldn't find anything appropriate that wasn't vulgar, so I used this.

Keep in mind – this is my experience with my not-so-normal brain processing everything.

High school was the beginning of a confusing roller coaster ride lasting a decade. I don't mean to say high school lasted ten years; the lost years of my life just started here and continued for five years after.

Aspies are considered little professors and mature in grade school. At the end of freshman year of high school, at about age 15, things start to unravel. By this time, the social skills apparatus in the normal brain is packed with 15 years of information, activating the ability to unconsciously or automagically handle social situations.

Normal people began to mature in this time period, and relative roles switched, where they began to mature, and I was left behind. I entered high school as a relatively mature child and left it as a clueless adolescent.

When you're a little professor, you can talk to adults as an adult. Many of them find it alternately amusing and fascinating. This characteristic of AS fits into the post-grammar school period, like screen doors on a submarine!

Those facilities and skills were never required, tested, or utilized before were suddenly needed. Emotions, less used, were less resistant to social drama. Study habits never formed were suddenly required to survive.

This happened so fast; it caused emotional whiplash and head-shaking confusion. Previously the *know-it-all* and mature one, I was suddenly off balance and out of touch with what was happening around me.

The complicated social structure hit me as though the rules, the language, and basically, the fabric of my world had suddenly been torn. I compare it to the times when the earth's magnetic poles are suddenly reversed. It was *that* sudden and traumatic. I could not process intellectually as fast as what the normals were doing automatically.

I hit a wall.

Everyone was reading from a new script, and I was without a copy!

Normal people were characters in a video game with guns that never ran out of ammo, while I had to stop, think, and reload the appropriate unique ammo every time a new monster appeared.

Social situations being the monsters, and they were everywhere – all the time!

High school is meant to prepare you for the work world, which is 60% social ability and 40% technical ability. I reached a peak of social development at 17 and remain there still.

Sure, I can cope, but I have to do this consciously with the front part of my brain, which is like a computer that never turns off with a constantly spinning hard drive searching for data.

In high school, things and events made less and less sense, and drifted from the concrete to the nebulous. Plans collapsed, footing became tenuous, morality started to flicker; the ground began to move, and there was nothing to cling to.

And, in the 1960s, there was no refuge. No one knew what was happening. Not I, not my parents, not the teachers, nor the doctors. I felt like I was banished to a raft and was furiously paddling to stay close to the shore while everyone else remained on dry land.

It started for me at the end of freshman year. It got worse and worse as the years progressed and didn't slow down until I entered the police academy at 23, when, although I was still living on the raft, I was finally able to tie it to something solid.

All I could do now was hold on and try to negotiate the hell that was high school.

Chapter 31

Homeroom

I didn't want to hate high school. I moderated expectations, as I now knew that I was endowed with more than those after the kindergarten and grade school lessons, and am tempted to say that in that comic comparison of degrees of BS, MS, and PhD as Bull Shit, More of the Same and Piling it higher and Deeper the same progression of confusion and disconnection was establishing itself in the way Kindergarten, Grade School and High School progressed.

I'm searching for a better word than abrupt, because to me, and perhaps simply because it's me, it's missing sufficient force. It needs added nuance of explosive, disruptive, and traumatic, because high school went to work on me even before I left my neighborhood and hit low, hard, and often.

It also wasted no time preemptively assaulting my senses - day one.

There is an urge that has to be constantly managed when you suffer from this condition. (See how I did that – used a word to elicit empathy, so I can proceed on to do something provocative. I learned this from normal people.)

Did you ever notice; people in certain professions appear pretty consistently different from those in other professions?

Reductio ad absurdum: The acting profession and modeling profession have folks with a certain appearance. Real life, not so much.

We walked into our first homeroom class, as the first class of our first day. As we settled into our seats, one of the boys went to the front of the room.

"Listen up!" he said, "My brother had this guy last year. Here's the deal. He'll ask everyone to meet him one-on-one. No one go alone! Take someone with you, and when he tells them to wait outside, tell him no!"

Then he sat down.

David and I looked at each other baffled. I had no context for what our classmate just said, until our homeroom teacher slithered in the door.

Dressed head to toe in black, sporting a greasy vampire hair-do, complexion to match, pants a size too tight, and shoes resembling black laced duck bills, his appearance evoked a visceral reaction.

Speaking with a lisp, he paced the front of the class, continually rubbing his pale hands hung from stooped shoulders.

When he walked, he held his thighs together, which suggested an image of him squeezing himself with each step he took. He held his upper thighs so tightly that they had to walk around one another.

If you got anywhere within reach, he would immediately touch you, and you had to forcefully remove his hands. I blanched when he called my name. Blanching for a redhead is like whitening chalk!

He had a note for me. The note instructed me to go to the vice-principal's office, and when I put out my hand to take it, he slid his rat claws over my skin, making me queasy.

I don't like to be touched generally, a stereotype with some validity. I especially didn't like being touched by certain people. This guy was their archetype. I pulled back my hands in an involuntary revulsion and left with the note. (When I proofread this – I shudder involuntarily.)

This creep show was our introduction to high school, and the day had just started.

Chapter 32

Forcing a Square Peg

The Vice-Principal had a strikingly Gollum-like appearance, which I suppose could have allowed him some acting opportunities, but that's a bit off-topic.

I mentioned earlier that everything had a nickname. This includes people. In a coming chapter, I'll draw some distinct lines between generations that were in close proximity during my early years. Among these generations, sometimes only a few years apart, there were significant differences.

Differences in the way we thought – subsequently in the way we acted.

One of the norms that shifted while I was young was the idea of nicknames. It seemed to me the generation before ours gave everything and everyone a nickname. I'm not talking about shortened names like Dick for Richard or Bob for Robert but descriptive, often belittling nicknames.

This practice seemed to wane in our generation or at least soften into descriptive but neutral, often affirming - sometimes complimentary nicknames, but most were just shortened names for someone's proper name.

Kathleen was Kathy, Richard was Rich, Miriam was Mimi, and Claire was - well, Claire.

There were a few with unique nicknames like John Fadgen, whom you'll read about in my cop book, whom we affectionately referred to as Fudge – a twist on his last name. Some of us, for whatever reason, were always called by our full first names – David was always called David, and some were addressed by our entire name – even now, folks from grade school call me by my full name, but few, if any, had a pejorative nickname.

I think what was happening, as detailed in the NOTE ABOUT CLASSMATES chapter, was that these rude nicknames died with us. I went into high school fully briefed by my older brother with the existing nicknames of all of the faculty, but none of these nicknames survived the four years we attended the school. Not because we weren't clever enough to think of any. We were very creative and clever. The whole nickname thing simply got no traction with us.

I have to think; being called to the vice-principal's office on day one would rattle most people, but I'm not most people. I was preoccupied by something my brother had said about his appearance.

When I walked into the office and all the while he prattled on about how he was going to push a square peg (me) into a round hole (engineering), all I could think was – Chicklet Teeth.

He had large spaces between each of his teeth. He had a tooth, then a space where there should have been a tooth, then another tooth. This was so pronounced; he was known as Chicklet Teeth.

And while I never heard any of my class use this expression; my older brother referred to him exclusively as Chicklet Teeth. When I first met him, the vice-principal, that is, I found it hard to concentrate on what he said.

My instinct was to laugh, but I knew that would initiate something extremely bad, so I focused. When I focus - people think I've zoned out. This is among the AS world, something labeled legendary focus. I can sit and monitor everything going on on a street corner in Manhattan, but when I focus, it's like a laser.

I was distracted because I was supposed to be taking this whole thing seriously, and all I could focus on was his teeth!

Since my two older brothers, bless their electrical-engineering-math-and-science-award-winning-hearts, had graduated from my high school a few years before me, the vice-principal was familiar with the family and was now helping them with the grand design.

I had looked forward to the first day of high school as I enthusiastically filled out the supplied course request form during the summer with my dream courses of art, music, and foreign languages.

I excitedly shared this with Mom. If I play back the tape now, I see an uneasy look on Mom's face, a clue I unfortunately missed.

I made the mistake of leaving the request form lying on my desk.

Mom had apparently called to preempt the whole initiative.

In the one-on-one with the vice-principle, he described the course of study I *would* pursue. He took the liberty of designing it personally, and efficiently crossed out my selections, and squeezed the correct course names between the lines on the original form, saving paper and time.

Why waste anything?

Taking the place of these useless courses were things like physics, chemistry, advanced English, and algebra. I was allowed to keep German, which surprised me, because it didn't seem to fit, but no other foreign language made the cut.

So began freshman year at The West Philadelphia Catholic High School for Boys. (And only boys.)

In various places around the school were small blue and white pennants with burrs on them.

That's because our school colors were blue and white.

And -

Our school mascot was a Chestnut tree burr.

No, that's not a typo.

The names of the streets in the center of Philly were named for trees; a chicken-and-egg scenario where one wasn't sure which was there first. Walnut Street was lined with Walnut trees, Locust Street with Locust trees; you get the idea.

Our high school was on Chestnut Street, and since ripe chestnuts are contained inside a prickly burr, we were The Burrs.

Other schools were named for cool predators like sea hawks, jaguars, or pirates.

We were named for tree flotsam, which clung to the soles of your shoes.

This led to confusion among us Burrs, but provided rival schools a war cry at sporting events.

At any given sporting event, the opposing teams' cheerleaders would initiate the chant, "What the hell's a burr?!" leading us to ponder, "What the hell was a burr?!"

I like to look for the positive side in every situation. The thought occurs; since we were a religious school, and the Burning Bush was a Shittah tree, had the school been on a street lined with Shittah trees, we could have been The Flaming Shitts!

Less bristly than The Burrs at least.

Among ourselves, our family, and in the neighborhood, we referred to the school as West. When asked by other Philadelphians where we went to school we would reply, West Catholic. I never heard anyone use the word Burrs, aside from the cheerleaders, of course.

Among the many places I would have liked to have been a fly on the wall, the meeting where they conceived burr as a mascot still ranks high.

Chapter 33

Meet Tigger

From what I've seen in teen movies, gym class is not something many folks enjoy. I was agnostic about it. It was just another wasted hour, the only difference being a shower at the end.

As I was assigned to an all-academic curriculum, the term used for STEM in the '60s, I had no time for art, music, or anything else time-wasting and non-academic, so how they got gym in there; I'll never tell you.

And, since the good brothers had used a top-secret algorithm to design my schedule, I also found myself the only freshman in a sophomore gym class.

I have to spend a minute on that logic. I can't get an exemption from gym, because the requirement is set in stone with some bureaucracy, but somehow I can be in the sophomore class. I'm in sophomore and junior math and science classes, so there must have been some thinking behind it, because the idea that it was solely schedule-based would just be silly.

Aside from a senate inquiry (tongue-in-cheek), it would probably be impossible to figure it out. And, it would probably cause some kind of irreparable damage to the logic center of the brain, if actually explained.

I argued that athletes should be exempt from gym, but you already know how that went.

As a freshman, I was an instant curiosity. Some thought I had transferred in, because the idea of a freshman in their midst did not compute. The treatment from the other students ranged from idle curiosity to outright shunning.

I had no issue with the latter.

One particular animated individual who would remind you of the character Tigger in Winnie the Pooh, in that he was constantly moving, bouncing, coming and going, was Frankie.

Frankie was short, vibrant, and wiry with limitless energy. His shirt was way too long, and he would pull his gym pants halfway down to annoy the teacher and make it appear as if he had six-inch legs.

He bounced up the first morning and said, "Who are you? I've never seen you before."

I had to revolve around an axis to keep the conversation going, as Frankie danced, bobbed, and weaved like a boxer. I told him my name and explained I was a freshman.

"You look like someone who just came back from basic training," Frankie said, indicating my physique.

Trying not to get dizzy, I followed him as he circumnavigated my position. To explain the physique, I told him about rowing.

When he heard this, he exclaimed, "Do you know Sean? There is this kid named Sean who rows. He's in one of my classes."

When I responded that I did, Frankie declared an immediate bond. He made it a point to touch base with me at the beginning of each class and volunteered himself as my partner whenever some class activity required. He would also check on me, if he saw me in the cafeteria or the hall.

Frankie was the kind of good guy who took you under his wing and served as a sort of Archangel. Whether I felt I needed it or not, if Frankie saw someone interacting with me in a way he deemed inappropriate, he would immediately insert himself.

My physique apparently had been noticed by the gym teacher as well. Just after Frankie bounced away, the gym teacher Mr. Exercise, approached with two questions: He wanted to know why I was there and what had I been doing to look as I did.

I told him about the scheduling issue as an explanation for a freshman in his class, and told him about rowing. He took an immediate interest.

Picture F. Lee Ermey, remove all the cursing and shouting, and you have Mr. Exercise.

He said, "I have only one requirement for you. Show up for roll call."

"But," he added, "If you could do me a favor."

I'm a sucker for a favor.

"What?" I asked.

He said, "Each year, there is a competition at the Marine Base at the Navy Yard. It consists of all of the PT exercises the Marines do at Boot Camp. I would like you to enter this competition."

"Ok," I said.

I gave this my best shot, but apparently, I wasn't built for this. I was always active physically and got athletic beginning around age 10. I tried all kinds of sports. But it wasn't until I began rowing that I found my niche.

My body was purpose-built for rowing. There was a popular book out at this time that had an image on the front cover. When I first saw the picture, I thought it was a picture of me!

It's a picture of a man standing naked against a desert background, as I often did – not! He has a clearly defined muscle structure and is thick in the arms and legs. Notable are the large calves, thick upper legs with just enough swell at the hips to accommodate them. It is also notable that although his arms are thick and strong, he does not have the conventional wide shoulders.

The picture shows someone reminiscent of Michelangelo's David vs. the then popular "V" shaped chest, huge shoulders, and tiny waist of a body builder.

While an asset in rowing, a set of legs this size worked against the regimen designed by Mr. Exercise. Marines are big into pushups and pullups. They include these in their competition, along with a rope climb and other exercises meant to demonstrate upper body strength.

So, although somewhat disappointed that I was not a good candidate for the calisthenics competition, Mr. Exercise still appreciated that I was health-minded and honored a requirement of just showing up. This allowed me the option of checking in at the beginning of class and then going to study or to work in the bookstore.

As long as I showed up for the required PT tests, I was good to go.

Chapter 34

Ripples from the Greatest Generation

The ripple effect metaphor is genius. You easily see the ripple created by a stone thrown into still water move away and touch everything in its path. And, you see, the effects diminish with distance and time.

Throwing another stone into the water accentuates the metaphor, as the new ripple moves out and effects everything in its path, including the ripples created by the first stone and, the secondary ripples created by everything they touched, and so on.

People go through life being affected by many ripples. Where they were raised, how they were raised, and by whom. I was raised by the Greatest Generation. That came with responsibilities.

I mentioned earlier that most of my interactions growing up were with adults, and most of them were members of the Greatest Generation. My parents were part of this generation, with my dad born in 1912 and my mom in 1920. Both lived through WWII. The confluence of events culminating in that perfect (shit) storm created ripples on the largest scale in history.

I'll paint a picture…

The term baby boom is thrown around like it was a singular event. There were actually two baby booms. The minor boomers were WWII babies. The BOOMERS were Korean War Babies. Many in both tiers of the boom were parented by the Greatest Generation.

The Greatest Generation was preceded by the Lost Generation, those unfortunates who were the primary participants in WWI, the great war, the war to end all wars. They were born between 1883 and 1900. They were lost in the sense that they were considered disoriented, wandering, and directionless in spirt after surviving WWI.

I would add, that if the lives and characters in movies representing the era are at all accurate, many were also cursed with dubious moral footing.

The incessant shelling within the confined spaces of the European trenches rendered many WWI veterans shell-shocked, and many presented the appearance of shuttering zombies.

My wife's grandfather came home from WWI, went to bed, and never got out!

Others exhibited the behavior that begat WWII, that is, unflinchingly amoral and monstrous. Some noteworthy WWI vets include Adolph Hitler and Benito Mussolini, both coincidentally corporals in that war and heads of state in the next one, hmmm…

Joseph Stalin, one of the architects of the Soviet Union was also a WWI vet, as was Herman Göring, the creator of the GESTAPO.

The greatest generation lived through the great depression, which we never stopped hearing about, and were also the primary participants in WWII, which we heard little about.

Primary participants mean they were the ones who did the work.

Just after the great depression, when WWII was being fought and the men were away, the birth rate in the U.S. dropped, creating the Silent Generation. These were the folks born between 1928 and 1945, sandwiched between the Great Generation and the BOOM.

Keep in mind the minor boom started when the men came back from WWII.

The BOOM started in 1950 when the men came back from the Korean War.

With both the WWII vets and the Korean Vets all home in the early 1950s - BOOM!

So, several things were at work, creating ripples. WWII was a time when the most horrid people in the world were in a position to do their horrors on a global scale. This was the first time in history that war could be brought to any place on the earth, with sufficient numbers of troops, with devastating weapons, in real time.

The Nazis and the Imperial Japanese were a real threat to everyone. They were committing atrocities on a scale never before imagined or possible, essentially committing industrial murder. And, since their leaders were part of the lost generation, their morals were non-existent.

The Greatest Generation, who were expected to vanquish these monsters, had to evolve the skills and mindset required to slay dragons. They were not powder puffs.

When they came back home they were not disoriented, wandering and directionless. They were aggressive, driven, and limitless. They drove the greatest surge in the U.S. economy ever seen, with the Silent Generation the initial beneficiaries.

Life was good for the Silent Generation with new houses with new cars in the driveway, vacations, new bikes, new clothing, plenty to eat, and schools, well laid out, with lots of resources and appropriately paid teachers.

And, they were growing up with the expectation that plenty-of-extra would continue. They expected their classrooms would never be overcrowded, trollies and busses would have enough seats for everyone, and there would never be a time when theaters were full.

Then we were born!

There are things requiring thought and study. There are paradoxes requiring contemplation and explanation. Enigma to be unraveled. But there are some things that do not require a rocket surgeon or brain scientist to figure out.

There were 2,785,456 U.S. births in 1945. A number, steady since 1930. When we were born in 1954, we were part of the BOOM of 4,078,000, representing a 45% increase in the number of children competing for everything.

Suddenly, more desks had to be crowded into the classrooms. The trollies and busses became standing-room only. Theatres that once had plenty of seats were now sold out on a regular basis.

And guess who got blamed for this! Not the people who created the situation, noooo!

It was our fault!

And, guess who our teachers were. When we reached high school, the Silent Generation was just coming into the workforce and having children of their own. They were heavily impacted by this influx of pests. Those most impacted by it were also the least able to deal with it.

The children of the Lost Generation were being invaded by the children of the Greatest Generation. They were expecting to continue reveling in the economic benefits of the post-WWII upturn uninterrupted. Here we were, gobbling up all the surplus and then some.

They expected class sizes matching theirs. And being the children of the lost generation, were reacting in much the same way as their shell-shocked formers. Caught between the greatest generation and the baby boom, they expected we would adhere to the training they received: be-seen-and-not-heard.

We were having none of it. We were being raised by slayers of dragons who were not subjected to the incessant shelling and shell shock of WWI but were routing out fanatics in the Pacific and jumping from airplanes to free Europe.

So, high school, with all its hype, was being taught by men who, by their own admission, were looking for themselves and were acting out by either being overbearing or going out of their way to try to be different.

Being someone who is different; it gets easy to spot a poser, and high school was full of them. Remember, this is still the '60s, the era of horned-rimmed glasses, loafers, skinny ties, and short hair with parts on the side.

I showed up in the uniform of the day: dress shirt and tie and shoes, no sneakers. Short hair and no facial hair. These were requirements.

And one of the first anomalies I encounter is a teacher with nasty long hair and a beard - home to a nest of birds. He reminded me of the guy living in the closet in Real Genius, and - since smell-surround is not available in theaters, his physical presence brought the BO.

I had this champion for a linguistics class. He spent several days arguing; the ing should not be pronounced in the word f-ing. His argument was that the inner-city dialects omitted the ing, rendering it moot. If he had ever actually entered the inner-city, where I would later work as a cop, he would have known; the c and k were also replaced with g's.

He was my first encounter with this generation's idea of different.

Chapter 35

Austerity in Education

When I mentioned ripples earlier, I neglected to note that ripples come in different sizes. There are little mincey ripples, and then somewhere along the continuum, they turn into multi-story tsunami-sized plows.

Austerity and scarcity are bedfellows. Prior to the BOOM, the available resources could be allocated lavishly. When the BOOM put strictures on the time and availability of teachers and strained budgets for books and supplies, certain costs could no longer be justified.

Opportunity Cost is the cost of one thing relative to another. Here's an example:

If gumdrops cost a penny and chocolates cost two pennies, the opportunity cost of a gumdrop is ½ a chocolate, and the opportunity cost of a chocolate is two gumdrops. If your goodie budget is two pennies, you have decisions to make and complications to overcome.

Purchasing a chocolate makes it necessary to sacrifice two gumdrops. Complications come in, if you want a gumdrop and ½ a chocolate, because now you need partners.

We put an additional 40% strain on teacher resources, book resources, supplies, time, transportation, and everything else utilized in our education.

One of the first things to affect us was the elimination of the teaching of printing. By going straight to cursive, printing primers were eliminated, as was the time required to teach the subject. Children were taught cursive, assuming they would pick up printing on their own by mimicking the writing in books.

Did this also adversely affect hand eye coordination among children denied the opportunity to learn this skill?

In high school, it got worse.

I had been exposed to the textbooks of my older siblings. Notably missing from my high school curriculum were the books for language instruction in Latin and Greek, as well as the recognition of German script. This eliminated the need for teachers to teach those subjects so they could be reallocated to teaching something else.

It also reclaimed all the time necessary to teach those subjects. Time was twice a victim. There was time itself, and there was the relative amount of time needed for certain subjects vs. their alternatives.

David and I were invited to work in our bookstore, starting in the summer between freshman and sophomore years. We came in in the summer to prepare for the coming year by unpacking and inventorying the books and supplies.

As we shelved the new books; I found, covered in a fine layer of dust, all those tomes for subject matter no longer taught. These included classics written by Homer and Plato, as well as, noted English authors such as Dickens.

We witnessed the transition from these hard-bound treasures to paperbacks written by Vonnegut, Heller, and Golding. The original works of Darwin were supplanted by recent works by Morris.

It took less time and effort to teach the latter, and the books themselves were much cheaper.

Luckily, I was able to rescue these orphaned classics for myself, the first a lovely hard bound copy of On the Origin of Species and the Descent of Man by Charles Darwin. The other boys, for the most part, were unaware they existed.

When you build foundations out of tested materials meant to enrich students, they tend to be stronger than those built on materials chosen solely for economic reasons. When the budget becomes more important than the students, something has to suffer.

Reading and writing are basic needs and have to be taught. Filling that basic need for 40% more children placed the opportunity cost of learning to print, understanding Latin, and a foundation in the classics in an untenable position.

Their opportunity costs were too high.

Since education budgets are never the first consideration, we got the leftovers and hand-me-downs.

Bonus Eidetic Memory Demo: Charles Darwin and Abraham Lincoln were both born on February 12, 1809.

Don't even ask ...!

Chapter 36

Love Them High School Dances

When I mention I hated high school, the conversation invariably wends its way to the exclamation, "Really, there must have been something you liked about high school!"

I have to honestly answer, "I really looked forward to the dances!"

Dances seem like the ideal venue for me to avoid. They are loud, crowded, full of strangers, and capable of harshly assaulting all five senses. It's just one of those paradoxes that they were my favorite part of the entire four years!

We attended a half dozen held in our auditorium. I recall some version of a soph-hop, a theme dance or two and one of the first ever computer dances where we were matched with girls via computer profile.

Our school's admission boundaries bumped up against the city limits, so the closest high school, Monsignor Bonner, had been identified as our rival school.

Our school was a one square block inner-city campus with Spartan amenities, read that, no amenities. It was bare bones.

Bonner, however, was located in the suburbs on a multi-acre campus with all the amenities, including the girls' school, Arch Bishop Prendergast. Although they attended classes in different buildings, they shared facilities, including a huge gym.

Weekly dances were held in the gym, and the best part was: only boys with a catholic school ID were allowed to attend, but there was no restriction for girls. With the largest public high school in the state a block away, there were always many more girls!

A smart person had somehow infiltrated their system.

Their dances were held every Saturday, and were better organized. Excellent memories were born on those Saturdays.

Conversely, something unexpected always happened whenever West held a dance, after which there was a cooling-off period before we could expect another.

The dance I most vividly remember was the first. Sean and I piled into his dad's car, and he dropped us off.

The dance itself was wonderful! The otherwise plain doors of the auditorium mysteriously became portals to a unique and mesmerizing cave with softer – nebulous social rules. It created an environment for us in which the teachers were mere postscripts, and we students could connect on a friendlier level.

It was the only place for me where non-verbal communication made sense.

It was also a place to shout, if you liked. Hold hands and feel each other's warmth, or dance by yourself, like no one was watching. You could be yourself here for a little while and make new acquaintances.

I was awestruck when I got tapped on the shoulder by a girl who took my breath away! She had an angelic face, iridescent black eyes, and blue-black hair to her waist. She asked me to dance a slow one, and we did.

Then she disappeared - I still see her face.

There were older girls who were rough and would push me and say, "Hey, you wanna' bump?" which scared me to death!

Overall, the experience was like a dream, and like a dream, it ended all too soon.

Like some dreams, it transitioned into something much less pleasant.

We normally arrived and departed from school in bright daylight. Assuming we rode the dedicated busses, we had only one street to cross, and we did it in numbers. During the day, our school grounds were safe territory.

This dance ended at Midnight.

We stepped out into unfamiliar surroundings.

Our ride home was late, and for some reason, Sean suggested we take the bus. The bus stop was just across the street, but it required leaving the well-lit, clear-cut side of 49th Street beside our school and entering the shadowy neighborhood proper with its thick Chestnut tree canopy, dimming the street lights.

There was a large crowd on the corner alternately waiting for buses, rides, or milling about smoking. I was standing just off the curb as a bus pulled up, and I was reading the ad on the side.

Suddenly, everything went fuzzy, and I found myself up against the bus. Something had hit me in the back of the head! I was dazed, and the ad on the bus was blurry.

When I was able to shake it off, I spun around to see Sean in boxing stance, with his back to the bus, facing down four of the locals. A beam created by the streetlights found its way through a defiant void in the canopy of trees, spotlighting a crimson line of blood snaking from his mouth.

A fist from the shadows hit me a second time, and again, I had to steady my wobbly legs against the bus.

I recovered and again looked frantically for Sean. He was gone, but three of the locals were still there, lying unconscious in the street. I ran through the knot of boys and girls at the front of the bus just in time to see Sean finish the fourth one.

Sean's speed and strength were legendary, and as the unwary fool stepped to him, there was a loud crack, as Sean feigned right and delivered a haymaker. His opponent's body spun from the sudden impact, bounced off the corner mailbox, and flopped limply to the asphalt.

Other skirmishes were breaking out and our boys were introducing me to their unique defensive tactics. The boys from one parish, who had to navigate sketchy neighborhoods more often, were known for their large brass belt buckles. Denied other forms of defense their belts and buckles served as modern maces.

The sound of shouts, invective, and blows was now joined by the buzzing sound of these belt buckle maces fending off other assaults by the locals. The violence was intensifying.

Suddenly, there was a gunshot and screams! All eyes turned to a stocky local who occupied the intersection and had fired a gun in the air! He was alternately holding it over his head and waving it at the crowd. The crowd moved alternately toward him and back in a macabre line dance.

The defensive arc ebbed and flowed as the vanguard of boy's belts, and the gunman menaced each other, when something started the crowd inching back toward the curb. They saw something the gunman didn't.

As he stood in the middle of the street, waving his five-dollar .32 caliber revolver, and we inched back, I saw the headlights. The crowd allowed the gunman to maintain his stand-off.

As the headlights grew larger, they were joined by the growl of the '57 Chevy gaining speed south on 49th Street. Cautiously inching back, we watched the gunman.

The gunman mistook our movement and, feeling hubris, cursed loudly, leveled the gun, and the Chevy hit him from behind!

He bounced onto the hood, cracked the windshield, and flew over the roof like a ragdoll! His gun landed about ten feet in front of me, and one of the boys kicked it down the corner sewer inlet.

The gunman hit the street with a thud and lay still as the tail lights of the Chevy disappeared down 49th Street.

As it passed, I glimpsed a familiar face.

Just then, a horn beeped. Sean called out to me, and we ran across the street and hopped into his dad's car.

Sean had suffered a broken tooth. One of the attackers had been wearing brass knuckles. This front tooth was actually a replacement; he lost the permanent tooth in a sleighing mishap as a kid.

Everyone's parents were miffed that we had been attacked and it was announced that, "Never again would we go to a dance at West!"

On Monday, those of us who had been there compared notes. Those who stayed wryly related details of the accounts they gave the responding police.

Frankie was missing from gym class on Monday and Tuesday. When he returned on Wednesday, he approached me sheepishly and asked, "Were you at the dance?"

I said, "Yes."

He said, "Anybody looking for me?"

I related the stories given to the police. Either a yellow cab driven by a clown with red hair, or a spaceship in the shape of a trash truck, hit the man in the street.

He said, "Really?"

I said, "Yes, that's what I saw."

He smiled.

I said, "Where's the Chevy ?"

"In the garage, getting a new windshield installed," he replied.

"Nice job, by the way!"

"Thanks!"

"No, thank you! From me and everyone else," I replied.

He smiled and bounced away. His Tigger smile the last part of him to leave.

Chapter 37

Mister Meyer

"To judge me by normal standards is like judging a fish by its ability to climb a tree."

- Albert Einstein

High school housed hormones, violence, angry people, and ignorance. Add teachers expecting normal students.

Teachers are human, and so, like anyone, they eventually succumb to the dullness of life—most people do, regardless of their job. And so, it's no surprise that many teachers, despite our expectations and theirs, having gone into a career with the best intentions, become drones.

A well-known psychologist, widely admired for his erudition, if not his tearaway personality, is fond of saying: if you're the smartest person in the room, you're in the wrong room.

Ouch!

The average IQ for a high school teacher is 120. This is often referred to as the sweet spot of IQ, because you are able to learn most things and still get along with most people. It occupies the 91st percentile on the Gaussian curve. (You're smarter than 90% of the population.)

To give some perspective, the average IQ is 100, the 50th percentile.

Medical doctors are found among the 95th percentile.

I've heard folks with higher IQ learn faster, but sometimes have trouble socially. I happen to think this is a nasty rumor.

Hank Meyer taught Creative Writing and was marketed as a standout among our other teachers because Hank had a master's degree. Most of the teachers made do with a Bachelors.

The average IQ of someone with a master's is 117, which occupies the 87th percentile, but since our man Hank also smokes a pipe, we're giving him the benefit of the doubt, awarding him the 120.

Remember, I warned about literal speech? I'm wondering about someone with an IQ in the 91st percentile teaching someone in the 98th percentile. And I'm not talking about learning something solid, like a trade. He's teaching something requiring intellectual weight, and we haven't even considered creativity.

Creativity is a gift; you either have it, or you don't. Creativity can't be taught to someone not naturally creative. The psychologist I mentioned earlier characterizes this as proven science.

Many of the silent generation were struggling to be different. When you are different; posers stand out, and Hank was the sore thumb of posers. He was in a near meltdown because he was missing the boat on which Bob Dylan, Paul Simon, Donovan, and other various and sundry artists of the time were sailing to millions.

Hank couldn't decide if he wanted to be Shakespeare, Chaucer, Ringo, Howard Hughes, or Fuzzy Wuzzy. He had a huge Mark Twain mustache and hair to match, with black wires replacing the matured white mane of Mr. Clements.

He sported a wardrobe the fashion police would consider a felony, and props including a Sherlock Holmes pipe and cigarettes that could gag a goat, which he smoked – in our windowless classroom.

He was an embodiment of non-verbal-TMI.

Now, I really don't know if he had everyone bamboozled into thinking he had it all going on, or they were schmoozing him for a grade, but there was always an admiring throng around him.

This is a hallmark of my condition: not being sure if someone is genuine or not.

The throng - that is.

I sensed something with Hank from the start.

He belched platitudes like they were diamonds and had an opinion on everything.

Most of these were mimicry of his personal favorites, Jack Kerouac - famous for showing up drunk on Firing Line, Kurt Vonnegut Jr., and especially and incessantly Jean-Paul Sartre, whose name he constantly threw around but oddly never quoted.

Most of the time in class was spent suffering Hank's platitudes and references to Sartre's existentialism. He said the word existentialism sans context in every class.

He would enunciate 'Jean-Paul Sartre,' and make it a point to tell us how his name was pronounced.

He would say, "Say, Sar-traaa…" then let his voice trail off and smile contentedly - dead air filling in for the missing context.

I felt like I was being taught by The Music Man.

I allowed myself to be halfway convinced he was legit. I was used to the gap in the continuum, but thought maybe he was at least sincere. He sounded really open to creativity, and I thought that perhaps I'd gotten lucky and found someone who could appreciate something really different.

I mean, it is high school, after all, and things are supposed to be different here—not like grade school, where they push you into a box and all.

I know - I'm doing it again.

I really wanted to be able to subscribe to the image the other students had, but the whole idea was gaining about as much traction as a rear-wheel drive car with bald tires and no chains in an uphill climb during a snowstorm.

But, I fell for it, wrote a piece, and submitted it to Hank. I was looking forward to getting some constructive criticism and maybe learning something new.

I learned something, but it wasn't new.

The next class started as usual, as Hank rubbed his chin and looked to the ceiling for inspiration, or daydreamed. Then, he distributed our papers.

He made a comment here and there about, a nice turn of phrase or an appropriate simile or nebulous reference or whatever and then went to the front of the room to ponder and wax poetic, adding the usual reference to Jean-Paul Sartre and existentialism.

He hadn't given me my paper, and I began to realize he was going out of his way to avoid eye contact with me.

This is hard to do, because I can stare a hole through people!

I have to interject here; for me, at least, being particularly stress-resistant is a real asset. If I had not been as I was, this type of behavior would have unhinged me.

This happened often when someone would withhold something, making me wonder if I had forgotten to hand it in. It was a subtle form of gaslighting. An inside-out version of inclusion. Luckily it did not hit me the way it would a normal person.

I caught his eye a couple of times, but he quickly looked away. I put my hand up, but he waved me off, communicating with a look representing, "I'm saying something important here - whatever you want will have to wait."

When class was over, you always had to wait till the admiring throng dissipated. When they were gone, I approached his desk. He was seated with his hands flat on the desk and his head down. His hands were on the closed folder that held our papers.

His body language communicated anticipation of gastrointestinal distress.

I said, "Ah, Mister Meyer."

He half looked up, raising his head just enough so his eyes, if he held them at the top of their orbits, had minimum vector to see me. The look you give someone you wish was not there. Someone who was giving you pain.

Dagger eyes!

He just looked and said nothing.

I said, "Did you read my paper?"

He said, "Yes, I did." and opened the folder.

There was red pen everywhere - question marks, exclamation points - sometimes multiples, and squiggly lines everywhere! But, oddly no comments, just random marks and no grade.

He said, "You crossed the line!"

I said, "I didn't think creativity had boundaries. You instructed us to be as creative as possible, so I was."

He continued to stare.

"Was it not creative?" I asked.

His reply was painful. He said, "I wanted you to be creative, but not this creative!"

I had a physical reaction, taking a step back! I looked at him as my mind raced. His words didn't compute.

Then it happened - like it always happened.

I looked him in the eyes and said, "Oh, you mean. Not more creative than you!"

He wasn't half looking at me now! He stood and started around his desk. When I didn't back away, he stopped and rethought himself. He was not what one would consider svelte.

He picked up the paper, threw it on his desk, and said, "Take this and get out of here!"

I picked up the paper and left.

I don't know what to think about this side of the condition. Do normal people have an internal alert to stop them from my reaction?

But, that would require the level of creativity - creating the issue.

It's too elliptical a problem.

What if we did have an alert. Maybe a claxon. "This is an alert! Your sensitivities are about to be assaulted!" "Something you don't expect and won't understand is about to happen!" "Prepare yourself by internally rolling into a ball!"

Would it be better to roll into a ball?

There are few good movies about AS. One I like, however, is the Swedish series *Bron or The Bridge.* The protagonist is a female detective with Asperger syndrome. Her character's name is Saga.

"Say, Saaah-ga…"

The depiction of the condition is pretty good, and Saga is well-played. Her coworkers are constantly making fun of her, usually behind her back, making me wonder how often this happened to me.

In one particular scene she is in a meeting with her ersatz boss, as her normal empathetic boss is in the hospital. She's suffering from the absence of her usual boss, who appreciates her talents and smooths the way for her, because, despite her clumsy social presence, she's an excellent detective.

The ersatz boss has just insulted her.

Saga says, "You make the same mistake that many people do. That I have no feelings."

People assume that since our social skills appear stunted, so are our feelings. This may be true, but they are there. It takes a lot to get to them sometimes. People often have to work hard at it.

So, when a popular teacher outwardly and callously discarded me, he reopened a wound, causing me to wonder why I had let my guard down yet again.

That disk-spinning effect I explained earlier was happening inside my brain.

'…Creative, but not this creative. What does that even mean?' I thought. And then it hit me; he didn't like it because he didn't think of it!

Wow! Here I thought I was finally meeting someone who could walk the walk, not just talk the talk!

I thought about not going back to his class, but then I thought, *'Forget him! He's not going to deprive me of the grade for the class*. I found a formula for giving him just enough crap to get an A for the class, and to his credit, he did recommend me for the experimental linguistics class in the following year, so even though he couldn't stand me, he didn't stop me.

He just couldn't stand to have it right in his face - sad.

Was that my fault - I wonder.

He did not have the intended effect on me, but his behavior was attempting to condition me to:

- Not color outside the lines
- Not to have expectations outside the norm

BTW: Here's an excerpt from the paper:

> *Jean-Paul Sartre sat down for breakfast at his favorite café and ordered his usual, "A cup of coffee with sugar but without cream."*
>
> *The waiter said, "I'm sorry sir; we are out of cream this morning. Is it ok without milk?"*

Well, at 15, I thought it was creative.

I ran into Mister Meyer years later in a center city bookstore. He really looked defeated. I believe he said he was out of work. I know it was in the '80s, but not sure when exactly. I'll have to think about it.

But not too long.

Chapter 38

One Teacher's Insight

Here's an outline of what I was taught in school:

- Cursive
- Long division
- Fractions

That sums up what I was taught in grammar school.

I learned quickly in high school never to be late for the bus home, but that's a bit off-topic.

During a fourth-grade final exam, I learned about the giant blue whale in the Smithsonian. I couldn't wait to go see that. I've since seen it often.

I also mined information from a geography book, that diamonds are processed in Amsterdam. I mentioned this to my dad, who said, "Diamonds are stepped on four times before they reach Philadelphia."

I took my wife to Amsterdam to get her diamond. That's another story.

Aside from that, grammar school was an eight-year-long waste of time. (As far as academics go.)

In high school, it was the same story in all but one class.

Mr. Parsons, our psychology teacher, was different. He was interested. It makes sense that he would recognize an anomaly. He also possessed a master's, but was the only teacher who displayed emotion other than anger.

The other teachers' continuums went from neutral to angry with little West of neutral.

Remember! I'm not writing about your normal high school kid. It was tough enough for the teachers to deal with them, so they really couldn't stand me.

I was an unknown quantity, and the opportunity cost of dealing with something out of the ordinary was too high. Since they didn't know what to make of me, they either steered clear or sent me away.

Mr. Parsons looked past the red hair, the flat affect, and the princely countenance. He sensed something else inside. Instead of blowing me off when I asked a difficult question, he would take the time to answer.

If I screwed up, he would express his disappointment and let me know he was upset I wasn't realizing my full potential. He encouraged me to engage it for better things.

It's a sticky subject to proclaim the other teachers had nothing to offer. But, as promised in the intro, I'm writing here as myself. They had nothing new for me. Everything I learned in that four-year interlude, with this one exception, was on my own.

Mr. Parsons suggested I read Gamesmanship. He talked about this in such an engaging way, that I made a special trip to center city to the big bookstore under Wanamaker's, where all the good books were hidden. If they didn't have what you needed, they could get it. It's one of the few things I miss about the '60s. (Well maybe White Castle hamburgers.)

I read this book many times. It was a quick read, written by an Englishman in their patented tongue-in-cheek fashion.

Here's the premise:

In any sport or game, you need a psychological advantage. No matter how good you are, you still need this advantage. In many cases, if you have this advantage, you can beat your opponent, even if he is much better.

The proper title of the book is *Gamesmanship or How To Win Without Actually Cheating* by Stephen Potter.

I have used the tenets every day of every year since I first read it 50 years ago. I've collected every title the author wrote, including an untouched first issue of Gamesmanship wrapped in tissue paper.

This is how much regard I have for this and the teacher who led me to it. One of the few, over my entire formal learning, who taught me anything useful. It was not part of the curriculum. He saw an opportunity to help me and just did it.

I believe he sensed something was missing and provided this tool to help me overcome it.

There is an excellent example of the tenants of Gamesmanship in the *BUD AND JACK* chapter later on.

I synthesized this stratagem to win national championship races, win contracts in business, initiate relationships (read into that however you like), end arguments, win promotions, acquire employment, get raises, and negotiate the release of hostages in multiple armed encounters.

What Mr. Parsons gave me, helped get me through the morass of life that was mine prior to my diagnosis, kept me employed, helped me get and stay married (no mean feat for one of us), and while I was in the PD, stopped crimes, saved lives, averted disasters and diffused riots.

It also taught me to look for other areas to seek advantage.

I'm talking about legitimate advantages, nothing Machiavellian!

It became a method guide for talents I did have to compensate for what I lacked! It was one of the few tools that got me through the time prior to my diagnosis of Asperger syndrome. Without it, what follows would have been impossible.

It is no surprise to me that Mr. Parsons went on to become Dr. Parsons, PhD, expanding his obvious counseling talents as a college professor teaching Counseling Theories and Helping Skills.

He's written numerous books on the subject and developed a seminal series of over 20 texts devoted to counseling, receiving the Pennsylvania Counseling Association's Counselor of the Year award.

He could see something in me, and in the short time we had together, he took the time to provide me with an excellent tool to help develop my own native talents.

Chapter 39

High School Rowing

Every day after school, we went to the river to practice until the river froze around the end of November. Tuesdays and Thursdays during the winter, we lifted weights and ran three miles.

I hated the runs.

The crew was small at this time because funding was weak, and our coach was volunteering his time. When we started, there were three of us. I recruited two more and we were five.

The word got out, and when we hit the water in late March, there were enough for three boats: a four, the double, and me in the single.

I had worked myself into a position of being so different from the others - a single was a natural boat for me, which I reinforced at every opportunity.

I didn't realize I was making myself irascible, but I was. It was a natural state for me to be alone, and I wanted to win. If I was in a single, no one could hold me back, and if I lost, there was no one else to blame.

Now started an intense spring season of workouts. Since our school didn't own any boats, I was relegated to using the one single, allotted to a freshman-smart-ass-oarsman - a heavy, fiberglass work boat. It mimicked a racing skull except for the weight.

Single racing sculls are light and can be carried over your head with one hand, but not this thing. It took two of us to lug it from the boathouse and sit like a pig in the water.

I rowed that thing back and forth in the Schuylkill from March until the beginning of May against the double and the four, always playing catch up.

All things being equal, the more oars in the water, the faster the boat. I was competing with boats with four oars in the water, but I had two.

The others were in boats they would eventually race, rated for their weight, but I was in the practice boat waiting to see what I would use for race day. I was 135 pounds in a boat rated for a 200-pound oarsman.

There were a number of wooden racing boats in the boathouse. There were several Pococks, a heavy-duty American-made boat, the standard for U.S. crews. There was a Phelps made in England – nuf said. There were a couple of privately owned Donarataco, made in Italy. Slightly sleeker and lighter, but not what I wanted.

I wanted a Stämfli, made in Germany by the oldest racing boat manufacturer. The Porsches of the river; they were handmade like violins. They were delicate, sleek, and fast, sitting high on the water vs. in the water as the other boats.

The Manning, the best in the house, was privately owned. It hung isolated on the ceiling in the single shed and was for use by select proven oarsmen.

Near the beginning of May, it was decided I would use the Vanilla, a vanilla-wood colored Stämfli I hadn't seen before. When I picked it up I instantly liked it and couldn't believe how light it was. It was made for a 135 lb. oarsman like me - it was fast!

Rowing the Vanilla vs. the work boat was like running barefoot after months in lead sneakers!

I was keeping up with the double and passing the four! I worried I might actually be too heavy for it, because I was starting to put on muscle and was creeping up on 145 pounds.

After a test, the Vanilla was sent to the boat shop for a new coat of varnish. I went to the boat shop to visit it and talk to the repairman, who was getting agitated, as I came by every day, especially since it was two weeks and it wasn't done yet!

One day, Sean had bad news. The boiler in the repair shop had exploded, and the Vanilla was damaged. I went straight to the repair shop after school.

There it was, in front of what used to be the boiler. Set there to dry, it took the full blast. It looked like the end of one of those exploding cigars in the old black-and-white comedies on TV.

It was in halves, and what was left was shattered two feet back on either end – a total loss.

I was back to square one - no boat. My coach said I would have to use the practice boat for the races, because there were no other singles available. I was openly angry. There was no way I could win schlepping that lumpy thing down the river without an outboard motor.

Then the adult politics started - something new to me. There was a Donarataco available, but there were several people who wanted it. In my mind I was the obvious best choice for a win, so the obvious one to get it.

The treasurer of the boathouse, Ace, seemed to think his nephew, Buddy, was the obvious choice. Ace was also a new experience for me.

Physically, he was what was known as bandy in the 1960s. Short, in good physical shape, muscular, perpetually tan, bouncing off the walls. He was extremely verbal with an opinion on everything, and as an officer of the boathouse, he moved in rare company.

The president of the boathouse at that time was Jack Kelly - Princess Grace's big brother.

Making this all the more confusing was that Buddy was my friend. Buddy was one of those folks you instantly liked: outgoing, tolerant, and always in good humor.

He was always quick with a joke and quick with compliments.

He was a junior in another all-boys H.S. Although a few inches shorter, he was much stronger - with 15 pounds more muscle.

I marveled at how much weight he could lift.

The whole thing was a no-brainer to me.

Ace owned an identical Donarataco he used on weekends. It seemed logical that Buddy would use his boat, and I would use the other Donarataco.

I wondered, *'Why doesn't Buddy use Ace's Boat?'*

Apparently, I was thinking this out loud because my coach looked at me and said, "He wants you in the plastic boat."

He wanted me in the plastic boat, so I wasn't a threat to Buddy. He wanted me in a boat rated for 200 lbs., while Buddy rowed in a boat rated for 150 pounds, essentially me competing against his nephew, despite his age, weight, and strength advantage, with an additional 55 lb. handicap.

He would hold his boat back so Buddy would be in contention with me for the house's boat. My coach held considerable sway in the boathouse and remember, Walter? He ultimately decided who got what boat.

Walter's cure was simple. Buddy and I would row off for the Donarataco. A row-off was an internal race to determine who would get some position within the boathouse, a seat in a particular crew, a chance to row in a particular competition, or the privilege to use a particular boat.

Buddy would race me using Ace's boat. I would use the house's Donarataco. Since they were identical boats, it would be a fair race. Whoever won, got the houseboat.

The voice inside my head said, "That boat is mine!"

The behind-the-scenes politics continued, and just before the row-off, my coach said, "It's been decided; you'll use the Manning for the racing season."

I couldn't believe it. Everything was falling into place. I was outgrowing the Vanilla just as it got blown up. And was getting the nicest Stämfli in the boathouse.

Life was good!

Chapter 40

Buddy and Jack

Nach dem Spiel ist vor dem Spiel!

The first race of the season was the City Championships, and I was nervous. This was unusual because I don't do nervous. I can't remember all the entrants in the race, but I know both the top contenders were Juniors.

One was Buddy; the other, Jack.

Jack, a junior from another school, was the favorite. He was 6'2" and weighed in at 185. That's 2" extra reach in the water and 40 additional pounds of pull. I learned these stats later, as I had only seen him from a distance at this point.

When I finally did meet him face to face, or more accurately, my face to his broad shoulders, it startled me how big he was.

The race went off with about a half dozen boats, and I had a sloppy start. Jack easily took the lead. I played catch-up all the way down and nearly had him, but he beat me by six-tenths of a second.

He beat me by six inches!

Brother Emory, the head of the athletic department, told me later that I had lost because I kept turning around, and had I just put my head down and rowed, I would have won.

Since you're going backward when you row, the boats beating you are actually behind your field of vision. You have to turn to see where they are. I kept turning to see where Jack was, which checked my forward movement and ruined my concentration.

Some of my earthy friends made other comments about the six inches. They wish!

I congratulated Jack and watched him pull over to get his medal. I was flattened. I had a really empty feeling watching that.

But, I knew something. If I could get that close…

The one-and-a-half-mile row back to the boat house from that race was the longest and loneliest of my rowing career. I kept castigating myself about the six-tenths of a second.

When I got to the boathouse, there was no one there but the coach.

I thought, "Uh, oh. Here it comes."

He came to the edge of the water to grab the blade of my oar to guide me into the slip. I thought he was going to dump me over into the river. All the work, and all he did to get me the boat and - six-tenths of a second!

He pulled me in, made eye contact, and said, "You know what to do next week?"

I said, "Yes sir, I do."

I knew exactly what he meant.

He said, "Ok." And turned and walked away.

There was only one way to erase the six-tenths of a second!

The next week he was referring to was the Philadelphia Catholic League Championships. For us, one of the biggest races of the year, us catholic boys, that is. Philadelphia had a huge catholic school population, so the turnout to this race was always impressive.

The buildup to the next week's race was awesome. The bets were on as to who would win. I knew who was going to win and had my whole family come to watch.

The Catholic League race was always on a Sunday, and it fell on Mother's Day that year. It was also the only race any of my family ever attended. There was no way anyone else was going to win.

Remember Ace, Buddy's uncle? He announced - Buddy was going to win! He had a film crew set up to capture the moment. A real film crew like in the movies with those big Hollywood cameras with mouse ears.

There was money being laid on the race too! I overheard the conversations.

The line was: Buddy was going to come in first by a large margin; then Jack would come in second, closely followed by me in third place.

Apparently, they had been holding Buddy back because he wasn't in the race the week before. I had never raced him, but I had him pegged as a sprinter, powerful in a short race, but someone who couldn't keep up with me for a full mile.

Length in the water was a big factor in the long race. A quarter-mile sprint was won by powerful oarsmen who could achieve a high stroke count. The schoolboy races were one mile where length in the water became an important factor.

The taller you were, the longer your reach. This translated into the oars being in the water for a longer distance each stroke – an incremental difference accumulating over a mile.

Ace was ramping up the gamesmanship. I had to be careful what I said. He was the adult; I was 15. All week long, I had to listen to him tell everyone how the race was going to unfold. Buddy in first place, Jack in second and me third.

"Maybe next year will be your year." he jibed.

"After all, you're just a freshman."

As though it meant something to me.

'Yeah, we'll see,' I thought.

Not recognizing authority or rank was actually a strength for me in these verbal games. It didn't sink in; it just bounced off. (Assuming I kept my mouth shut. Thanks, Kathy!)

He even hinted I should lose because it wasn't my time yet, and tried to use my friendship with Buddy against me, indicating I had four years of competition ahead of me, whereas Buddy had only two.

He opined it was wrong for me to win!

He didn't realize the effect he was having; pulling out all the stops - killing a fly with a cannon - was intensifying my resolve. I had read Sun Tzu. He was coming at me from every direction and leaving me no option but to fight with everything I had.

Since the race was on Sunday, instead of the usual Saturday, I had to listen to Ace rant for an extra day.

When race day finally came, I was on the slip bright and early, rubbing lemon oil on the Manning. It was a perfect May day - sunny, light breeze, not a ripple on the water.

Please excuse the crude reference, but a perfectly flat river with no wind and no waves was dubbed piss-on-a-platter. When the river was like this, I did my best.

I was a finesse oarsman by necessity. With bigger and stronger competition, I had to finesse every last inch out of my boat. My style had to be near perfect: no back check, no sloppiness in the water, but light and precise application of power to the oars.

The big boats, like the Olympic eight I coxed at 12, tore through the water with muscle and power.

I skimmed the surface of the water, leaving little disturbance in my wake.

I looked up the river.

'Piss-on-a-platter,' I thought.

My coach, thinking the same, motioned with his head at the river and just nodded. I nodded back utilizing the type of non-verbal expression cops and soldiers exchange.

People sometimes preferred this type of interaction with me, the non-verbal kind of interaction. It spared them anxiety.

Buddy came out of the boathouse and saw me oiling the boat.

He asked, "Do you think I should do that to my boat?"

I said, "Yes, it will make your boat look nice!"

The play had begun!

Chapter 41

Pre-Game

Ace's wordplay was harsh like cannon fire, Buddy's weak like a slapfight, mine pointed and subtle. I wouldn't engage in verbal combat first; someone else had to start it. When I engaged in gamesmanship, I fired back in short, succinct bursts meant to penetrate and linger.

I liked Buddy and didn't want to needle him, but I did have to engage in some wordplay with him. Telling him that it would make his boat look nice was a noodge.

What I was saying was, "You're going to lose, but at least your boat will look nice."

Ace would have said, "You need to do anything you can to help yourself." - harsh.

I didn't want to talk to Buddy close to the start of the race, especially since I intended to beat him badly. I had to. Ace had been setting me up as a dupe, and if I had four years left, I had to stop this now.

Buddy had also made some remarks about me being a freshman asking, "Do you really think you can beat me? I mean, you're only a freshman."

I finished up the oil job, admired my work, and decided to play it just a little more, so I rubbed my oars down with lemon oil. Made the oars nice and shiny but really did nothing to help me go any faster - just something else to make Buddy wonder.

(When people asked me why I oiled the oars, I told them, "The lemon oil makes them smell nice.") (If they asked why I oiled the boat, I told them, "It clears the way of fish, because they don't like the smell.")

Being non-verbal and stoic adds to my style of gamesmanship, unnerving normal people. If they get angry, I evoke Sun Tzu - *If your enemy is upset, agitate him.*

Quiet agitates normal people. Take my word on it!

I finished and took off for the race, found some shade under a tree opposite the starting line, and watched other boats gather. I liked to arrive early and check out the competition. The Schuylkill Navy boathouse bulletin board told me to expect a seven-boat race.

I knew Jack and Buddy but didn't recognize the additional entrants' names.

There are ways to tell how long someone has been rowing - the way they handle the boat, move the oars, react to certain commands. Something as simple as how they lift their oars off the water tells you how savvy they are.

Observing their shirt untucked, how white their sox are, how worn their trunks appear, and the lack of new grease on their oar sleeves on race day are valuable clues.

I left the shade and turned the boat with the oars tucked under my arms, which turns the skull into a surfboard. It takes years of practice to do this because the oars are what keep the boat from flipping over; it was a non-verbal taunt to test reactions.

A klatch of four singles were in conversation. I assumed they were the owners of the four unfamiliar names. One of them tried to copy what I had just done, which was always fun to watch. After he had tried several times and failed, I knew he was new and just dismissed him as a novice, which was good, because he had cannon balls for biceps!

But, if he was the trendsetter among them, they were all in trouble.

Then he made a really bad move - he spoke!

Remember the adage in negotiating; "Whoever speaks first, loses." It works in gamesmanship too.

I was pretend-adjusting my foot-stretchers when he came within earshot and said, "How long have you been rowing a single?"

"Two years," I replied.

I asked him, "How about you?"

"Not long," he responded.

"I see!" I said with a toothy smile.

As a group, Aspies are often accused of pedantry, especially in speech. I agree, as I said earlier, with Sir Winston and learned to curb it, but I still retain the skill. All the reading I've done, added with the instinct for pedantry, provided me with a considerable verbal arsenal.

I knew the nuance in the expression, "I see."

When I said that, accompanied by my fetching smile, I left a lot of room for interpretation.

That vagueness was now preoccupying my four adversaries when they should have been focused on the race.

I was using the norms of social interaction against normal people.

It was only fair!

And, as often happens, instead of taking The Wise Old Owl's advice, my man opened his mouth again.

Rowing is full of rules and traditions, each school having their own. Our school's rule on the tradition of betting shirts was, "Never ask, but never say no." The idea being; asking was foolish, but declining was cowardly. A kind of spin-off of the old, "Never start a fight, but never walk away from one."

We also had another somewhat controversial rule that fit an AS personality so well, I often wondered if somewhere back in Goode Olde England, some Aspie started it. Maybe at first out of pure innocence - picked up later by normals as killer gamesmanship. My man rowed right into it.

He called out, "Good Luck!"

I looked right at him, summoned my most cordial smile, and said, "Thank You!"

This actually came naturally to me, but it had evolved into the school's rule already in place when I arrived. The rule was: never wish another crew good luck! Be polite, say thank you, but don't wish them good luck. Wishing them good luck was wishing yourself bad luck, or voting for your opponent in an election!

The others heard the exchange and weren't sure if I was being polite or snarky. I watched their reaction and officially crossed them off as contenders as they moved back together to continue their conversation.

Now, I had only two boats to worry about.

Nach dem Spiel ist vor dem Spiel!

Chapter 42

Sit Ready!

This race was a floating start, so instead of lining up at boats anchored on the starting line, we would line up by commands of the starter, and when he thought we were all even, he would start the race.

I had to give this everything, so I intended to outdo myself in every way I could. I was, however, preoccupied and couldn't think of anything clever to say to Jack and Buddy. They had arrived and were at the starting line.

When most of the boats were in the area of the starting line, I slid into my lane. Jack was in lane one, closest to the shore; Buddy was in lane two, and I was in lane three – my lucky number.

The new guys were to starboard – my left – remember we're going backward.

I still couldn't think of anything pithy to say, until I heard Jack call Buddy.

I could hear Jack as clearly as if he was sitting next to me, asking Buddy if he wanted to bet his shirt on the race. Buddy agreed to bet.

Jack then said with a condescending toss of his head, "Ask him!"

Not Mike, but him, telegraphing his state of mind and level of arrogance.

Buddy asked Jack, if he should ask the other boats.

Jack said, "No!"

Actually, he didn't say no; he said, "No, forget those guys." Except, he used another word in place of forget.

I was pretending not to hear them by fussing with the laces of my foot stretchers when Buddy called out, "Mike, Jack wants to know if you want to bet shirts."

I called on the rule and immediately replied, "Ok!"

The fact you didn't have to think about it communicated a heightened level of confidence and experience. The reaction of the other competitors was visible and obvious.

I said, to Buddy, as if I hadn't been listening, "How about these guys?" pointing to the boats to my left.

Buddy replied, "No, forget those guys!"

Only, like Jack he used another word in place of forget.

I nodded in affirmation.

Buddy relayed to Jack the deal was done. That he, Jack, and I would be betting our shirts on the race.

They didn't realize it, but they had just given me what I needed! All of this emotional nonsense meant something to the others.

Jack was irked that I was in the race, that a freshman was threatening what was, by rights, his.

He was thinking, "This guy has a nerve."

I did, and now I had his goat.

Let's tally up:

Jack is sure he's going to win despite the humiliation of racing a freshman.

Buddy is sure he's going to lose. Despite all the pressure from his uncle et al., he's already beaten, as his subservient behavior toward Jack revealed.

If Jack had ordered me, "Ask him!" I would have responded, "Ask him yourself!" Buddy saw Jack as superior, whereas I saw him as just another self-important pin to knock down!

Add the fact that neither one of them wanted to bet shirts against the unknowns spoke volumes about their overall confidence!

I could hear the previous race coming to a conclusion down the river by the level and intensity of the shouts and screams of the spectators gathered in the stands near the finish line. I could also see familiar activity at the starter's station.

The starter had his megaphone under his arm and was looking at a clip board his assistant was holding. We had about ten seconds before the race started when the starter would eyeball the line, make sure everyone had their keels even, make adjustments if necessary, and give the commands to start.

I took a quick survey. The new guys to my left looked scared to death. On the right, Buddy's head was on a swivel between me and Jack.

Jack, ever confident, was looking at his foot stretchers, making final adjustments.

I watched the starter. When he took the megaphone from under his arm, I let them have it!

I turned toward the bank and shouted, "Hey Jack!"

His head jolted in my direction. His body shuddered, reflecting in ripples around his boat.

I shouted, "Where are you going to be after the race, so I can get my shirt?!"

I told the both of them - they were going to lose!

Jack looked like he just saw a ghost. His mouth dropped open, and his eyes bugged like Buddy's. Buddy's head was swiveling back and forth like he was watching girls' volleyball.

I forgot the both of them, turned my head to the stern, and got in the ready position just as the starter called out the starting command, "All Boats, Sit ready - ready all - ROW!"

Chapter 43

Another Two-Boat Race

I didn't look at Buddy or Jack for the next few seconds, and exploded off the line! I was known for bad and sloppy starts, but this one was poster-perfect.

I was pounding a Power-Ten, checking the puddles of my oars, which were flying way past my stern. I made a quick check for the lane marker on the bridge, made a minor adjustment, and went back to pounding the oars, hitting an early stride putting my powerful legs to work right from the start.

The boat was sliding through the still water like an arrow through the air; the only motion a thin line of wake and my puddles. Muscle memory was in full gear as I made my way into the shadow of the Strawberry Mansion Bridge.

As I emerged on the other side, I checked on my friends.

The new guys were already lengths behind and were having trouble keeping to their lanes. My assessment, thank goodness, had been correct. They were not ready for this level of competition and not a concern.

The race became a three-boat race of Buddy, Jack, and me.

By now, I had a clear one-length lead on Jack, who was frantically trying to catch up, and a length and a half on Buddy. I knew that if Buddy hadn't taken the lead, being clearly built as a sprinter, he had no chance in the long race.

Now it was a two-boat-race – the best kind!

The race was one mile long, and as we moved into the open from under the bridge, we approached the three-quarter mile mark. There was a slight adjustment to starboard for a small dogleg in the river then a straight shot to the finish.

I had to be careful. The middle half mile of any race was the worst part for me, unlike most oarsmen who absolutely hated the last quarter mile. The first quarter mile always disappeared in a flash, and I loved the last quarter mile, because I could see the finish line.

It was the middle half mile that slowed the clock.

I knew that if I was in the lead going into the half-mile, it would be almost impossible to catch me. Remember, when you're rowing, the losers are where you can easily watch them.

I had Jack where I wanted him - behind to the right, where I could monitor every move. When he made a power move, I could counter; if he raised his stroke count, I could raise mine. With lanes 4 - 7 out of contention and with Buddy already faltering, my job became simple: "STAY AHEAD OF JACK!"

His head was on a swivel because he couldn't see what I was doing and adjust his strategy. I sat on his bow, demoralized him, and ran him into the ground. With each stroke, I added an inch to my lead and had no doubt, unless I was attacked by sharks, that I was going to win.

I checked the lanes, made the adjustment for the turn, and turned back to monitor. The referees in the motor launches were way back behind the boats in lanes 4 - 7, so I didn't have to be too concerned about my position in my lane and could give Jack my full attention.

Jack turned and made eye contact. I met his gaze and felt my face smirk. He made a move to power up, so I powered up. When he raised his stroke count - I matched it. I had him boxed, and could see panic starting.

At the half-mile mark, I could hear shouts at the finish line beginning to build. I heard someone, probably Brother Emory, shout from the bank, "Don't look at him!" but Jack was doing all the turning and looking now.

I saw my coach on the bank. He was beaming and pointing at the finish line. We were rapidly approaching the quarter-mile mark, my sweet spot and the nemesis of other oarsmen.

I pulled out a Power-Ten to test the movement in Jack's boat. The motor launch with the referees had actually passed the last four boats and left them knowing they were out of contention.

I could see the effect of my Power-Ten on Jack. He was broken. He tried to match me, but he was spent trying to catch up.

As the ¼ mile mark inched closer, and the roaring cacophony of thousands of spectators' cheers swelled to a thunderously deafening symphony of screams, shouts, and calls, I recognized one unique voice.

My coach ordered, "FINISH HIM!"

I did.

I hit the quarter-mile mark, my sweet spot. I lengthened my stroke, which had a profound effect on Jack, and panic took him as my stroke got longer and my boat moved away.

I calculated I could put an additional inch between us for every stroke, if I did it right. I laid into the oars, incrementally increasing my stroke count covertly, so Jack didn't know what was happening.

I never relaxed when I was ahead. I made the lead bigger. This is something that infuriates and demoralizes opponents.

My normal racing stroke was 24 strokes per minute. I was now at 26+. My plan was to move to at least 28 if I could get there without losing form or checking the boat. I was now at 27 with over one length of open water between my stern and Jack's bow.

I wanted more!

I took one last look behind me, checked the position of the motor launches behind Buddy, put my head down, and went, "Balls to the wall." I pushed my body to row harder and faster than ever before. The pain and burn were excruciating, but I wasn't going to stop until the finish flag went down on my boat and up on Jack's - first and second place!

Ten strokes to go! I couldn't feel my arms anymore. Jack's face was as red as a beet, as his head swiveled in disbelief.

Nine - and I was moving the stroke count even higher. I was at 28 and pushing for more.

Eight - and I was even with the walk leading to the viewing stands full of spectators jumping up and down, the thousand shouts a hum in my ears, with focus on the race and blood pressure off the dial!

Seven - I had a full length and half of open water now, and Jack was broken, but I didn't want him coming back, so I pushed harder to eliminate him in this and future races.

Six - I pulled even with stomping feet in the stands!

Five - I glimpsed the striped pole and flag marking the end of the race.

Four, three, two, one - the flag goes down, I continue to pull, two strokes and the flag comes up, and I hit the back of the slide and let the oars fall flat on the water!

The momentum took me through the opening of the bridge 30 yards past the finish line, and I came out of my trance.

It's only now that I've stopped the motion of moving to the end of the tracks and pulling those oars through the water that the crushing sound of the thousand people cheering hits like a wave.

I heard the announcer call out lane number two as Buddy crossed the finish line - lengths behind Jack.

It hit me - I won! At fifteen, as a freshman, I was the Philadelphia Varsity Catholic League Single Scull Champ! The crowd was still on their feet, and the cheers were thundering over the water, drowning out the announcer.

What we treasure as legendary focus, demeaned as: "... the all-encompassing pursuit of a circumscribed interest involving a topic to which the individual devotes inordinate amounts of time..." just paid off.

Chapter 44

Post-Game

Normally I would be at the slip now, receiving my medal, but the four lagging boats were so far behind I had to sit off and wait for them to cross the line. I saw the flag move for the last time as the time keeper recorded their times.

I admired them for having stayed in the race and finished.

The crowd rallied with a round of applause.

Shortly, the judges would announce my name, and I would move over to the slip to receive my plaque for winning the race. The plaque I would give to my mom for mother's day, but something was not quite right.

When you are beaten in a race, the sportsman like thing to do is to congratulate the winner, with "Congratulations, Good Race!"

Buddy had already come by, congratulated me, and rowed off toward the boathouse. The other boats had come round and said, "Good Race." They weren't sure who had won because they were so far behind, and Jack was still lingering between me and the winner's slip.

Jack wouldn't leave. Even after the announcement calling me to the slip, he lingered. This is why I like lots of open water between me and the next boat. It eliminates the confusion Jack was obviously suffering, challenging the win.

Jack had his boat in a position where I had to row around him. Only a nimble single skull can do this maneuver. The psychological effect of rowing circles around someone is hard to calculate. It was a move I reserved for only the most arrogant opponents. He had actually given me license to do this by blocking the way back to the slip.

I had to do it!

I backed through the arch of the bridge and swung my boat in a clockwise circle around and behind Jack's position, like it was normal, but the effect on the crowd was palpable, and they went nuts. It completed the perfect spectacle: the two-boat race, the little guy coming back to win, the upset and surprise, all exciting stuff for the spectators.

When I slid into the slip, another cheer went up from the crowd as I circled Jack. I looked right at him so he could do the right thing. He stared at me for a second, turned his head away, and rowed off.

But, now was time for basking. I pulled in, received my plaque, and received my congratulations from the judge and my coach. I handed him the plaque, shook his hand, and thanked him. After a quick wave to the crowd, I pulled away from the slip.

And, did the Aspie-pause.

I just sat and drank it in for about 30 seconds.

I smiled at the crowd, waved, scanned the crowd for familiar faces, then, with perfect form, dipped my oars and disappeared in the shadow of the bridge.

I couldn't wait to get back to the boathouse. There would be people there who would be surprised, happy, and angry. Buddy would be chief among the surprised. Walter would be one of the happy ones, and Ace was going to be pissed!

By some strange coincidence, the film got ruined in the cameras Ace had hired to film the race.

Imagine that!

The row to the boathouse went so fast, I hardly remember it. The excitement was overwhelming, and my mind was racing.

What will people say?

Will I get a school letter for this?

I wonder who I'll be racing next week.

Where are these people with my shirts?

By the time I got to the boathouse, Buddy had already showered and gone. I knew he would meet up with me at the grandstand. I wanted to get back there to bask and see what was happening.

My coach met me at the slip and congratulated me again. He told me to shower quick, so he could drive back up to the stands. I showered and dressed in record time.

On the way to the grandstands, he discussed the race. He told me I did it right this time. Keeping my head in the boat was the way to go and the way to win. The trip was short, and we were at the stands in no time.

When I walked into the stands, there were lots of congratulations—from my team, from other crews, and from my family. I shook lots of hands, met a lot of new people, and was generally overwhelmed.

The next race was approaching the finish line, so attention was drawn back to the river. I strolled in the general direction of Jack's boat house to intercept him and get my brand-new crew shirt. I was anxious to add it to my collection.

Buddy was at the edge of the stands. He congratulated me, shook my hand, and handed me a brand-new school tee shirt.

We were talking when I heard a voice to my left ask, "Are you Michael Cubbage?"

I looked, expecting to see Jack with my shirt, but something seemed out of place. This young man looked like Jack, but smaller, and had red hair like mine.

The closest I had seen Jack was 20 yards, but I was sure he wasn't a red-head.

Then it hit me. This was Jack's younger brother.

Handing me my new shirt, he introduced himself, "I'm Jack's brother. Jack asked me to give you this."

He extended his hand and said, "Congratulations," and smiled.

As I shook his hand, I got the feeling that he appreciated in some way that Jack had gotten knocked down a peg or two.

I said, "Thank you. Where's Jack?"

He said that Jack couldn't come down and had asked him to deliver the shirt. Apparently, Jack hadn't fully absorbed the lesson yet. He still wasn't beaten.

I appreciated what his brother had done. He was a sportsman. I asked him what year he was in because he was dressed in racing attire.

"A freshman, like you," he said.

Although I felt bad for the position he was in, I couldn't let this lie. I was going to have to race Jack again and Buddy too, who was watching this unfold.

I wanted the brother to know that he had done the right thing. I couldn't really think of the appropriate thing to say. "Where's Jack?" had said it all.

I noticed a young girl about nine or ten years old watching all this - probably the sister of one of the oarsmen come to see the races. She knew the significance of the shirt, and was soaking up the drama.

I turned to Jack's brother. I told him I appreciated him bringing me the shirt - I expected Jack, but that's ok.

While Buddy and Jack's brother watched, I turned to the young girl - still at arms-length, unabashedly eavesdropping.

I said, "Hi, would you like a shirt?"

Her eyes lit up! She really did know the significance of the shirt.

She beamed a smile and held out her hand as I proffered the shirt. She took it and said, "Thank you!" and ran off into the stands to show off her new trophy.

I turned to Jack's brother and said, "Thanks again." Shaking his hand, I added, "Tell Jack what I did with his shirt!"

He nodded, looked knowingly from me to Buddy, then turned and walked away.

Buddy was at my left elbow the whole time. He stood stunned, bug-eyed, with his mouth open. I made eye contact.

"Forget him!" I said.

But I used another word in place of forget.

Chapter 45

NYAC And Annapolis

The week after the Catholic Leagues was the Stotesbury Cup Race, which the coaches used as a testing ground for the Schoolboy Nationals the week following. A sophomore from a school in New York was entered in the race, as were Jack and Buddy.

The sophomore was from a school I had never heard of - somehow thinking this made him someone who couldn't be too much of a threat, so I concentrated on beating Buddy and Jack again. I shot off the line into the lead just like the previous week.

The sophomore must have been confused because he didn't start when we did and had to play catch-up, so I just wrote him off.

Initially, we were in the same position as last week. I was first, with Jack in second and Buddy in third.

Suddenly - the sophomore was moving up! I increased power to stay ahead of him, but he came on like a Diesel engine.

I could not maintain the lead.

He gained on me with each stroke and passed me at the half-mile mark; he was a real animal.

A normal race plan included blocks of power strokes at strategic milestones. A Power-Ten off the line, a Power-Twenty at the ¾ mile mark, and so on.

This kid did a power one mile! His plan was to give it all he had from the time he started, until the race was over.

Well, he won that week and the following week at the nationals, but I maintained my place ahead of Buddy and Jack, whom I noticed fell further behind.

I was learning new lessons. They weren't falling further behind; I was getting faster.

I was also learning; although I was immune to most social deficits, I was not immune to hubris, so I inoculated myself against it for the future. (The hubris bug must have been on the shirt Jack sent. I wasn't worried about the little girl. Hubris mostly affects males.)

When I entered the Stotesbury Cup race, I left the realm in which Buddy, Jack, and I were competing and was now competing against someone much better. I was now in the big pond of national competition.

The sophomore was challenging me to a new level. I was getting further and further ahead of Buddy and Jack as I tried to catch him. He was just too good for me to catch at this point in my career, but I was definitely getting faster.

Although I knew I had no chance of beating him this season, I now had his formula and could create a long-term strategy.

Buddy and Jack were defeated.

I was evolving.

I wasn't too upset, because this was what was supposed to happen. I was supposed to be beaten in these races as a freshman. I had beaten the locals and was moving against national talent. I still had plenty of time, and second place as a freshman in the schoolboy nationals is an acceptable first showing.

My efforts were recognized, and that summer, I was invited to the New York Athletic Club Invitational Regatta, a rare honor, especially at fifteen. There, in my first 2,000-meter race, I placed second in a field of six to a college student in his 20s!

This was conducted in the yacht basin of the New York Athletic Club.

It's an athletic club so big it has its own yacht basin! I rowed to the starting line past scores of motor yachts, some as big as 100' long!

The racing course was man-made, a 2,000-meter-long swimming pool!

As I was making my way to the starting line, a motor launch pulled up behind me and took a position about 30 yards back. This was a signal to primp. When this happened, it was often someone scouting you for some crew or college, so I struck my best form.

As the boat got closer, I recognized my coach in the passenger seat animatedly speaking with the captain of the boat. They passed me to get a better look, and I acknowledged him. He nodded in return. As they sped off, I noticed the small flag but couldn't quite place it.

When I finished the race; my arms had been reduced to rubber.

I congratulated the winner.

"Thanks! How old are you?" he asked.

"15," I answered.

"Was this your first 2,000-meter race?"

"Yes."

"I thought so," he chuckled. "You ran out of steam at the mile mark." He added, "You weren't going to win, but I had to work to stay ahead of you! Keep doing what you're doing!"

I was satisfied with the outcome. I was satisfied with even being there, and I rowed back to the slip.

My coach was on the slip when I returned. He helped me in by grabbing the blade of my oar and leaned in.

"How would you like to go to the Naval Academy?" he asked.

It hit me. That's what the flag was!

I said, "Sure!"

He said, "That was the coach. We were in the Navy together. He said to just keep doing what you're doing. He'll do the rest."

The plan was working.

But, according to a lot of folks I was too young to be doing this. I didn't deserve to be doing so well because I wasn't old enough. Like Mozart should have waited until he was thirty or so before composing.

If Wolfgang had waited until he was in his twenties, we would have been deprived of half his compositions, including the most beautiful piece of music ever written, K-41, Piano Concerto 4 in G Major, composed when he was eleven years old!

Chapter 46

July 20, 1969

This is not a trick; all I did was search the internet for the first moon landing for the date. I do remember what we were doing, though.

David, Kathy, Sean, and a handful of chosen few were camped out in David's living room watching One Giant Leap for Mankind.

It was the only memorable thing that summer not rowing related. Ten or so 15-year-old kids sat in front of the tube contemplating whether we were actually seeing a moon landing or a skit on a moonscape-like set in some Hollywood back lot.

That girl from the schoolyard was there too among her entourage – in a transparent mist.

Chapter 47

The ASVAB

I've always been interested in the military. I think my interest started young when mom wallpapered my bedroom with a 1776 revolutionary theme. The dates, locations, and names of battles, and images of Washington, Cornwallis, and others were threads to pull, leading me to details of the revolution and resulting war.

This was also a time in my history when the greatest concentration of war stories could be gathered: from my grandfather's memories of conversations with Civil War Veterans, David's grandfather's recollections of the Great War and the 1917 Flu Pandemic, my next-door neighbor's experience jumping into Normandy with the 101st Airborne in WWII, my buddy's dad's reluctant Korean War memories and the ever-growing number of vets returning from Vietnam.

The accounts of their adventures mesmerized and excited me, so much so that I set my sights on a military academy and would not miss an episode of West Point, a popular TV series based on actual real-life occurrences at the academy.

The show was well done and, as a point of trivia for true aficionados, was written by Gene Roddenberry and featured - wait for it - Leonard Nimoy as one of the actors!

We were back at school now for the sophomore year when an army recruiter appeared in some random class to announce that anyone interested in the military could take the Armed Services Vocational Aptitude Battery or ASVAB.

This was my introduction to the soup-sandwich of bureaucracies.

At this point, I'm in high school in one of the oldest and largest cities in the greatest civilization extant; the high school is part of an elite system within that structure. I'm in the all-academic advanced section of the school, and

I'm now about to interact with the most powerful organization on the planet, The United States Army.

See if you can follow the logic!

I signed up and took the test. When the results came back, the same sergeant returned. He called each student by name and handed them their results. When he was done, he called my name, and I approached the desk.

He asked, "How old are you?"

"16," I replied.

He said, "How did you get here?"

"On the bus," I replied. (This was during one of my more literal periods.)

"No, how did you get into the test."

"I was in class when you told us we could take the test. I filled out the form and received an admission card for the test in the mail."

He said, "But the test is only for seniors; you have to be at least 17 to take the test."

"I'm a sophomore taking senior classes," I told him.

He shook his head. See how irritating I am!

He said, "You'll have to take it again next year."

I didn't even bother to push back. Something about the uniform.

But I did ask, "How did I do on the test?"

He referred to his list, then came the familiar strange look. He said, "You got the highest score in the class."

"Good!" I said, which was rewarded with a new version of the strange look.

Any volunteers to explain the logic?!

My instincts kicked in, though, and I researched all those things from the test with which I was not familiar. They were in my eidetic storage area we spoke about earlier.

I learned about the special sparkplug sandblasting machines, how carburetors worked, how brake systems worked, and what a torque converter was.

The next time I took the test, I scored highest in the class again and higher than before. The army called me at least once a month until I was over 30.

Chapter 48

The Nationals in Junior Year

After freshman year, Hugh asked me to row the summer season for Vesper in a pair, a shell with two oarsmen, each with one oar. This is a tough boat to master, requiring both oarsmen to be well matched, so Hugh identified another oarsman, also a redhead, with basically the same build, and began to coach us.

We were like a pair of twins. (Get it? Pair of twins?)

One blisteringly hot and humid Philadelphia summer day, a few weeks into training, I forgot to take my salt pill and was overcome by the heat. I spent two weeks flat on my back with nervous heat prostration, ending the summer season for me.

I still was not myself when the sophomore year started and sat out for a year. I played on another sports team to keep in shape, but I didn't row at all.

This wasn't just physical. The symptoms of AS were accelerating, making wise decisions almost impossible. I watched myself drag my disconnected body to school each day against my will.

When junior year rolled around, I realized my mistake and approached Sean to intercede with his dad for my return to the crew. This didn't seem likely because I had also blown off the entire winter workout prior to hitting the water in the Spring.

Sean told me his dad wanted to talk to me, so I went to the boathouse.

The coach met me in the locker room and said, "Suit up and meet me on the slip."

I did.

In the water at the end of the slip sat a four-oared shell. In it were three oarsmen and, standing by the stern, a tiny coxswain. The stroke seat was empty.

Sean's dad said, "There's your boat, if you want it. I don't have time to coach you; you're on your own."

I felt hollow, but there was no time to think. With the little wind I could muster, I said, "Ok, thank you."

He smiled wryly and went off to coach the other boats. He would devote his attention to the boats with fully seasoned and tested oarsmen to prepare them for what was expected to be a winning season. He was a man of his word too, and left us completely on our own for the entire season.

He knew I would bite. He actually had them put an oar in the stroke seat for me.

I stood for a minute contemplating the four. I recognized the two-man. The bow and three-men were unfamiliar, so I assumed they had the one year's experience acquired during the year I was gone.

All of us were juniors.

The cox was a brand-new freshman named Rob.

I felt like I was on the Titanic - staring at the one empty seat in the last lifeboat, and one of those nebulous religious concepts took shape as I approached my own personal Purgatory.

I got in the boat and told the cox to do the same, asking, "Have you ever done this before?"

He said, "No." but had an eager look about him. This boat had the classic setup with the cox in the stern facing forward - facing me.

I said, "I'll take command. Listen to me, and you'll be fine." Adding Hugh's admonition, I further said, "Just keep us straight and don't hit anything."

"Ok," he replied.

We pushed off - before the first-mile marker, I had them turn around. We put the boat away and met in the meeting room.

I said, "The coach told me he won't be coaching us. We have to do it ourselves. Is that ok with you guys?"

They shook their heads in the affirmative.

I said, "Ok, there are some things I have to shake out of this boat. I don't have time to be sensitive, so I'm just going to point out what I see, and we'll work on it together, ok?"

They agreed.

The dynamics were obvious. The other boats had been rowing and racing for three years. My guys joined the team late and were inexperienced and new - especially the cox. The coach did not have sufficient time to teach, train, and season them for a race.

He left me to shake out the boat, determine what I had, and fix it, and I had no surplus; I had to deal with what I had. I had to fix whatever flaws I found among them, get them coordinated with one another, get them in physical condition, determine the best race plan for the resulting boat, and train a cox from scratch - all from the stroke seat!

Fortunately, the reputation I created prior to their arrival still held enough weight to carry me with these guys. They hung on my every word.

After the nationals in freshman year, I had bragging rights. This manifested itself in an unfettered mouth. I never hesitated to add to a discussion to the point it appeared arrogant, but it was just a manifestation of an inability to filter expressions as normal people do.

The coach was giving me an opportunity, in normal people's terms, to put my money where my mouth was. He was aware I had coached the quad that beat Ken's boat (It just so happens that Sean was in the other boat we beat that day), and he knew that I gave David his initiation to the single skull in which he won the nationals sophomore year.

I asked for a second chance, and he gave it to me along with a huge responsibility. He was teaching me a valuable life lesson.

He stood back now to see if I could walk the walk.

We spent the next few weeks on basic oarsmanship. They were frustrated, but I told them to be patient, and it would pay off. Something drastic was needed if we were going to make any kind of showing.

Actually, at this point, I felt it was necessary just to avoid embarrassment.

I threw out the standard workout plan and instituted one I learned from Walter. We needed an edge, and a unique plan was as good a place to start as any. I regressed to basics to force out the most obvious problems.

All boats initially encounter a problem with coordination, but they get used to each other during the season. We didn't have time for this.

One of the crew couldn't complete a stroke without skimming the surface of the water before squaring his oar.

Another had trouble keeping time with the other three.

None of them were used to taking orders.

I employed another of Walter's tricks: I made them row for the first two days without using the slide. They could only use their backs and arms. I would not let them feather their oars, forcing them to clear the water for each stroke with a full 90-degree blade.

This accentuates the issues with balance and identifies anyone who leans.

This works different muscles, so when they went back to the normal stroke, it was almost a relief. But, I still would not let them feather their oars. Each time someone leaned and his oar skimmed the water, everyone got sprayed with Schuylkill Punch.

At that time of the season, the temperature of the water was about 40 degrees, so each time someone jolted everyone with freezing spray, he was subjected to a litany of abuse. Occasionally, an oar would hit a wave, forcing the knuckles of everyone on the opposite side into the gunwales, upgrading the abuse to invective.

Chapter 49

The Crew

Each school's workout routine ended in a run. Our standard was a three-mile run to the stands and back.

U of P, our next-door neighbor, ran the steps of the Art Museum - Rocky style.

Maniacs ran hills!

I introduced my crew to Lemon Hill. Opposite the boathouse was the cut-back road to Lemon Hill. It was a 35-degree angle climb. With little time to polish off much beyond the most obvious rough edges, we were going to have to forgo finesse and resort to power.

Running ten hills, instead of the usual three miles, would bulk up our legs and give us extra power. I told them it would hurt like hell but for a much shorter time, so they agreed.

I had a boat with three rookies and a brand-new coxswain. None of us were really big, so there was that, and there was noticeable slop in our style. That was as good as that part was going to get!

What we did have, I discovered, was a crew who were naturals at gamesmanship!

Over the course of the months we spent readying for race season, the different personalities began to emerge. The bowman, Ron, didn't say much, but expressed himself by sporting a knit cap with the colors of the Kenyan flag.

It's not uncommon to put your power in the middle of the boat, so two and three were our heaviest and strongest.

The three-man Matt was the biggest - a sort of quiet giant who, although outwardly stoic, revealed himself to be quite emotional on race days.

Rob did what he was told for the most part and learned quickly. I wouldn't let him give many orders, because of the time constraints, and being a freshman, he was naturally intimidated.

I maintained the position of in charge which went surprisingly unchallenged, but quickly relinquished my gamesmanship duties when a specialist emerged. When you encounter someone who can combine speedily delivering a witty remark with the skill of the game, it's priceless.

Our number two man, John, was an expert! I didn't inhibit conversation in the boat if it didn't interfere with the workouts. Not much inhibited John's repartee in any case. His wit was something I could only admire, and he assumed the position as our ambassador so I could concentrate on coaching.

The idea of the two-man as the boat's spokesman disoriented other crews, because the main communicators in any big shell were typically the coxswain or stroke.

When the two-man responded to hails from the other boats, there was a physical reaction among them. It took them a second to comprehend; this boat's spokesman occupied the two seat. It made no sense to them.

We augmented our physical regimen with gaming strategies. I don't know where it originated, but we came up with the idea of the four-man push-up. Rob would stand in a spot and order us into position. One man would get into a push-up position, the next would put his feet on that man's shoulder blades at a 90-degree angle, and so on, until there were four men forming a square with their feet on one another's shoulders.

Rob would begin to count, and the rectangle of oarsmen would rise in a pushup with him standing in the middle. We did this on race days where the other crews could see us. It had little value as an exercise, but the looks on their faces were priceless!

When we found ourselves in a venue where other fours were on display and their crew was nearby we would walk near enough to their boat to actuate an awareness zone. John looked intently at some vague area and, gesticulating loudly, pointed this out to the rest of us.

A pantomime routine would follow focused on the imaginary area of concern. When the other crew would react, we would look at them with blank faces and quickly withdraw.

The other crew would turn their boat inside out, trying to figure out what we found.

But our best routine started after we realized our three-man had something of a nervous stomach.

He would throw up before the start of every race without fail! Each race started with his breakfast dripping from the riggers. At first we reacted to it with some concern, until he assured us - for him, this was normal.

On the starting line other crews would invariably call out, "Is he ok?!"

Nonplussed, our ambassador in two would say, "Yes, why?"

The other crew would say, "He's throwing up!"

John would reply, "Yes, he lightening the boat. Don't you do that? We all do it before each race to make the boat lighter!"

The persona of our boat had other crews thinking they were dealing with the ultimate rowing fanatics!

Our coach entered us as senior oarsmen in the first three races of the season. We didn't embarrass ourselves, but it was quite obvious; the other crews had been together for most of their four years of eligibility and were well-seasoned.

The nationals were held in Syracuse, N.Y., that year. After the Stotesbury Regatta, our coach told me that since we had a year of eligibility left, he would enter us in the junior event at the nationals. I didn't realize the full wisdom of his move at the time, but I had way too much respect for him to ever question his decisions. Nor did I have any strong opinion either way.

I think his logic was that we had trained against the senior field for 75% of the season, so we might have a chance in the junior field for which we all still qualified.

Syracuse was super disorienting. We were packed into some random hotel four to a room, so Rob had to sleep on a cot. I was experiencing my usual lower GI issues, so I spent a lot of time in the loo, and sleep was especially challenging as an Aspie in unfamiliar surroundings.

We were informed that 20 boats had entered the race, so there would be qualifying heats the day prior. That meant we had to race two days in a row;

something I had never done. I usually slept 'til noon the day after a race; I was sure I would be exhausted on race day.

We wide-eyed the race course with awe. Instead of the normal corralled river race course, this regatta was held in a huge lake near the university! It was so wide that ten boats could race abreast. I had never seen a race like that. It seemed ridiculous.

Chapter 50

Ready All!

On heat day, we were told there would be two heats in which five boats would qualify. Those five boats would join the winners from the other heat, and ten boats would race for the championship the following day.

Rob was trained well enough to give all the commands to the boat, but they were still coming from me. I was no longer giving direct commands to the crew, but through him.

Face to face with me, he relayed actual commands to the boat. He was nearing the point of taking full control, but however ready he may have been, I was not yet ready to relinquish it.

The morning of the heats, we had an unfamiliar breakfast in an unfamiliar restaurant which had familiar results on me, and I had to be summoned from the hotel bathroom to go to the lake.

The lake was overwhelming, huge, filled with all sorts of boats, and, to my great dismay, windy and choppy as hell! We figured out how to get to the starting line, lined up, and I got to row in my first heat.

It started off like any other race, with three's breakfast dripping from his rigger and us executing the plan we had been practicing until an idea surfaced.

In the heat with nine other boats, at about the ¾ mile mark, I realized we were in fifth place in a field of ten but far ahead of the last five! I took a quick look around to see the four boats ahead of us furiously competing for first place!

When I realized the boats in our wake were never going to catch up, Jack Kelly's words came to mind, "Know the rules!"

The rules of the heat were: the first five boats qualified – period!

And, that insubordinate Aspie thought surfaced - This is stupid!

I had Rob ease the boat off into a paddle. He looked like he had seen a ghost.

He said, "We can't do that!"

I calmly said, "Just do it."

He ordered the boat to "Take it to a paddle."

I made the mistake of not telling him to whisper, and the officials heard the command.

Officials follow every race in motor launches to enforce the rules. Their concerns are keeping boats in their own lanes and keeping uninvolved traffic off the course.

If boats leave their lanes and interfere with other contestants, they may be disqualified. Motor launches are prohibited in the area, so they don't create wakes and upset the racing boats.

Normally, the officials stay at the back of the pack and follow the race. In rare situations, if they determine some boats are so slow, they actually prevent the officials from officiating the boats likely to win; they can pass them and catch up with the dominant boats.

With the field of 10 boats stretching out over a large swath of the course, they were getting frustrated, trying to decide what to do, and when they heard the command to paddle, they passed the last five boats and came up directly behind us.

The one in the passenger seat began to shout at us through a megaphone to row faster!

He was trying to speed up the heat.

I mumbled, "Forget you!" just loud enough for Rob to hear.

His head spun on a frantic swivel. The official was having no effect on me, but he was visibly rattled.

The official reiterated emphatically, "Row faster, or you'll be disqualified!"

Rob reacted by shouting, "On the next stroke, Power-Ten!"

I said, so only my boat could hear, "Don't listen to him. Continue as you are."

I barked at Rob, "Don't listen to him. Listen to me!"

He was visibly shaken and said, "We'll be disqualified!"

I said, "No we won't! All we have to do is come in fifth to qualify. Let me handle the official."

I shouted to the official, "We're rowing as hard as we can!"

He replied, "No, you're not!"

I repeated, "We're rowing as hard as we can!" Then I added, "Sir, you're swamping the boats behind you!"

I had him.

In their anger, they had abandoned caution when they passed the slower boats and were zig-zagging behind us in an attempt to herd us to the front of the pack. He looked back and saw his wake was adversely affecting the following boats.

This is a major no-no! An argument started between him and the captain culminating with the captain pulling out of the way of the trailing boats.

I said to Rob, "Problem solved. Forget him! Just keep us on course, and let me know when we've crossed the finish line."

He needed something to do.

We crossed the line in fifth place, securing our spot in the finals, without sapping our strength simply to place in a heat. I could never understand why the first four boats did that.

Chapter 51

Row!

Normal race plans call for a Power-Ten off the start. Almost every boat in the U.S. Schoolboys practiced this plan.

I remember someone telling me once: every boxer has a plan, until he's been hit. I liked plans, but I didn't consider them constitutional.

I had some good experiences behind me. I knew that unless you were a physical animal like my sophomore friend from NY, you needed to capitalize on every advantage. You had to combine the ingredients required to win into the right recipe to suit the particular race.

I was able to synthesize lessons and draw on them when needed, and this race was the perfect proving ground. I had already used Jack Kelly's lesson of knowing the rules to help us conserve our strength for the actual race.

The next morning started better, with the usual unfamiliar meal, but this time, the multiple visits to the head were not necessary.

I got a shock when I ran into my sophomore friend from NY whom you'll remember from my first national attempt. He was a senior now and a shoo-in for the senior singles championship.

Apparently, he misjudged the finish line and stopped short during his heat. He had been disqualified.

This did nothing to help our nerves, and as we rowed to the starting line to give it our all, our expectations were conservative. We were ready to make a good showing at best. The mood in the boat was a quiet resolve as we sat near the starting line.

The silence was broken by the two seat, "Matt, what are you waiting for?!"

Matt said, "What do you mean?"

John said, "Throw up on the rigger!"

Matt said, "No, I'm ok."

John said, "No Matt, you have to throw up on the rigger. It's good luck!"

Matt said, in his understated way, "No, I feel ok. I don't need to throw up."

I turned around to see a panicked look on John's face.

Much of what normal people do is hard for me to grasp; superstition is way out of reach.

In what seemed like extremely well-organized confusion, we lined up, the race started, and we hit the water with a Power-Twenty.

Since most crews' plan began with a Power-Ten, as much as it was part of our different style; it also served to disorient the other crews. When we did this it was not unusual for us to pull ahead at the start, but our previous efforts were overcome by the bigger - more experienced seniors invariably overtaking us.

This day, however, something unexpected was developing. We were ahead as expected, but the other boats weren't moving on us. I had Rob pull another Power-Ten. When he did, we pulled a half-length ahead of the other boats!

I said, "Do it again!"

And we pulled another half-length ahead.

I told Rob to crank up the stroke a little. He did this by banging the handles of his tiller lines on the gunwales, signaling the change in stroke count. I picked up the stroke, and the others followed.

Suddenly, we were sitting at least a length of open water ahead of the next cluster of boats! I kept the stroke just slightly higher and watched the open water grow until we were at least two open lengths ahead!

The effect of being in the lead boat with open water cannot be overstated. This was the first time the rest of the boat was experiencing it. It energized them, and re-energized me!

A bit of optimism crept in.

At the half-mile mark, we were at least three lengths out, watching the real race - the race for second place. Five boats were now furiously competing with each other as though we didn't even exist. I could see their heads swiveling right and left to see their relative position in the field.

As we passed the half-mile, it hit me - we were going to win!

I got a funny look on my face, made eye contact with Rob, and said, "Look behind you."

When he turned back around, he blurted out, "We're winning!"

I said, "We are going to win!"

We had to struggle to control each other. This was a time when one or both of us could panic and blow the whole deal. I could see it in his eyes. I had to keep talking to him to keep him calm, and if I'm honest, keep myself calm as well.

I said, "Keep them doing what they're doing."

He instinctively executed our now familiar plan, adding a power stroke here or there, but nothing crazy. I stopped monitoring him and watched the other boats. I could see we were still moving ahead and knew at this point, as I like to say, "Unless we were attacked by sharks …"

At the last ¼ mile, I told Rob to pour it on. I could hear the men behind me grunting with pain. They were breathing hard and pulling furiously, because they had super energy from knowing we were in the lead!

I almost lost it. I remembered what happened to our sophomore friend the day before, and I was afraid we would misjudge the finish and be disqualified. I said to Rob, "Remember what happened to the guy from NY. Don't stop right away!"

He startled me with the command, "Shut up! I got this!"

It was his boat now! He took us into the last ¼ mile, leaving no doubt he was in charge. When this boat crossed the line, he was going to be the one to do it!

I did as he said and shut up - for a minute. Then Rob said, "We're across. We won!"

I said, "Don't stop! Keep going!"

I watched the flag at the finish line. The crew were loudly grunting at this point, fighting for every breath. This was my rule, not something normal people practiced.

They were over the line, so the race was done. They wanted to stop, but I wanted to see the flag go up on the next boat, so I was absolutely sure we were over the finish line.

I could hear people screaming behind me. I had forgotten we were on a lake, and at this point, we were well past the finish and almost at the beach. The shouts were cautions from spectators on beach chairs!

John shouted, "We're done!" and stopped rowing. We all crashed into each other, but we were so overwhelmed by the moment that we didn't care. We were now officially national champs!

And, to everyone's surprise we were the only boat from our school to win! In a lineup predicting a win for three of the four boats entered and a loss for us, we turned the tables and delivered the only win.

Most of the rest of the day was a blur as we packed up and headed home. The ride home went fast, and I ran home to give my family the good news.

Later, I stopped by Sean's house. I remember this clearly. His dad, his assistant coach, and Sean's older brother were sitting at the kitchen table. The coaches, both WWII vets, were tough customers, and they were enjoying a frosty beverage as I walked in.

When I came into the kitchen, the conversation stopped, and they all looked up. I stood alone in the middle of the floor facing this table full of Alpha males, who just sat back and looked at me.

My coach spoke first.

He said in his endearing affect, "Cubbage, you have got one big set of balls!"

The entire group broke into laughter and stood to congratulate me. There were handshakes and backslaps of recognition from some of the toughest critics in the sport. I thanked him for his help.

His son said, "No, this was all you!"

Their remarks were some of the best compliments I ever earned!

I sensed a reprieve from purgatory.

Chapter 52

Mr. Smith

"Knowledge is knowing tomatoes are a fruit; wisdom is knowing not to put them in the fruit salad."

– Albert Einstein

As high school progressed, if that's an appropriate characterization, my ability to cope with social issues continued to backslide. I reached the stall point at 17.

I spoke earlier about little professors and accelerated maturity at a young age. I also noted the polar switch in high school. 17 was the limit for organic social development for me. I'm told this is common. Social savviness remains a work in progress.

The experts have observed something about AS that baffles them. When attempting to diagnose someone with AS, their family members, if available, are questioned to see if the history of behavior fits with the criteria. They're looking for behavior that indicates AS, as well as, eliminates other possibilities.

A question invariably asked is, "Occasionally, does he get angry suddenly?"

When the answer is "Yes."

The next question is, "Does the anger disappear just as quickly as it came on?"

The answer is invariably also, "Yes."

I have a theory about this:

I was often met with a reaction of anger by adults when I said or did something they felt was inappropriate. A few examples are:

- A question they couldn't answer because they didn't understand it themselves

- Something I wasn't aware was inappropriate within society's paradigm
- Something said at the wrong time and place
- One too many questions
- The person I was asking was just an irascible SOB

I believe we've been programmed at some level, since we've had it directed at us frequently, to utilize this to warn someone off. It's not something we conscientiously do, like normals seem to, but a learned behavioral reaction - like shooing a fly - the feeling I got when it was done to me - I was being shooed away like a fly.

Something they miss, however, is the substitution of something as a surrogate for anger. This can be something obnoxiously snarky-and-over-their-head, flippant and dismissive, or, as a last resort, something purposely rude.

I had a teacher in some obscure subject, nothing STEM-related, begging the question, "Why is it on my roster?"

He had also been an oarsman, coincidentally in our main rival high school. He mentioned in class one day he had won a nationals when he was in school.

He was a big guy, several inches taller, with a 40-pound advantage. He was still in good shape with big arms and broad shoulders.

Since he had attended the rival school, this alone was a license to noodge him, and some of the other students did, but I didn't have their sense of boundary.

He had a chip on his shoulder over me from the start. After I won the nationals in Junior year, the chip became too heavy.

I attended a dance one Saturday. I was taking a break from the auditorium, which could quickly become warm and humid, as there were always a thousand-plus teens in attendance.

I happened on a trophy case.

Guess whose trophy was behind the class! You guessed it: Mr. Smith's!

He was right; he had won a nationals. He won the third-eight as a senior.

I laughed!

Let me explain. There are two divisions in schoolboy rowing. Junior and Senior oarsmen. One could row as a junior oarsman until reaching senior year when you had to row as a senior oarsman.

There are only so many boats and so many races, and large crew teams have people who do not qualify to row in either junior or senior races. Keeping these oarsman in tune requires having them rowing, however, so the folks who do not make a junior or senior boat are sometimes put together into what is called a third-eight.

Some less sensitive folks call this a scrub-boat.

Our man, Mr. Smith, with his extra 2" in height, reach, and extra 40 pounds of muscle, had been relegated to scrubs! Now it made sense why he constantly gave me a hard time. I had won a local senior championship in freshman year and had just won a junior nationals!

In school on Monday, I told him I had had occasion to walk the halls at his alma mater Saturday, and saw his national plaque. His face said it all! He never missed an opportunity to dun me now. This all culminated one day outside the lunchroom, where he was assigned lunchroom duty, not a chore teachers enjoyed.

The school, for whatever reason, had relaxed the dress code. Although we still couldn't wear sneakers or jeans, we could grow our hair out any way we chose. Everyone had some version of a Beatle's haircut, representing some phase of their career, and everyone capable of growing facial hair had a mustache and beard.

I was sporting the Prince Valiant version.

As I waited to ascend the stairs outside the lunchroom for the start of the next class Mr. Smith was holding us back, waiting for the bell to ring. I was standing face to face with him, waiting for the bell. I said nothing, and since he had reconciled himself to try and stare me down, I stared right back.

He had a contemptuous look on his face as he looked me up and down. I still hadn't moved or said anything.

Suddenly, he said, "What a disgusting thing. An oarsman with a beard."

To which I responded by belching loudly. (Remember, we just left lunch.)

He slapped me violently in the face! I parried as best I could, and recovered.

"Feel better?!" I asked.

Realizing what he had done - he backed up a half step, turned, and ran up the stairs!

He found ways to avoid me after that.

Chapter 53

Variation A - The Tipping Point

Not being burdened with a need to be dramatic enables me to identify root issues. After almost 70 years bumping around in the dark, one thing is consistent and abundantly clear. Humans have to eat, sleep and poo, and to facilitate this they either have to hunt bears and build houses, or get jobs.

Most get jobs.

I mentioned the work world requires 60% social ability and 40% technical ability, and by this point I would guesstimate I had 10% social ability. Assuming I was 100% technically able, and no one is, I was 50% ready for the real world.

Life was about to take an abrupt turn for me, so I have to take a quick break from the purely anecdotal to set the framework for the next phase of my life and the book.

It's hard to fix a problem with an unknown cause, and near impossible, when you don't know there is a problem. Problems didn't come to me in the form of academics, mechanics, science, theory or philosophy but in human drama.

When I submitted the paper with the tongue in cheek reference to Sartre and his ideas; I understood clearly what I was writing. I understood Sartre's overdone theory; in order not to have cream, cream would first have to exist as a possibility, and, that I was lampooning the whole idea.

My problem lay in an inability to process the teacher's reaction. I had done something socially unacceptable that had nothing to do with Sartre, his theory, or cream for that matter. When the teacher said, "You crossed the line." he meant some normal social line, normal people instinctively knew not to cross.

Since almost everyone has to have a job; they associate their persona or worth with their job - some professions more than others. It's more ingrained than we realize.

Many foreign languages say, "I am plumber." vs. "I am a plumber."

People are their professions.

I recently saw a bumper sticker: "I Change the World – I teach."

Hank certainly changed mine. I don't think that's quite what he had in mind though, when he thought about his work. He had a vision of himself as the keeper of great knowledge, which he imparted to us to validate to himself that he and his profession were making a difference.

I made him feel like Spain's Regent for Flat Earth Studies when Columbus returned from America in 1493.

I have to deduce this retrospectively, because those nebulous social rules did not allow for any redress or what the military call after action report where your mistakes are laid out, so you don't repeat them.

There's a quote attributed to Abraham Maslow: "I suppose it is tempting, if the only tool you have is a hammer, to treat everything as if it were a nail."

Normal brains seem to operate in agreement with this axiom. Whereas, AS brains work along the lines of the axiom:

There are many ways to skin a cat.

Which normal people refute with, Stay inside the lines!

I had come to the point where I had to decide if I wanted to stay inside the lines or follow my own path, and I was being pushed to do this with no clear idea of where the lines actually were.

When Dr. Hans Asperger encountered AS, he viewed it from the perspective of a medical doctor, as a corporeal problem. Excerpts from his paper indicate:

- A particularly interesting and highly recognizable type of child.
- All have in common a fundamental disturbance that manifests itself in their physical appearance, expressive functions, and indeed the whole behavior.

He was describing the discovery of a type of child with a different physical appearance – he goes as far as to describe a common princely countenance in their consistently narrow faces.

He was describing a variation.

I call it: Variation-A.

Dr. Lorna Wing, also a medical doctor, treated the discovery as a medical issue. Her paper, Asperger syndrome: A Clinical Account, continued along Dr. Asperger's line of inquiry into the tangible.

Dr. Uta Frith as a psychologist works with a different set of tools. She wrote at a distance in Asperger and his syndrome moving from the clinical to the theoretical. The titles of the papers say it all.

Asperger syndrome is currently stuck in this nebula.

Brain scans showing the Asperger brain is significantly differently structured than a normal brain, and that normal brains and autistic brains have more in common than the Asperger brain, have been pushed aside for a fuzzier approach.

Asperger brain scans look like an arial photos of New York City at night. Scans of normal brains look like Nebraska at night.

There are lights on - just not as many.

Cool your jets!

Let me explain.

Normal brains have structures purpose built for social interaction. Asperger brains have 10% more grey matter. And, whether by design, available resources, or simply a matter of space, the parts meant for social interaction are either missing, are smaller, or just don't function.

Normal brains are equipped with mirror neurons, a fully functioning amygdala, and more or faster white matter that automagically processes and reacts to social situations.

We have to do it all on demand, in the front part of the brain, which never stops processing.

I can solve problems faster, but small talk escapes me. If the girl in the cloakroom in seventh grade had asked me to calculate π I could have readily accommodated her, but when she smiled at me; it almost caused a short circuit!

I still maintain that I do not want to be normal, but I would have gladly traded the π knowledge for a few mirror neurons and the ability to understand what was behind her smile.

Chapter 54

Fixing an Unknown Problem

"A man cannot know what he does not know."

– Someone quoting Plato

There are several places in the U.S. where one can take a scenic ride on an old locomotive train. There are two nice ones in Pennsylvania: one in Strasburg, and another in Jim Thorpe. These old locomotives require constant care and maintenance to keep them running.

Since the factories that produced these engines are long gone; companies have to rely on existing documentation, assuming they're lucky enough to find any. One such enterprise was lucky to have found an original manual, but were constantly blowing gaskets on the engine.

They followed the manual exactly, and although the manual called for a six-month replacement, their gasket would not last a month, requiring a teardown of the engine, putting the train out of service for at least a day.

They were incurring five times the normal cost for the gasket replacement and losing five days of revenue, a nagging and expensive problem.

One day, an elderly gentleman riding the train engaged the conductor in a conversation in which he noted having worked in the factory that produced these engines at the turn of the 20th Century. When the conversation turned to the problem with the gaskets; he asked to see their repair manual.

He went directly to the chapter on gaskets and noted a typo in the original manual. The wrong gasket was recommended.

The manufacturer, realizing the mistake, had mailed each original train owner an insert instructing the installation of a different gasket. This manual was missing the insert.

When the new gaskets were introduced to the maintenance schedule; the gasket problem miraculously disappeared!

At 17, I knew I had a problem but didn't even know what it was. At least the train company could replace the blown gaskets, but I wasn't even that far ahead. I just knew there was some kind of problem.

I had to constantly invent workarounds for each social encounter without knowing the root cause for either the social problem or the root cause for my not understanding or recognizing it.

Recall, for a moment, the chapter about The summer of '68, when in the locker room, Ken was trying to belittle me, generating a response from me that appeared clever and on point.

I checked the faces of the crowd, turned to Ken, and said, "You mean like this race?"

In the early stages of pre-reading for this book, I provided trusted friends with one free-standing chapter, The Summer of '68. I chose the chapter with no direct reference to AS, which I wasn't ready to disclose, because I needed input about my style in a vacuum, without the AS distraction.

It was brought to my attention; when the story jumped from me clumsily coxing the new eight to the seemingly mature and clever interaction with Ken, the transition was too abrupt. Readers needed a smoother transition.

This was powerful feedback, which I appreciated and took seriously. I did an extensive rewrite to that chapter, and others, to provide better transitions.

But here's the onion; when I asked Ken, "You mean like this race?" I wasn't engaging him in clever repartee; I was seriously asking him, "You mean like this race?"

I wasn't focused on Ken's comment for its intended content; I was focused on his comment for its literal content. I wanted to know the implication of intermediate oarsman because, I was not only not aware of what the implications of changing my standing were, but wasn't even aware it had happened. I didn't know I had just changed my standing, nor did I know prior to the race; this would happen as a result of winning.

I was not sufficiently self-aware at this point to even attempt (if I even understood the concept) the type of behavior Ken was displaying. I was just seeking additional information which appeared as clever and witty repartee - an understandable interpretation without this context.

This has always happened, happens now, and will probably continue to happen. People find some things I say humorous when it was not my intent. And even now, it is often the case; I have no idea why they are laughing. This is the obverse of the often cited stereotype noting Aspies have no sense of humor when we don't laugh at someone's joke.

Hans Asperger observed about his boys, "(He is)…only himself. And is not an active member of a greater organism which he is influenced by and which he influences constantly."

In the interactions with Ted and Jack, I was practicing a precise game, tailored to the situation and would continue to build upon the skill, but with Ken, it was all literal.

Unless I feel something is really clever and I have the right venue; I don't usually attempt to engage normal folks in humorous banter. I'm just not good at it in normal social settings, and wouldn't even attempt it in a business setting.

I don't have regrets. (Well, maybe the cloakroom thing…)

I've done just about every crazy thing a person can do, except jump out of a perfectly good airplane.

My son said it best:

He told me when we attended his jump week at Ft. Benning, "Jump school is three weeks long. The first week, they separate the men from the boys, the second week, they separate the men from the fools, and the third week, the fools jump!"

Not me, brother! I had enough to do on the ground keeping his mother from getting on the plane with him!

Chapter 55

Mr. Connard

Ok, we're back to the anecdotes, but keep the last chapters in mind. This next incident marks a turning point which for me was the beginning of a five-year free-fall. As much as I would have liked to forget this chapter; I had to include it or leave too many questions unanswered.

Much of what happens in anyone's life is timing, but most of this situation was due to the devastating handicap. A normal person might have been able to work around it, but my world was too black and white at 17, and I couldn't see this coming.

I was nearing the end of junior year in a class where the teacher was also the coach of the alternate sports team I had joined in my sophomore year. He became visibly angry when I went back to the crew team and ordered me not to. He was not at all happy with my response.

He gave weekly tests, and I was in the habit of keeping everything at this time, because I might need it later on, and I'm glad I did. My average at this point was 96%.

After I won the nationals and two weeks before report cards, he handed me a failure notice without having previously given me the required failure warning. He was failing me in the course for the entire year.

When I confronted him with my test scores he said, "You didn't have sufficient class participation."

I pointed out the violation of protocol, as he had not given me the failure warning required by the school board in enough time to reverse any potential failure. He completely ignored me.

Remember the Naval Academy? Their rule book, which I had read so many times by now it was tattered, read; failure of any year-long course was disqualification for entry to the Academy.

I tried to talk to him, bringing past tests to demonstrate he was wrong. He didn't care and walked away from me. I followed him all the way to the main office where I grabbed him by the right shoulder.

Apparently, I had been communicating with him quite loudly along the way.

A voice in my right ear whispered, "Not a good idea." The disturbance had attracted the attention of the disciplinarian who had come up behind me and was now holding my arm, gently shaking his head.

The disciplinarian had a reputation as a particularly physical individual, but with me, he was using kid gloves. I could see no anger or aggression in his eyes but an imploring and empathetic look. He was telling me he was concerned for me, not the teacher. His concern was negative consequences for me.

I let the teacher go, and he ran into the office.

I went with the disciplinarian to explain what had happened and showed him the test grades. He said it was up to the teacher, so there was nothing he could do, and suggested I speak with the principal.

My family had a history with the vice-principal, so I spoke to him. He gave me the same line, "It was up to the teacher."

The next day I had my mom come with me to the school to try and convince these people to fix this problem. Here's how the meeting with the vice-principal went:

I explained the issue in detail, showing the test grades. He reiterated it was up to the teacher, and that he could not change the grade. I pushed back, reminding him; that as vice-principal; he had the power to do just that, emphasizing this as a matter of right vs. wrong and his duty to do the right thing.

He said, "Ok, you're going to have to go to summer school to make up the grade."

The thought of going to summer school hit me like a train! I thought, "How do I explain; I'm on the honor roll and in summer school?"

My intellect was my only tool in the social battle being waged around me. Attempts had already been made to take away my creativity, and now they had come for my intelligence.

It would be like a star ship giving up its force field.

It was never going to happen.

I said, "I won't go to summer school."

My mom put her hand on mine.

I looked at her and said, "I'm sorry, but I have an A in this class. I'm not going to summer school."

Negotiating with educators is what I like to call Che Guevara negotiation. This was just my first experience. This type of thing is what causes many Aspies to think they've been mistakenly dropped on the wrong planet!

Educators' negotiations are pretense leading to a predetermined outcome where authority trumps object.

You're the object.

We negotiated for a half hour. Finally, he decided he had had enough and as a way to break the stalemate said, "If you don't go to summer school; you can't come back in the fall."

I answered, "I don't need to come back here. I'm 17. I don't have to attend school in Pennsylvania past 16."

"If I fail this course; my plans to attend the Naval Academy are ruined, and if I can no longer go there; there is really no reason for me to come back."

He said, "What will you do?"

I answered, "Walk into any governmental office and take the GED exam. I could pass that in my sleep."

I continued, "At 17 ½ I can join the Army. They accept a GED in lieu of a high school diploma. They want me there because I got the school's highest score on the ASVAB."

"So, I really don't need to come back here next year, actually I can't because this time next year; I'll be in Vietnam. I've already mapped it out with the Army: Basic Training - Advanced Infantry Training - Jump School - Vietnam."

There was a lot of silence in the office for the next several minutes, and I was upset at this point my mom had not thrown this pipsqueak around the room a couple of times to back me up. She was certainly capable, but that generation was so brainwashed about the position of religious people she did not contradict him.

My jaw was set about summer school, and the meeting ended on that note.

The next morning; I was called to the vice-principal office. He had come up with a plan to get me out of the situation.

He sat at his desk and said, "I compiled a list of ten books. Prepare ten book reports over the summer, hand them to me, and you may return in the fall."

I said, "And, that will change my grade on the course for the year?"

He said, "No. The grade stands as a failure for the year, but an additional course will be added to fill the requirement, so you can graduate. The book reports satisfy the requirements for the course."

I said, "So what is the value of the added course?"

He said, "You'll be able to graduate."

I said, "That's not the issue." (In retrospect I should have emphasized not more forcefully!)

I explained, again, "The issue is a failing grade in a yearlong course making me ineligible for the Academy. With that on my transcript, I can't attend. If I can't attend, graduating holds no value for me. I can get just as far with a GED, and not have to spend another year here."

He stood extending the list of books - signaling the end of the meeting. I accepted it, as an automatic response.

It made it as far as the trash can in the outer office.

I made plans for the GED. I had at least six months before I needed to have that, so I didn't run right out and do the paperwork. I had to have it done by September, but around the end of July, my mom told me she had spoken to the vice-principal, and I could come back even though I hadn't done the book reports.

This was 1971. The failing grade showed up on the report card at the end of Junior year. It's the only report card I don't have because I tore it up.

I graduated in 1972.

I didn't attend Annapolis.

So, why not just go somewhere else?

The syndrome had me confined in that time and place to society's paradigms, and their paradigms had fuzzy boundaries. The outcome of the negotiation was determined by authority alone and no amount of logic, right, reasonableness or truth can combat authority bereft of fairness, impartiality, and dare I say, empathy.

I had not only those strictures to navigate but also those inherent in the syndrome. When I had exhausted logic, circumnavigated the wall of educators' itinerant version of the truth, and been denied empathy and sympathy, I could only withdraw and reevaluate.

Chapter 56

Final Year – The Last Straw!

I was being forced back inside the lines. Inside the lines everyone wanted me was engineering. Not the fun kind involving trains either, but the really boring kind.

I watched my older brothers study to become engineers and I didn't like the silos within which they were being taught. When I studied a subject; I needed to see the cross value among the courses.

I also needed similar relationships to see the value of individual life lessons. I had learned to navigate winning boat races but hadn't yet synthesized it fully to apply it to life holistically, or I would have just taken the retroactive advice of, "Why not just go to another college?"

Waiting for senior year, I stared at the growing mountain of letters from college rowing programs. Harvard, Yale, Columbia, Georgetown, Lehigh, Lafayette, Princeton, UCLA Berkley, if they had a crew; they wanted me there!

The coach of U of P would physically stop me on Kelly Drive and take me into his boathouse for tours to encourage me to row for him.

When people ask what would you change in your life, if you could, I would have thrown out all but the letters from Stanford. But, that assumes pre-knowledge of Stanford; I didn't have at that time. If I had seen Stanford's campus; nothing could have stopped me from attending!

The letters continued through the summer in a snowstorm-like white-out, and they came every week. After a while I got so overwhelmed; I couldn't even read them. My desk at home was covered with a six-inch high pile.

In September, I robotically dragged myself to school to begin the final year. I was looking forward to a great rowing season paired with David in a double. We would have been unbeatable.

Then the other shoe fell. When we walked into the boathouse for our first practice, we found out our coach had retired and a new coach met us in his place.

I'll never forget his welcoming speech. He called the entire crew into the trophy room and announced, "I'm the new coach. Nothing you have done in the past means anything to me. As far as I am concerned, you have zero accomplishments!"

I had one question, and I watched myself ask, "Nothing we've done counts for anything to you?"

He answered, "That's correct."

I turned around, got dressed, cleared out my locker, and left the boathouse for the final time. I went home and did something a normal person would never have done. I tossed the pile of letters in the trash.

No one ever approached me about it. No one tried to stop me, talk some reason to me, or point out the mistake I was making.

I'm still not sure who let who down. Did I let them down, or did they let me down?

I do believe to whom much is given, much will be required, but at 17, I really do think; someone else should have stepped in.

Maybe I'm wrong, though. Maybe it's always been me.

I was still at a disadvantage as a literal, logical animal. I had knowledge but no wisdom. Future events like the one described next would help me accumulate some.

A few years after high school, I was at an event at an all-girls college. These were still allowed in the '70s, and as one can imagine, they attracted boys on weekends. Attending such an event, I noticed a group of midshipmen from the Naval Academy and struck up a conversation. The subject of the failed course surfaced.

One of them said, "Why didn't you just do what Joey did?"

I said, "What do you mean?"

He said, "Joey, tell him about 13th Grade."

Joey said, "I failed two classes in high school, so the Academy has a program for that. I went to the Academy right after high school graduation. A bunch of us took classes during the summer before the rest of the class started in September to retake the classes we failed."

I said, "So you failed two classes and they provided a way for you to get around it."

"Yes," he answered.

One of the other midshipmen laughed and said, "Yeah that program is full of athletes!"

They graduated from the academy in 1976; the year I would have graduated.

It gets better…

In 1983, my wife and I bought a house just after our first son was born. I was in the attic unpacking boxes and found the transcript from my high school. When I initially received it in 1972, I just threw it into a box where it lay unopened for 11 years. Just for shits and giggles; I sat on the bare wood floor and opened the transcript.

End of year grade for English in Junior year = 73.

You could see where someone had changed it to a passing grade.

Probably should have let me know, huh?

Chapter 57

Credit Where Credit Is Due

The natural state for an Asperger hovers around that trait which leads some to believe it is some form of autism (I don't – just for the record).

That trait is the self-focused state of being.

When I recall the events of the past; I see them as I did then, at whatever age I was, and I wrote many of the stories here as I was when I lived them – meaning I remember with my teenage mind the stories of high school, and I wrote them in that mindset.

I now have the benefit of many years of hindsight and am lucky enough to be able to apply that and realize there were other people in the picture at the time. I may not have been aware of them and still may not know who some were, but the change of the grade on the transcript is just one existing piece of forensic evidence – they did exist!

I've learned most people who help do so from the shadows vs. stepping directly in front of the bus as was my wont to do - a habit for me often counter-productive.

These people, like Doctor Parsons, were those who had long vision and could make moves designed to subtly provide help or provide accommodation long before the term took on today's meaning of help for someone with a disability – longer before it was twisted into a pejorative.

Looking back from today's perspective; I see those folks.

Chapter 58

Brother Larry

Brother Lawrence E. Oelschlegel, FSC, taught freshman English. He taught traditional English vs. the creative sort our previous friend struggled with. His erudition and confident commanding voice, unique among the faculty, got my respect right from the start.

In other words – he got my attention.

His manner of speech made my head snap in his direction because I didn't want to miss anything he said. Originally from Philly, he had obviously worked to mitigate the nasal twang and sounded like someone from that clean-speaking area of the mid-West.

A mutual respect formed and at the end of freshman year, he invited David and me to work for him in the school's bookstore, which he managed.

In the summer after freshman year, we worked daily in the store to process the incoming shipments of books, receive and recycle the usable texts from previous years, and account for the necessities of high school life: pens, pencils, notebooks, and tokens for the busses and trolleys.

When school started in September, Larry asked us to stay on to work daily in the store during those hours it was open, to accommodate the student's needs for those necessities. Provided our own individual keys; we would open early, before classes started for an hour or so, at lunch time and any other time our class schedule permitted.

So what?

Well, here's so what: Among the several hundred students Larry taught, he singled us out to trust to help him in the store. It was a brilliant accommodation on his part and a boon to all three of us. He got help in the store from people he could trust and we got perks.

We got, basically, the run of the school. He provided us with permanent-hall-passes, so anytime we were in the halls between classes and were challenged; we had a free pass. After a few weeks in sophomore year, everyone in the school knew who we were, including the faculty and staff.

And, since we both had good grades, we could leave class early or beg off entirely if there was a need for us to be in the store.

I had a constructive outlet for my endless energy and some level of prestige, trust, and recognition in the school. As well as, a brilliant place to hide and recharge, if the occasion arose, which often does with my condition.

Sometimes, just eating my lunch inside the store away from the great unwashed was enough to get me through the day.

Larry moved to LaSalle University in later years and was there when I attended classes in the '80s. I would often go to the brother's house for mass and then breakfast or dinner.

The other brothers had funny stories about him always having what they needed, or didn't need, in the way of those little necessities of life such as extra socks, gloves, toothpaste, snacks, and of course, #2 pencils!

I was looking forward to having him read this book, but unfortunately, he died in 2022 after 58 years of service to the community.

He was one of those who provided accommodations for me to sustain me through high school long before I knew I needed them. His many kindnesses and strong advice were pivotal in my survival during those years.

Chapter 59

Brother Gerry

When Larry was reassigned after our sophomore year Brother Gerald stepped in not only to pick up the reigns of the bookstore but as a confident mentor as well. He could have easily picked his own crew for the store, but he kept David and me on. We worked in the bookstore for Gerry for our junior and senior years.

Gerry had a completely different but equally likable personality. I can't remember ever seeing him when he was not smiling. Gerry taught accounting but did not present a stereotyped accountant's persona.

Quick with a joke or funny story; he loved the interaction in the store and found us as enjoyable as we found him. He was always ready to listen to whatever drama I needed to vent and was always quick with advice and a cheery sendoff.

He also allowed us to continue to enjoy the perks of book-store-guys and validated our permanent-hall-passes, so we could come and go with much less stress and anxiety.

It was Gerry who facilitated my acceptance at LaSalle University when I was still struggling to complete my BA.

He liked to poke fun, and Larry and I were particularly good to poke fun at. Larry could get serious at times, and Gerry could always be relied upon to get him to ease up and relax. One day at Sunday mass in the brother's house I didn't see him, because he came in late and sat in the back.

When I asked him where he was he said, "In the back. I saw you up there in the front with all the other bald guys."

I found myself thinking, "What the heck?" Until I got home and looked at the back of my head in the mirror!

He always had too much hair anyway!

Gerry is still active at LaSalle University, still as cheerful as ever, and still has too much hair.

Chapter 60

The Ladies of The Office Staff

For some reason; I've always gotten into trouble for this type of thing: Why is it; the faculty got all the space in the yearbook, spots in the newspaper and on T.V., awards, and accolades presented at rubber-chicken lunches and dinners, and the folks who ran everything sat in the shadows?

The people who knew everything and everybody held all the secrets and did all the work got one measly page in the yearbook.

Well, if it wasn't for Alice Dougherty, Mary Sweeney, and the other ladies of the front office and their accommodations; the place would have been much, much worse. They sat on the other side of those doors where meetings with the principals were held and screened all the calls.

They intercepted the deluge of late-to-schools each morning and had to filter stories related to late public transportation from the BS of those chronic offenders, you know, the ones you ran into in middle management later on.

I don't know who actually changed the grade on my transcript; first ideas run to the vice-principal, but the idea of a conspiracy-of-moms among and including mine, crossed my mind. A silent conspiracy which was their wont - no recognition, just a wink, a smile, and the satisfaction of knowing they averted yet another disaster for us.

The teachers (all men BTW) got things done in spite of themselves, because behind the scenes; the ladies got things done in spite of them.

I do appreciate all the hard work and help from these folks. I still reserve my right to kvetch, but I have to give credit where credit is due.

Chapter 61

When High School Was About to End

When high school was about to end I figured I should probably attend college. It seemed like the next step.

I applied to The Philadelphia College of Pharmacy & Science.

I watched David artfully craft the essay for his application to the University of Pennsylvania. He printed his response in the allotted space. Actually, he drew his response, entering each letter carefully.

I don't remember an essay requirement for PCP&S. Maybe they weren't really concerned about personalities, just academics.

Anyway, I intended to attend in the Fall of 1972, but as usual, the world had other plans. I applied for a grant from the state, because I didn't have enough money, and I had decided early never to take a student loan, but there was a flood in Harrisburg, PA, the capital, and all state business stopped for a time.

I couldn't find out if I got the grant, so I didn't attend college that year.

The grant came through in November, but it was too late. When I applied the next year, they told me I should have gone to college assuming the grant would come, and since I hadn't utilized the grant when it was first issued; I was not allowed to apply ever again for a grant. I was on my own.

This is why I love government bureaucracies so much!

This type of situation was not uncommon. I took things literally, so I couldn't process the idea of negotiating with the school to wait for the grant, nor negotiate with the state for the grant for the second year.

David and I had taken a summer job at the same place after high school. When he went off to U of P in the fall; I didn't sit on my hands, I stayed on at a car rental working as a chauffeur.

Don't let the title fool you. We had to join the chauffeur's union to get the job, but it had nothing to do with driving people around. That year, I cleaned rental cars and shuttled them back and forth between the Philadelphia International Airport and the base located two miles away.

Chapter 62

Travel, Rental Cars and Arlo Guthrie

"Travel is the enemy of prejudice"

– Mark Twain – The Innocents Abroad

The nuns always told us to apply ourselves. In the year before college, I applied my ass to car seats at a car rental.

Here are some things I learned:

- There are adults in the U.S.A. who can't read or write.
- One can achieve membership in the Hundred Mile an Hour Club on the stretch of road between the airport and the base.
- Circa 1972 American cars hydroplane at 57 MPH.
- You shouldn't pass gas when people are eating lunch, or any other meal for that matter.
- If you can grow a mustache at 18; you can get into bars and clubs.
- There are things called After-Hours-Clubs that operate all night long.
- If a union goes on strike, you have to stop working, because your health will suffer if you don't.
- People who rent cars, leave coins in the crack at the back of the seats and bills on the sun visor.
- If you turn the ignition off while the car is running and then turn it back on; the car will backfire.
- If the alternator dies, putting a rubber band on a cotter pin and sticking it in the hole in the back makes it a generator and you can limp it to the shop.

- If you put the two bumpers together; you can jump-start a dead car with a coat hanger.
- Being able to retrieve cars when they've broken down makes you popular with management.
- People call off sick most often for the first shift. If you can wrangle yourself onto a Midnight shift; you will get an almost unlimited opportunity to work a double.
- If you never cash your check; you'll save money.
- The higher a person's level of education; the more likely you'll have to show them how to operate the rental car.
- The Roach Coach has the best coffee and doughnuts. (Never eat anything else, though.)
- If you don't pack a lunch; you'll spend one-quarter of your pay on food.
- The rental company made most of their money on mileage charges.
- Rental cars have extremely shortened life spans.

I fed my wanderlust during this year by retrieving our cars when customers drove out of state and left them at other airports. There was a charge for this, but they didn't care, because their company was paying for the rental. Private individuals didn't rent cars then; only corporate and business people did.

This naturally happened to other cities as well. Someone would come into D.C., for instance, and they would drive the D.C. car to Phila. We would have a collection of these foreign cars in our lot at the end of each week.

If we had a NY car, I would call NY and ask them, if they had any Philly cars. If they did, I would tell them to hold it, and I would drive the NY car there on the weekend and exchange it for the Philly car, and bring it back.

This was the best of both worlds because I not only got to travel for free; the company also paid me a fee based on miles driven for the return of their car!

I traveled all up and down the eastern seaboard in brand-new cars for nothing. I got to visit all the museums and points of interest in NYC, D.C., Baltimore, Allentown, R.I., Maine, Connecticut, and others. I actually had a trip to L.A. lined up, but it came too late in the summer, so I didn't get to L.A. 'til years later.

I was always looking for extra money to save for college. Eventually, I developed contacts in other states and turned this into a side business. I would identify a half-dozen cars in D.C. or NYC and have my guy hold them for a promise to return their cars.

I accumulated a group of drivers who would come in on the weekend, and we would pile into a car, drive to that city, and bring our cars back to Philly. The job lasted an entire year until I attended college in the fall of 1973.

I did wrangle my way into a midnight shift the summer before I left where I would service as many cars as possible for the day shift morning rush. Frequently, a call came from the airport for a special car, so I would drive it to the airport, drop it off at the front desk, and take a returned car back for service.

During one of these trips, I was leaning on the counter talking to one of the attendants when I heard a commotion behind me. I turned and saw a man who seemed to be upset, sitting on the bench in the middle of the hall.

I looked at my friend behind the counter and said, "Is that Arlo Guthrie?"

She said, "Oh, yes. He's here with his group."

I walked over to where he sat down, as several of his crew left.

I said, "Hey, Arlo!"

He looked up and said, "Hi!"

I said, "What's the matter?"

He replied, "We've been waiting close to an hour for our cars."

"What cars?" I asked.

He said, "We rented three station wagons from the other rental company, but they're telling me they're not ready yet. Which is BS, because we reserved them weeks ago."

I said, "Hold on."

I went to the other rental company counter and said hi to the clerk. We all knew one another among the various rental agencies. I asked for the phone, which she knew was the direct line to the garage where they serviced their fleet.

Jay answered the phone.

I said, "Hey Jay, its Mike Cubbage."

He said, "Yo, what's up Cubbage?"

I said, "Do you have three station wagons ready back there?"

He said, "Yeah, but there's a poker game on."

I said, "This guys a friend of mine. Can you bring them up here?"

He said, "No problem, man. Be right there."

I hung up and returned to Arlo.

I said, "They're on the way."

He smiled and said, "Really?"

I said, "Yeah, these guys are friends of mine. They'll be here shortly."

He said, "Thanks a lot man. Is there anything you need?"

I said, "Yeah an autograph for my girlfriend."

He wrote it out with her name on it and gave it to me.

Five minutes later I was watching him and his guys load their instruments into the three station wagons which had been brought directly to the front door, so they didn't have to drag their stuff to the lot.

He thanked me again, and I went back to my lot.

A socially savvy person would have gotten an invite to his gig, party, and what-all-else.

I settled for an autograph.

Chapter 63

College - Leaving the Home Planet

Grade school and High School had been tedious social issues aside, a simpler confusion, because they were regimented and represented the same social collective as me.

Grade school was populated by kids I grew up with and knew. In High School, the others were all catholic from similar backgrounds.

College was a new kind of chaos. The Philadelphia College of Pharmacy & Science or, PCP&S, was a small college on the edge of the U of P Campus. Many folks thought it was part of U of P, but it was its own entity.

It had a small and limited enrollment, 230 freshmen each year. 184 were pharmacy majors, 27 med tech majors, 10 biology majors, and I was one of nine chemistry majors.

It was also known as the hardest college to get admitted to. You had to have a high GPA, show particular aptitude for the sciences, be recommended by a pharmacist and an M.D., and have four years of high school German behind you. It was also the most expensive college around.

The main building housed the administrative staff, the dean's office, and the lecture hall, which seated exactly 230 students. This was the reason given for the enrollment being limited to 230.

Each day began in the lecture hall with every freshman present. Relationships grew concentrically from where I sat, so I accumulated a dozen relationships with those close by, but unlike the homogenous classes I knew; this class consisted of people from around the country.

Coming from an all-boys' catholic high school to this diverse mixture was exciting, but also fraught with confusion. The laissez-faire attitude of the teachers about your performance was also a shock.

Another unique thing was every teacher at the school, with the exception of one, was a PhD. The rumor was he refused to change one section of his dissertation, so the university refused to grant him his PhD. It was said this was ongoing for the past ten or fifteen years, and neither side would budge.

He taught vertebrate zoology.

Some notable incidents included a call to the dean's office so, he could show me a bullet hole in the hood of his Cadillac. Apparently, someone took a shot at him with a hunting rifle, as he was driving in that morning. The dean called me by my first name and somehow found out I had some knowledge of ballistics. I would often see him outside his office and discuss this or that.

People will find fun things to argue over. After our first exam in vertebrate zoology, an argument erupted between the professor and one of my classmates. This professor dictated copious notes, and his rule was, "The text is always the tie-breaker." Meaning, if your notes differed from the text; the text won.

After my experience with Mr. Connard, my expectations weren't high, but since the competition was alive in this school; students closely monitored every question on every test.

You should also know there were no multiple guesses in exams. There would be a question and a blank. And, any misspelling made the entire answer wrong.

After the first exam, a number of students decided to test the text vs. notes rule. The test question was, "How many species of boney fish are there?" Everyone's notes read, "16,000" but, the text read "60,000."

I had the right answer on the test, so I wasn't paying much attention to the argument building in the front of the room until it got loud.

It got loud when the professor proclaimed, "I did not say, 16,000!" and wouldn't budge even though half the class had the wrong answer.

It got louder still when a student produced a tape recorder and played back the part where he did say, "16,000"!

I was startled and looked up when the screaming started. The screaming match stopped with the professor directing one student to, "Go to the Dean's office, and don't come back to my class!"

The dean sorted this all out, and the student was back the next day.

The prof announced, "Tape recording is not allowed in any of my lectures!"

This meant all the tape recorders, and most had them, had to be hidden now. I had a view of half the seats in the room, so each successive class started with a display of creative recorder-hiding, while the professor whipped his head back and forth trying to spot them.

I guess anyone stubborn enough not to change a minor part of their dissertation to get their PhD can't be expected to give up a single question on someone else's exam.

Another shocker for me was the socio-economic diversity in the class. The well-off people in my social niche were the ones with the newer cars or those who had a nickel each day in class for a pretzel.

The continuum of wealth in the lecture hall started in small towns in the Pennsylvania slate belt and ended in Beverly Hills.

One of my acquaintances brought back a photo album from Christmas break. He had been to visit his mom. He grew up in Long Island New York where his dad practiced medicine, but his parents divorced and his mom now lived in Beverly Hills.

He said his mom had a party while he was there and this album was from the party.

During my break, I picked up some extra cash shuttling cars for ten cents a mile. I was in the middle of the socio-economic continuum.

There was a girl in my class from central PA who sat in her dorm room for spring break and rotated through three outfits during the semester.

My man flew, I have no doubt non-stop first class, to California. There, he attended a party at his mom's house (I guess a mansion is a kind of house) at which there was a professional photographer.

Note: at this time, for the great unwashed, it took over a week to have a roll of film developed.

He not only had the film developed the day after the party but the photographer put it into an album for him!

Oh, the best part is, he gave me a look at the album, and pointed out his mom seated next to Charlton Heston! - just one of the notables at her party.

After a few months of freshman year, I began to rethink my decision. I had met some of the people in the class destined for research or pharmacy, and thought the direction they were going was not the one for me.

I don't know, I think the word I'm looking for is boring!

The whole social thing was exhausting too.

Before the semester ended, however, my guy said one day, "Mike, I want you to come to a concert my friend from high school is giving for us in the auditorium this Friday."

I thanked him and said, "I'll try to get there." and promptly forgot about it.

So, I missed the Billy Joel concert.

Tick off yet another blown opportunity.

Chapter 64

ROTC But Different

When I started freshman year in college; I was dating a girl whose sister was married to a Marine Corps pilot. I always had an interest in the service, but I had seen some disappointing things in the Army and Navy, so when he said the Marines were different I thought; I'm different; maybe I should check it out.

He had gone through a program called PLC, or Platoon Leader Class. It was like ROTC but without the uniforms or classes.

I searched the phone book for the nearest Marine recruiting office and found one on the Navy base by the barracks. Everyone in Philadelphia knows the Philadelphia Naval Shipyard, active in the '70s as a refit and mothball center.

I spent time there when I was younger; in fact, I attended the christening of Kitty Hawk, the non-nuclear sister ship of the aircraft carrier Enterprise. I would never miss the yearly open house and would often go just to walk around. The gate office personnel on duty would just wave me in. It wasn't like it is today.

My red hair was a real asset in this place and soon everybody knew me. I was invited onto almost every ship I passed. I got tours of ships, barracks and other attractions as a boy.

The navy base was much as I remember it, but now I was driving, so it was a different entry procedure. I parked my car and signed in at the desk, got my pass and drove to the recruiting station where I met Staff Sergeant Brown.

Sergeant Brown was respectful and dressed in an impeccable uniform in a stark contrast to some other military recruiters. His initial impression made me think I was on the right track.

This is an Aspie thing for me - the focus on the uniform. I found later; while the Marines were focused on the uniform the Army was focused on other, which they considered, more important things.

He welcomed me in and showed me around the station - introducing me to the cadre of Marines running the program.

After all of the preliminaries; we sat down and he explained everything:

PLC was a program where college students could become Marine Corps officers. There were no drills, no classes to take and no uniforms to wear. He explained, if I joined now I had a choice to attend a summer camp between junior and senior year, which would initiate me into the Marines and enable me to be commissioned right after graduation from college.

If I joined after college, I would attend the camp after graduation and then be commissioned after the camp.

It sounded good. He said I could start some paperwork now, but nothing would commit me before I was actually commissioned.

We started the paperwork, which was like any other mound of paperwork except for the list of subversive organizations. There were hundreds of them, which I had to read and sign to acknowledge I had never been a member. Aside from that, the rest was normal stuff.

Then there was a test, and before I started the sergeant asked if I had ever taken the ASVAB. I told him I had taken it twice. He looked puzzled. I didn't mention the scores.

The test was timed, so the sergeant came in and gave a two-minute warning. After I finished; the sergeant said he had called down to the central record center and gotten my ASVAB scores.

He had one of those weird looks on his face.

He said, "You scored really high."

I said, "Thanks." - I'm nothing if not polite.

He scored the test through a card reader. After a quick buzz; the card popped out my score.

He turned with a funny look again exclaiming, "You should become a pilot!"

I said, "No, I'd rather stay on the ground."

He said, "But pilots get paid more."

I said, "No, that's ok."

He said, "Do me a favor."

This always gets my attention.

He said, "Look, you don't have to become a pilot, but if you qualify you have a choice few others have."

"And" he said, lowering his voice, "We have to qualify a certain number of pilots each month, and it's hard to get many to pass the exam. I think you would pass, and it would be a favor to me."

I'm a sucker for doing a favor. It's the sympathy vs. empathy thing.

I said, "Ok, if it will help you." - and was rewarded with a big smile.

I had a problem with, "No".

I had a girlfriend once, who couldn't say "No" but I don't mean it that way.

I know how to say no it just doesn't come across well.

There's no build-up, I just say, "No."

Apparently, most normal folks don't like that. Some need it delivered softer and some just don't like to be told, "No." Either way, it comes out wrong.

The sergeant produced a new test about twice as long as the first one. It had puzzles, directional questions, and visuals with related questions.

Things like:

- A picture of a stick in a helicopter asking which way to move the stick to go, forward right, or left.
- A picture of a map with questions about obstacles.
- Pictures of compasses and dials with questions about direction and graduations.

As a chemistry major, this was all cake. Within an hour, at least from an intellectual level, I was qualified to be a Marine pilot.

The sergeant was happy now and took me to the captain's office. The captain was a pilot who had flown F-4 Phantoms in Viet Nam. He jumped up and pumped my hand, sat me down, and told stories about flying in Viet Nam.

By the time the sergeant came back, I was convinced to become a pilot.

Chapter 65

Getting Physical

Now, I needed an aviation physical. Ground Marines get ground physicals, but aviators get aviation physicals. I had to go to a Naval Air Base for my aviation physical, which was scheduled, as all of these were, for a Wednesday two weeks away, giving me enough time to inform school I would need the day off.

The physical was eight hours long and included a thorough inspection of everything. I was to report at 7:30 AM and expect to be there until 4:00 PM. I would lunch in the officer's mess.

When I reported there were about a dozen other folks in the waiting room, which was set as a classroom. In addition to the potential aviators, there were also some folks taking a physical for the Marine Reserves. A doctor in a navy uniform told the reservists; they would be an hour or so, and to wait in the back of the room in their undies.

Another navy doctor came in and said, "What's up?"

The original doctor said, "These kids are here for aviation physicals."

The new doctor acknowledged with a nod and looked toward the back of the room.

The original doctor said, "Be careful what you say – there are M-A-R-I-N-E-S in the back of the room." - spelling out the word.

I had heard about the rivalry between the navy and Marines, but what shocked me more than the teasing laughter shared by the two doctors, was the confused look on the Marines in the back of the room. It was a little scary.

The physical was highly organized and thorough. First were measurements to determine we had the correct symmetry and our weight was in proportion to our height.

We were weighed, measured, peered into, poked, prodded and pinched. They checked skin, bones, alignment of spine, and then took some blood. They had us get naked for one doctor who checked our goods and made sure we had all our parts.

He even checked behind to make sure we were using it as nature intended. (This had to be explained to me. My imagination didn't go far enough for it to be intuitive.)

There were eye tests, physical agility tests, and a test for hearing. Everything belonging to me was inspected and examined. Just before lunch, we went to the dentist who checked our teeth and made an assessment.

Lunch was served in the officer's mess on bone China utilizing real silverware. I was starting to see this might really be a nice gig.

Several things stood out, particularly during the eye and ear exam. There was a separate doctor for everything; no shortcuts here.

The eye doctor told me I had really good vision, 20/15 which was the highest this particular scale measured. He also said my depth perception and color recognition were 100% on all his measurements.

He sported a big smile, so I thought, "Good."

The afternoon was spent finishing up the tests; the hearing test took some time, and then the psych doctor, who asked questions like:

How many in your family?

Where do you fit in?

How do you get along with them?

How about your parents?

Why do you want to be a Marine?

Nothing too intrusive.

At the end of the day, another doctor reviewed the results with us. He made sure nothing had been missed, and told me everything looked good, pending review by the flight surgeon, but before I left he noticed the hearing test results, and said, "You know, you have really good hearing."

He added, "Your hearing is above and below normal human thresholds. You can hear in ranges normally only dogs can hear."

He was smiling, so I felt good about it, thinking I'll be better able to hear the bad guys coming.

Later I started to think maybe that explained some things.

I had a new mission - finish college and be a Marine. This had a lot of appeal because there were people there who seemed to think like I did. It was organized and regimented, had routine and great food. I still wasn't too sure about the flying thing, but the Sergeant said I could still go Ground, so all was good.

A few days later I stopped by the base to see how I did on the exam. I passed the physical, so everything was finished.

Nice, I thought. I'll just finish college and I'm all set.

The next call from PLC was a real thrill; I was qualified as an aviator and could participate in initiation flights with Marine pilots. This would test whether I really wanted to be a pilot. It was also a way for the Marine Corps to winnow out anyone with a fear of flying or other issues.

There were several other benefits for the flights. The pilots who were doing the initiation flights were reservists, who could get the requisite hours in to keep their wings. It was a good thing all around.

Chapter 66

Get Ready to Taxi

The first initiation flight was scheduled with enough lead time to schedule the day off from school.

When I arrived, the front gate was expecting me, so things went fast. Soon I was in a briefing room for pilots with a few other students. We were briefed on flight prep, emergency procedures, that we'd be suited up in flight suits, fitted for parachutes - pilot stuff.

We also got an overview of the planes we'd be flying, T-28s. These were essentially a design resembling a WWII fighter plane updated with the latest technological improvements to keep them reliable and flying. They added a seat to accommodate a pilot and a student.

The pilot sat in the rear cockpit with the student in the front. It was a big single-engine airplane, which would have looked right at home in the Pacific theater of war in WWII. It had a 1,500 HP engine out of a B-17, I was told.

After the briefing, we were fitted with flight suits. We were told we'd be strapped into the plane and a parachute, which would come with us if we had to bail out. I don't know why, but this didn't seem to bother me, because we were told this was unlikely, and again, being literal, I believed them.

The planes stood over fifteen feet tall at the cockpit. The propeller was a gigantic three-bladed monster that looked twenty feet high. MARINES was painted in big bold block letters across both wings and both sides of the fuselage –Awesome!

The pilot climbed up the left wing with me to help me into the cockpit. There was a Marine ground crewman, an enlisted man, standing outside the cockpit on the opposite wing.

I climbed into the cockpit while the pilot explained how to release the harness in case of an emergency, noting the parachute would stay attached to me, as the crewman strapped me in.

The pilot showed me how the radio worked and pointed out how the microphone and headphones were attached to my helmet, noting these had to be detached first, before detaching the harness.

As the pilot talked; the crewman was pulling the straps on the harness tighter and tighter, until I finally looked at him. I guess that's how he knew they were tight enough because he chuckled and stopped. I felt like I was part of the plane. I could hardly breathe, and could only move my head, legs, and arms.

I can't say enough about how much a part of the plane I felt. We, the plane and I moved as a unit. I pressed and pulled things and the plane and I went places.

The last thing the pilot said to me was, "Ok, I'm going to take off and when we get up, I'm going to turn it over to you."

I looked up at him.

He said, "I'll walk you through what to do."

"Remember this!" he said.

"If I say, 'I got it!', take your hands off the stick and throttle and lift your feet off the rudder pedals. I'll take care of everything from there, OK?"

I nodded.

The pilot went to the back cockpit and, while he was being strapped in by the ground crewman; I inspected the cockpit. There were instruments in a cluster in front of me like a large flat dashboard. There were dials indicating altitude, RPM, fuel levels, and other things I didn't recognize. These were centered around a large instrument resembling a globe floating in clear liquid.

After a few seconds, I heard the pilot's voice in my earphones.

He said, "Do you see the black button on the throttle? To talk to me you push the black button. You release it when you're done talking."

Then he said, "Do you remember what I said I would say if there was an emergency?"

I pushed the black button and said, "I got it!"

I released the button.

He said, "Good."

"What did I say to do if you had to bail out?"

I pushed the button and said, "Pull the plug on the headphones and release the harness by hitting the round button. Stand on the seat and dive at the word MARINES on the right wing."

He said, "Well done! Let's go."

Verbal directions are easy to remember when given like this with all the visual and physical cues. Without them, they are just a lot of noise.

I hadn't realized at the time but he was multi-tasking. While he was talking to me he was exchanging hand signals with the ground crew. When I play back the video I see the ground crewman standing by the propeller.

I could see the pilot in a little rearview mirror above the dashboard. I think it was really for him to see me, but it was doing double duty. The pilot made a motion, and the ground crewman replied with a rotating motion with his index finger; there was a low rumble and then a boom and all 1,500 HP of the engine sprang to life with the sound of the front row of a muscle car rally.

The ground crew sprang to life and pulled the chocks from the wheels. They gave the pilot a thumbs up and we started to roll.

Being strapped in was not like the seatbelt in a car. I've been in muscle cars where you can feel the power and vibration through the seat, but I felt like I was actually a part of this machine. The power was going through my whole body.

The pilot spoke continuously now.

He said, "Ok you're going to hear me talking to the tower. You'll recognize the difference in the way I talk and the sound through your earphones, so you'll know when I'm talking to them through the radio and when I'm talking to you through the intercom. Stay off the intercom, when I'm talking to the tower, Ok?"

"Ok," I said.

I could see him smile in the mirror. And, I could feel the power of the plane as he throttled up. We were instantly rolling at about 30 MPH.

He was talking to the tower, "Marine 245 to Willow Grove tower."

"Willow Grove tower" came the response.

"Permission to taxi…" said the pilot.

"Taxi to runway 9." came the response.

We were the first crew ready and there was no one in our way.

It was a perfect day for flying. There wasn't a cloud in the sky and it was warm and calm.

We rolled past hangars and other planes at rest, a unique perspective. Usually seen from outside the fence; we were in the center, on the runway, rolling past the shops, hangars, and other planes.

Some of them were the Marine's A-4 attack jets, a single-seat jet which was rapidly becoming my favorite.

The Marines had OV-10 observation planes which were two-seaters used for forward observation, large cargo planes C-130s that could carry a platoon of Marines, Huey Helicopters, Sea Knights, and Sea Stallions which were huge helicopters.

They also had, which was the most coveted, the F-4 Phantom Supersonic Fighter.

However, each of these had a design flaw. They had more than one seat.

The A-4 was by default my choice.

By this time, we had reached the turnaround for runway 9 and the pilot said, "Ready?"

"Ready," I said.

The pilot said, "Marine 234 to tower on runway 9, ready for takeoff."

"Marine 234 you are cleared for takeoff." Came the reply.

Chapter 67

Takeoff!

We swung to the end of our counterclockwise 180-degree turn onto runway 9, the engine roared to life, and I was pressed back into my seat. Roared doesn't really do it justice, because the engine was producing so much power I could feel it in my bones!

I was alternatively looking out the window and at the airspeed indicator. In a few seconds, we were doing over 100 MPH. Suddenly the plane made an unusual movement. The landing gear is not as forgiving as automobile suspension, so you can feel every contour and bump in the runway.

Then, the plane was weightless! The unusual feeling was the plane getting ready to leave the ground and stretching, vs. pressing, the landing gear.

My senses were in overdrive. The speed indicator was at 130 MPH, and as the plane came level to the ground, I got a better view of the runway rushing under us!

Suddenly, I felt like I was being crushed, as the plane leaped into the air. It didn't take off or glide up like an airliner; it just jumped from the runway into the air!

The pilot said, "Look at the ground!"

I looked out the left side. The ground was moving away at a rate of speed I had never before experienced, and my mind raced to put it together.

The pilot said, "We are rising at a rate faster than our forward movement!"

We were going up at over 150 MPH. I had never been in anything going that fast in one direction - let alone forward and up at the same time. The pilot throttled forward and the engine returned a deep snarl!

I looked out the canopy and got my perspective. We were now at 2,500 feet, in a bank moving over the houses that had grown up around the base. The cars moving on Rt. 611 were getting smaller and smaller.

We went to 5,000 feet and leveled off 20 miles from the base.

The pilot said, "You want to fly this thing?"

"Yeah!" I said. I could see him laugh.

He said, "Ok see that thing in the middle of the cluster that looks like the earth?"

"Yes, I see it," I said.

He said, "That's called the horizon. See the line in the middle?"

"Yes," I replied.

He said, "That tells you your position in relation to the ground. When the line on the glass matches the line on the ball, you're level. When it's below the ball you're climbing, when it's above the ball you're diving, get it?"

"Yes," I replied.

He said, "Watch it." He turned.

He said, "See the horizon tilt?"

I said, "Yes."

He said, "That tells you when you're going right or left."

I could see how the horizon worked, and he explained it was necessary, because your senses get confused when flying, because there are other forces working on your body that you mistake for gravity, and you could actually be upside down and not know it, without these instruments.

He said instruments are especially important when it is cloudy or foggy and you can't see the ground and have to rely on your instruments and your senses.

Then he said, "Now, I'm going to show you how to fly."

He said, "Take the stick."

I took hold of the stick that had been moving on its own back and forth between my legs.

He said, "Can you feel it?"

I said, "I can!"

I could feel the heart of the plane through the stick. I was becoming one with the plane.

He said, "Ok here's how this works. When you want to turn left you move the stick to the left. When you want to go right you move the stick to the right. If you want to go up you pull the stick back, if you want to go down you push the stick forward, got it?"

"Got it," I said.

He said, "Ok; push the stick forward a little."

I did. I could feel us going down.

He said, "Ok now slowly pull it back."

I did and we started to go up.

He said, "Look at the horizon. When it gets level, level the stick out."

As I did; I thought, "This is easy!"

"Good," he said. "Ok, now we're going to try a turn."

He said, "Move the stick a little to the left."

I did, and the plane started to go left, but something felt wrong.

He said, "Look at the horizon and tell me what you see."

I looked and noticed we were going left but we were also going up.

"I said, we're going up."

He said, "Great, that's right. Ok straighten it out."

We were level again.

He told me, "When you bank left the plane wants to go up because the propeller is spinning in the opposite direction and the air is being slapped down, pushing the plane up. You have to compensate by pushing forward on the stick a little."

He added, "Ok let's try again. Bank left a little and at the same time push forward on the stick."

I did, and could feel the difference. I learned how much to push by feel and watching the horizon. The plane was now in a nice gentle controlled and level turn to the left. Again, I thought, this is easy, and fun! I was hooked.

He said, "Ok level out again."

I moved the stick, took a look at the horizon and we were again level.

"Ok" he said, "Now we're going to try a right turn."

He said, "This is a little trickier. When you turn right, you're going in the same direction as the prop is turning. The prop is going to want to pull us down, so in addition to moving the stick to the right, you'll also have to use the rudder to counteract. The rudder is controlled by the pedals under your feet. Have you seen them moving?"

I said, "Yes."

He said, "Good."

"Ok," he said; "Now start to turn to the right and at the same time start pressing the left rudder pedal."

I started the turn to the right and could immediately feel the plane start to dive. I pressed the rudder, but I didn't have the mix right and we kept diving.

I looked at the horizon to make sure, because I could feel the dive and see the ground but I wanted to make sure. Yes, we were diving. I pushed the pedal some more. Nothing!

I looked in the mirror, he was grinning. I thought, there must be something else. But, I took another look at the horizon and pressed harder on the rudder - still wasn't happening.

Then I realized I wasn't paying enough attention to the stick.

As I was turning right I was also moving it forward aggravating the dive. The stick didn't move forward and sideways on a true vertical and horizontal path like a gearshift, it moved wherever you pushed or pulled it.

I moved it back, eased off the turn, and increased the rudder. We started to level off. A quick peek in the mirror revealed I was on the right path. I was taking a quick look at the horizon to make sure what I was feeling was happening in the real physical world, when through the mike came the urgent command, "I got it!"

I let go of the stick and lifted both feet off the pedals!

Chapter 68

Small Traffic Problem

"Where the hell did he come from?!" boomed through the headphones.

I scanned to see what he was looking at.

"Holy Shit!" I thought.

50 yards directly ahead of us was an Allegheny Airlines commuter plane! We were flying at the right side of this plane at over 150 MPH.

Allegheny Airlines was the predecessor to USAir and operated short hops out of what was then known as Allentown Airport. This was a twenty-seater prop plane, and we were so close I could see the faces of the passengers pressed up against the window.

I can only imagine what they were thinking.

The engine of our plane made a tremendous and deliberate growl! Before I knew it I was getting an intense pressed-into-the-seat feeling again. I looked around to get my bearings and realized - we were upside down!

I thought, "But, I don't feel like I'm upside down."

I was looking at the ground through the top of the canopy, as the world quickly flipped over and righted itself again. Now it felt like we were sliding sideways like a car out of control in the snow.

I found out later; we were sliding sideways. The pilot had executed several maneuvers and had taken our plane over the other plane and come back down on the other side.

When I looked forward again; the Allegheny plane was ahead of us on the right.

From the headphones came the remark, "Now, if we were a fighter plane we would drop a couple hundred rounds into him."

The pilot had executed a maneuver to take us over and to the left rear of the commuter plane, rising a hundred feet and rolling over on our left wing. When he came back to the same altitude as the commuter plane we were in a blind spot on the left rear of the other plane.

"Very cool!" I thought.

It also occurred to me we were over 60 miles from Willow Grove. The speed with which we had done this was mind-boggling. We had risen to 5,000 feet in 5 minutes and traveled over 60 miles in 15 minutes. I think I had found my thing!

The pilot said, "Ok, that's enough fun for today. We're starting back."

He flew back, and we landed without incident.

Back on the ground we (I'm part of the crew now.) taxied back over to the starting point and the pilot swung the T-28 neatly around into its parking spot. The ground crew ran up and put the chocks behind the wheels, as we throttled back and started the shut-down procedure.

The pilot said, "Sit tight, the men will be up in a second."

The canopy started to open and I could see the men coming up onto the wing, as the engine slowed and wound to a stop. They looked at me and around the inside of the cockpit expecting something, but were disappointed; they looked at each other, shrugged, and laughed.

I found out later; they heard what happened with the commuter plane and expected the front cockpit to be splattered with vomit. Apparently, I had passed another test!

They unstrapped me and showed me how to get out of the plane. The pilot was waiting for me at the bottom of the wing with a smile across his face.

He said, "Kid, you're a natural!"

He added, "I was really surprised when you figured out how to get out of the right turn dive and how you reacted when I took the stick. But, anyone else would have lost their lunch all over the cockpit when I pulled the evasive maneuver."

"When I looked at you in the mirror you were watching and learning from what happened instead of holding your head and throwing up. And, believe me, the last few cadets launched all over the cockpit!"

I said, "Oh, no. It was cool! I just wish the flight had lasted longer."

He laughed, "Yeah, you're a natural, alright. None of us can ever get enough time behind the stick! Come on, let's go in and debrief."

Back inside the briefing room, the other cadets came in looking like they had seen a ghost. None of them had their flight suits on. Their pilots looked at mine and rolled their eyes. He chuckled.

At the front of the room there was a locker full of equipment, and still dressed in our flight suits, he pulled out two small airplanes on sticks. They were like pinwheels, but there was a small airplane on the end of the stick.

He used them to simulate the situation with the commuter plane. Using the sticks; he showed me how he had taken our plane up and over the other plane and come in behind him, adding, "This is a typical fighter plane maneuver."

He explained several other maneuvers, the Immelmann, named for a WWI German Ace, Max Immelmann, a roll, and others.

After the briefing, we shed the flight suits and talked about flying in the locker room. He encouraged me to stick with the program.

He walked me to the mess hall and said, "The other cadets are in here having lunch. I'll leave you here. See you next time!"

He shook my hand and joined other pilots already at a table.

The other cadets were at a table together looking alternatively green and pale. I came up and with my usual filter announced, "Wow, that was great! Let me tell you what we did!"

I recounted the story to them in detail, and they looked at me like I was nuts! Apparently, their flights didn't go as well.

One ended abruptly when the pilot couldn't get the cadet to work the radio, and he could hear him retching even over the engine noise.

Another froze on the stick and the pilot had to scream at him to let go.

Another just found the whole thing kind of boring. Go figure.

Anyway, they listened to my story like I was making it up, but I'm used to that.

At the pilot's table, my guy was laughing with the other pilots. The others were just shaking their heads and wondering how they had gotten themselves into today's situation.

All in all, a great day for me and what I figured was the roadmap to a career and the next 20 years.

Class was no longer the mission but a means to an end. A new motivation to do well in school replaced the malaise I was beginning to suffer. Having a goal is good for me. The nebulous, we'll do this then do that, was not the best way for me to operate.

My girlfriend was happy, because she wanted to get out of Philadelphia and this was the ticket! Her sister and brother-in-law were seeing the country as a military couple, and we agreed this would be fun!

Chapter 69

Not A Party Animal

A week or so after the flight, a member of the cadre called to announce a party for cadets in the NCO Club on the base the following Friday night. Seemed like a good thing at the time, although I wasn't really a party animal.

The instructions were, "Bring five bucks." No further information.

The party was during the fall, so was already dark when I got there. I found the NCO Club, parked my car and went in. There was no bone China or silverware in this place.

Much less ornate than the officers mess with its posh atmosphere, maple wood chair rails, framed photos of famous people and winners cups from golf and horse competitions; the NCO club had plywood walls, squad pictures and shooting competition trophies.

It smelled like the corner tappy, which someone tried to mask with the smell of bleach and pine oil.

Where the former had been designed with fine dining and socialization in mind; this place was a simple watering hole.

The fare for the evening was pretzels, potato chips (the soggy kind-meant as props) and beer served in plastic cups, which quickly turned it warm. Tap beer in plastic cups was necessary to eliminate bottles and glass mugs that not only were a pain to clean but were great weapons when some folks got too much beer in them.

I arrived early, because I didn't want to miss anything. I was there to see the final touches being put on the setup and was introduced to the brownies who helped the cadre.

And, being a newbie, I was introduced to everyone else. There were no women in this operation. I guess their time hadn't come yet, because it was all college age men.

I asked if the captain was coming and got the weirdest look ever. The sergeant just shook his head and collected $1.00, "For the beer!"

He chuckled and walked off.

The party was just getting started when two young women carrying bags came in the front door. I noticed this and thought they were lost, but the sergeant was expecting them and after an animated conversation, ushered them to a back room.

Music started from somewhere, and the girls reappeared wearing robes.

Now, did you ever hear the sound of a hard drive, right before your computer crashes; or when you are doing a search of the entire drive looking for some obscure file? That noise started coming from my brain.

My mind was racing for context. Nowhere in my dBase was there any reference to girls in robes in an obviously all-male gathering, especially one with all college students preparing to be Marine officers.

The answer wasn't long in coming. There was a little dais on the side of the room - not quite a stage. It was probably for award presentations or some other mandatory fun.

Keeping time with the music, the girls dropped their robes - revealing scanty bikinis, stepped onto the dais and began to dance! Well, normally I have a flat affect, but I would like to have seen the expression on my face when this happened. I'm sure it wasn't flat.

I sat there frozen; wondering, "What in the world?!"

I stared at these girls for the entire first song. I had several thoughts: What the hell is going on? Is this some other kind of test? Am I in the wrong place? Is there a separate party for the aviators? Where are these girls from? How did they find two so skinny?

And, my favorite: Where did they go to college? (I'm especially glad I kept this one to myself.)

This was the time before the invention of mixing and when the first pause between songs came; I looked around expecting to find equally baffled faces. But, as usual, I was the only one who didn't get it. Everyone else was talking, laughing and drinking beer. Those who weren't drinking beer were getting another beer.

I thought, "Ruh, roh! What did I do now?"

I also thought, "I'm sure my girlfriend and her sister were not aware of this part of the program!"

My face was numb; and not in a good way. It wasn't the beer, because I still had 90% left. I could milk a beer for hours. When someone would remark I would say, "This one is flat or this one is warm, I'm getting a new one."

They would smile.

This served the purpose of me not drinking beer, and them being satisfied I *was* drinking beer. It was also observed by those who were constantly on watch to see who was getting *another* beer, because having only one beer was highly suspicious behavior.

I was alternately watching the crowd and watching the dancers. We were now on a first name basis; they were the dancers.

The dancers were also demi-gymnasts doing interesting things, like bending over, and flexing certain highly trained muscles. This got cheers and accolades from the platoon, but it was still early. They would devolve as the evening progressed and the beer disappeared.

I was in my normal party mode, off to the side, at my own table, with my back to the wall, so I can see the whole room. I'm people watching, which, all learned indications would preclude, is one of my favorite pastimes.

I do look disinterested I'm told, but I'm focused and fascinated. It's the flat affect, I suppose. My energy is focused elsewhere.

This went on for about 20 minutes and the girls took a break. I guess that's hard work coordinating all that activity to the sound of music!

The girls came back for their second set to the tune of everyone's fourth or fifth beer. Things got louder, and I began to think maybe I should call it a night, but I didn't want to give offense.

Usually, I didn't think or care about that, but I was really liking this pilot idea.

So, I stuck it out.

Then the hat came around. Now, I know when a hat comes around; you're supposed to put some money in it, but I usually know why.

I asked, "What is this for?"

I hadn't read the manual yet, so I didn't know not to ask.

The sergeant said, "The girls are going topless."

I thought he was kidding. I laughed.

He said, "No, really. Put $2.00 in the hat".

This is what the balance of the $5.00 was for! The full implication hadn't hit me yet. I just gawped at him, robotically did what I was told and threw $2.00 in the hat.

Sure, enough when the hat hit the stage, so did the tops. Now the two skinniest girls in Philly, were dancing 10 feet away in high heels and bikini bottoms. The thought went through my head, as I'm sure it was going through everyone's head, these girls need a good meal.

The music was playing, they were dancing and swiveling, and everyone was having one hell of a time!

Now, remember the remark about flexing certain muscles? One of the girls' special talents was flexing her pectoralis muscles independently. I was savvy on pectoraliseses from vertebrate zoology. She was skilled at this and did it in time to the music.

I thought, "I wonder if so-and-so can do that." I decided not to ask.

This picture was in my head for the rest of the year, every time that song came on the radio!

After another 20 minutes; the girls gathered up their robes and tops and took another break. I don't know what dancers do on break, but they were gone about 10 minutes or so, when the hat came around again.

I didn't have to think about it this time. They only had two things left to take off, and I was pretty sure they would keep their shoes on. When they came out I saw the sergeant talking to them outside the door of the break room. One was shaking her head and the other was nodding.

The one girl was packing up her stuff while the other was taking the hat and its contents to her bag. As one left and the music started up again I was doing two things. Calculating how much was in the hat (how much did it take for this?) and looking at the stage with my mouth open.

Halfway through the first song the bikini bottoms hit the floor.

I hit the door!

"What the hell did I get myself into now?" was the dialogue in my head as I drove off the base. There was nothing in my data banks for a reference. What happened if the hat went around for a third time?

Second thoughts again.

What happened to decorum? What am I doing with these people? Maybe these are just the Ground cadets, but Tail Hook would dissolve that idea some years later. How do these people have families? What do I tell my girlfriend about the party?

I went back to school with the disc inside my head spinning.

Chapter 70

The Bad Math

I wanted to start this chapter off with a rant about how math is broken. You can't divide by zero and the square root of -1 is an imaginary number? What is that all about? But, I decided to hold the thought for another day.

On to the anecdote.

I was back at school now with a melody stuck in my head for some reason or another zoning out in math class.

One of our required classes was algebra. I understand algebra; I just can't do it. This is typical and honest and always gets rolled eyes. How can't you do it if you can understand it?

One of my tricks is being able to come up with an analogy for almost anything and a proverb to negate any proverb.

I can come up with dozens of analogies to compare to this, but let's just take my word for it. My best guess is it has something to do with the numbers moving from one side to the other and from the top to the bottom of the equation. But I really don't know. It causes my head to spin.

I get the same effect when I work on a car. If, I'm on my feet; I have no problem with tools or nuts and bolts. If, however, I lie on my back and get under the car, everything is reversed; it makes my head spin. I have to do everything deliberately, or I'll break something.

My brain just doesn't like algebra. I can ace arithmetic, statistics, trigonometry, geometry, chemistry, bio, physics, accounting, economics and everything else they throw at me but algebra.

Albert Einstein had the same problem. Maybe that's why the idea of relativity came naturally to me.

But, back to the bad math. As a chemistry-major chemistry problems included algebra. Adding the algebra course to help with the chemistry, gave me the opportunity to do poorly in two classes.

The algebra professor pointed out; I had to do something fast, because my grade in the final at the end of the first quarter was hurting pretty badly.

There is always more than one way to do something. I can usually come up with ten. Some good – some not so good.

I needed a good one.

It came at Christmas.

Mankind had just moved from using the abacus at this point in evolution and was using the slide rule to perform calculations. The slide rule was a tricky device used before the calculator was invented to do all those cool calculations you now do on your computer.

The calculator was the device in-between the slide rule and the computer.

Someone like me realized; logarithms were the source of all truth and knowledge where math is concerned and put them on parallel rulers that slide back and forth and produced answers. It was a magic wand for algebra.

I got an early Christmas present, a new slide rule. Yeah, I know a slide rule for Christmas. What did Ferris say, "I was born under a bad sign." But it turned out to be what the Germans call Glück im Unglück; literally luck within bad luck.

The luck wasn't actually the slide rule itself; it was in the manual. During the Christmas holiday I studied the manual.

Yeah I know, but listen.

That manual was just what I needed. I learned; the logarithms on the slide rule could be used to solve binomial equations, the most evil of algebra problems. Just that should tell you to avoid them. They're purposely built to be problems!

The manual showed me how to take these binomials and solve them with the slide rule. I was killing them within a few hours. None of them were safe from me anymore! I went through all of the chapters covered to date and redid the problems, and got them all right.

I ruled algebra now, and slide rules were perfectly legal and permitted during the exam.

In the next exam; I solved those problems quick as Pan, and was in and out of the exam like the Marines! I don't think I was home an hour when the call came from my professor. I should have just anticipated it and stayed at school, because I knew why he was calling.

He said, "Mike can I ask you to come over to my office?"

"Sure, I replied. I'll be right there."

I went back to school and straight to his office, making sure to take the slide rule and manual with me.

He was wearing a look I had seen many times before. His face was a little hard to describe, kind of like he was trying to get his eyebrows to touch, also he wasn't smiling.

He said, "Do you know why I asked you to come in?"

I said, "Yes, you think I cheated on the exam." which sat him back in his chair.

He sat upright and said, "Why would you say that?"

I said, "I nailed it; didn't I?" He had it in his hand.

He said, "Yes, but there is no work on this exam, and you did so poorly on the past exams."

He asked, "Can you explain?"

I said, "Sure!" I pulled out the slide rule and the manual. I handed him the slide rule.

He said, "Nice!"

I thanked him and said, "I got this for Christmas. The manual shows how to solve algebraic equations with the slide rule. I found; all I need to do is keep track of the powers of ten and the slide rule does the rest."

He said, "I don't understand."

I said, "May I see the exam?"

He handed it to me, and I demonstrated how I could manipulate the slide rule to get the answer. I showed him how I counted the powers of ten and kept track of them, and highlighted scribbling on the exam.

He looked up at me confused.

I said, "See those numbers?" pointing to what appeared random on the test.

He said. "Yes."

I said, "That's the work."

I ran through the complete problem and pointed out the appropriate numbers and showed him the final answer on the slide rule.

He sat back in his chair again with his eyes wide.

He said, "I've never seen that before. Do another one!"

I did. He looked at me again.

He said, "I'm not sure I believe you."

If I had said that; it would have been catastrophic! I loved these reactions. If he didn't believe I was doing this, as I demonstrated right in front of him; how did he think I was doing it? Magic?

I said, "Do you have an exam we haven't seen yet?"

He said, "Yes." And turned to a file drawer next to his chair. He fingered through the files and produced a blank exam.

I looked at the problem, worked the slide rule, jotted down a couple of numbers and put the answer on the exam. He looked at me again.

He said, "Do it again."

I did another one.

Not being afflicted with creativity made it easy for this Professor Doctor to do what he did next. You would think I'd have learned by then not to expect a person with a PhD in math would be excited about this.

He said, "I've been doing this for twenty-five years, and I've never seen this before."

I thought, "Cool, we're on to something; something he would be excited about and maybe write a paper, but Nooooo."

He said, "Well, you didn't do the work, so I can't give you full credit."

I pointed out I had done the work, and showed the powers of ten on the paper.

He said I hadn't done all of the steps, so it didn't count.

I pointed out what I did was better, because it eliminated the steps and still got the right answer. He was adamant; he would only give me enough credit to pass the course, but no more.

A normal person would have called in the chits they had with the dean and had the professor's ass handed him, but what it did for me was to add yet another ounce to the bad side of the balance for staying at this school.

I would think anyone who is punished for doing the right thing would react with a bad attitude. What it did to me was to reconcile relative IQs and move on.

Between freshman and sophomore year of college I transferred from PCP&S to Temple University and continued working on my first degree, full time and part time, since a degree was just a rite of admission to the Marines at this point.

Chapter 71

Temple U

I changed my major to accounting and stayed at Temple, until my first real job seemed to render it moot. Within the first week of class, it was obvious I had again stepped into something I didn't understand but bigger and more baffling.

During orientation, we were given several standardized tests and were now getting the results in the packed 626-seat lecture hall.

A graduate student was in the front reading names and assigning room numbers. It took an hour for the hall to be almost empty, as those called left for their assigned rooms, until there were 50 of us left.

Then he said, "The rest of you can go."

I turned to the kid next to me and said, "What was that all about?"

He said, "They have to go to remedial reading and math."

I said, "What is that?"

He just laughed and left. When I found out what it meant; the idea of it scared me.

Accounting 101 was the initial class for an accounting degree, what they call Finance now. Temple U had a huge campus in North Philly into which 40,000 full- and part-time day and night students took turns shining the seats.

There were several lecture halls feeding us the initial tenants of the foundational courses for the degree: accounting, economics, marketing, and the like. I was allowing myself to be exposed to ever larger and more diverse venues and the effects were almost mind-numbing but exciting.

One of the things I found hard to adapt to was people calling out in class. We were trained to raise our hand, but the cross section in this environment was motivated by the desire to get what they needed, so they had to be assertive.

In the first week of Accounting 101 in a lecture hall with 300 other students; one student near the instructor was constantly calling out some question or other. It got so I knew his voice after a few weeks of this. I could clearly see his face.

Years later, I was watching a TV show called America's Funniest Videos and recognized my former classmate.

Yeah, Bob Sagat was in my freshman Accounting 101 lecture.

I never talked directly to him, but it was impossible not to recognize his voice. I fact-checked myself, and sure enough, he was enrolled at Temple the same years as me.

Chapter 72

Otherworldly Cheating

I have the ability to be accused of cheating in venues you didn't know cheating existed!

I was still mulling over the pass-the-hat incident when I got a message to call the base.

Sergeant Brown dryly said, "Can you come down to the base tomorrow?"

PLC was now my focus, so I skipped class and went.

Previously he would greet me enthusiastically and walk me to his desk. Today he just sat at his desk and beckoned me. He and the other cadre had a certain look on their faces.

I thought, "Oh, I know that look."

Something is wrong now, and we're going to have the talk.

Situations like this were often a surprise to me. With the math professor; I knew what was wrong, but often I either didn't know I had done something wrong or didn't know what I had done was wrong.

This time I had no idea what was wrong, and clearly something was.

Sergeant Brown started the bifurcated explanation, "Whenever someone changes schools, they audit all their paperwork and make sure everything is ok." adding "They also check the aviator cadets' physicals on a yearly basis just in case."

The two stories told me he was hiding something. I learned later in life; this is dubbed TMI - Too Much Information, and is indicative of deception.

I pushed for details and he said, "They were checking your physical from last year and found some irregularities".

Oh, those dreaded irregularities! When this weasel word joined the conversation; I knew he was fudging.

"Irregularities?" I said.

"What does that mean? A germ? An anomaly? What?"

He didn't know, but he was sure it was important, because they wanted me there on Tuesday, and no one ever goes for a physical on a Tuesday, only Wednesdays - the familiar lock-step pattern of governmental bureaucracies.

He had a mix of apprehension, anxiety and pissed-offedness on his face. The others in the office flashed that Oh, man – are you in for it! look as they went by.

Ok, whatever, another day off from class and another free lunch!

I was about to learn another lesson - TINSTAAFL. There is no such thing as a free lunch!

That Wednesday I got up early and drove to the base. I reported to the dispensary to weird looks. I couldn't tell if they were pissed off because, I was disrupting their normally quiet Wednesday, or something else.

I was the only one there for a physical. A navy doctor in a lieutenant's uniform met me at the reception desk and introduced himself. He told me he'd be taking me through the physical.

He had a clipboard!

This time the doctor walked me from station to station and recorded everything. I didn't get it, but if this is what they need…

I've since learned, from my wife; this is the point where you start to ask an exhaustingly long list of questions, but I hadn't met her yet, so she couldn't tell me.

Some of the doctors I recognized from before, like the eye doctor. He gave me a big smile and examined my eyes. This was thorough and included extra time on the optical machinery - a cross between a microscope and giant binoculars. The first time this test was quick, but now it lasted the better part of an hour. There were hmmmmms and ohhhhs and ahhhhs.

My doctor (I've come to think of him as mine by now.) was making copious notes and notations on his clipboard, taking this way too seriously.

The final part of the exam was the eye chart. Again, my score was 20/15, the highest this type of test measures. (It actually goes higher, but this was their cut-off point.)

Then there was a discussion. I wasn't paying particular attention to it, because it was just a routine eye exam, so I was looking around the room to see what I could see.

I remember hearing my doctor say, "That doesn't prove anything."

The eye doctor grimaced and told a corpsman, of which there seemed to be an unlimited supply, "Get the other charts."

"Yes sir!" he said and gave me the stink-eye as he turned his back to the doctors.

People hate an interruption to their routines. They hate anyone who is different and upsets their paradigm of the world - making me especially popular.

The corpsman came back with several other charts and replaced the one I already read. This one had completely different letters on it. The results were the same. They progressed through the other charts.

One had all three-legged tables decreasing in size, another had different shapes, there was one with clocks on it, and the final chart had arrows pointing NSEW.

Nothing changed. 20/15 each time.

At the bottom of each chart, the manufacturer's name and Philadelphia address were printed in smaller letters than the 20/15 line.

I almost said, "I can read the print at the bottom, if you want." But thought better of it.

Normally, I would have done this, but I had a heightened level of discomfort by this time which can stifle me – a little.

The eye doctor looked at my doctor and said, "Satisfied?"

He said, "Yes, let's go."

The eye doctor winked and shot me a smile, as we went to the next station.

There was a short discussion at the ENT Doctor. They left the room, so I didn't get that one, but when we got to the hearing exam things went pear shaped.

In the room where they do the hearing test is a large soundproof booth surrounded by desks occupied by yet more corpsmen.

My doctor asked the ear doctor to, "Please read the instructions to this candidate." with heavy emphasis on read.

He didn't want any mistakes made.

The doctor motioned to a corpsman.

The corpsman picked up a card and read, "The test you are about to take tests hearing acuity. You will be asked to step into the soundproof testing booth and place the headphones on your ears. The headphones are marked left and right. Please be sure you have the correct headphone on the correct ear. When the test begins you will hear a sound in one of the headphones. Please press the button when you hear the sound. Hold the button as long as you hear the sound. When you no longer hear the sound, release the button."

The corpsman looked up from the card and asked me if I understood.

I said, "Yes."

The ear doctor said, "Please repeat the instructions back to me."

I did.

He was satisfied and looked at my doctor, he nodded, and the ear doctor said, "Ok." to the corpsman.

The corpsman opened the sound proof booth and told me to take a seat. He picked up the headphone and showed me that it was marked right and left. He handed the headphones to me and watched, as I put them on. He handed me a stick with a button on the end attached to a wire that disappeared into the wall.

He backed out and shut the door.

He didn't have to back out, but he purposely backed out and watched me, until he was outside and could shut the door. For a few seconds he looked in at me through the window in the door, then disappeared.

Soon I heard a high-pitched noise in my right ear. I pressed the button and held it until the noise stopped. This went on for ten minutes, first one ear then the other, up the scale, down the scale. Some sounds lasted for a second some for ten seconds. Each time I heard the noise; I pressed the button. When it stopped I released the button.

Pretty simple, huh?

Wait for it!

After the noise stopped there was a two-minute discussion outside the booth before the door opened. When the door opened, the corpsman facing me had his back to the doctors. The corner of his mouth was curled up in an expression indicating angry frustration.

I got up and came out of the booth. My doctor and the ear doctor replaced the corpsman, who gladly got out of the way – the all too familiar weird looks on their faces.

My doctor blurted out, "We think you are cheating on the hearing test!"

Now, this is not the first nor last time I've been accused of cheating. When my math professor called me after the midterm I knew exactly why, but this made no sense!

Chapter 73

Catch-222

"... cheating on the hearing test!" hit my ears like a smack in the face! My mind raced for a millisecond and then they got the full treatment.

Brace yourself!

I said, "HOW, EXACTLY, does one cheat on a HEARING TEST?!"

This came not with my modulated humble let-me-hold-back-voice.

This was the quarterdeck, Noah, build me an ark voice!

Everyone shuddered from the impact and then stiffened. Those who had been pretending not to be listening couldn't help but stop what they were doing and turn around to see what was about to happen.

My doctor said, "We think you are just pressing the button."

I snapped back, "I AM pressing the button, isn't that what you", looking around at them all, "said I was SUPPOSED to do?"

He said, "Yes, but we think you just keep pressing and releasing the button in a rhythm regardless of what the sound is."

I said, "What the HECK would I do that for?"

He said, "That fools the machine into thinking you're hearing sounds you're really not hearing."

I said, "So, your machine is unable to tell the difference?"

He said, "Yes, that would give a false reading."

I said, "Well that's NOT what I'm doing. The instructions were simple and easy to follow. When I heard a sound; I pressed the button and held it until it went away. That's what you wanted, isn't it?"

He said, "Yes."

I said, "WELL?!"

He and the ear doctor went to the doorway. After a brief discussion they came back and he said, "We'd like to rerun the test."

I said, "I'm here all day."

He said, "We'd like to run it again and see if the results are the same."

I said, "Ok."

They ran the whole test again. This time however, a corpsman stood at the little window in the door and alternately looked at me and the corpsman who was running the testing equipment.

Ok, test number two was over, and results are showing an even better score. They're really baffled now leading to another huddle in the doorway.

"We would like to try something else." said my doctor.

I don't really like him anymore, but he's who I'm stuck with.

I said, "Like I said - I'm here all day."

This time the corpsman stayed in the room with me while I re-took the test, and again, the results got better. A new level of confusion entered the room, so the doctors called for another opinion.

A third doctor came in and the ear doctor, my doctor and he had a huddle. Then they approached me as a herd.

In addition to their nonsense; I have three corpsmen giving me the hairy-eye-ball. I'm really starting to dislike the navy. I'm beginning to realize why God didn't want me to go to Annapolis and why they don't get along with the Marines.

The third doctor was about a year older and outranked these two, so he was automatically the wisest. He was going to fix this, but now I'm at battle stations.

When this happens, my brain discards nonsense and gets literal and succinct.

He said, "Can you tell us what you are doing in the booth?"

I said, "Yes."

He just looked at me, and I looked back at him.

He said, "What are you doing in the booth?"

I said, "Taking the hearing test."

He looked at the other doctors.

He said, "How are you taking the hearing test?"

I said, "I put the headphones on. Sound comes out of the headphones and goes into my ears. When I hear the sound, I press the button. When the sound stops, I release the button."

He looked back at the others again. Not too many places to go from there.

I was in full AS mode now, really holding on, trying to forestall the meltdown. Cheating on the hearing test! Whoever heard of that. Who would even think of it. And why? Only reprobates cheat.

At this point the three of them huddled at the door again. The tie breaking doctor asked for the chart from my doctor. He scanned the tests and when he got to the eye test he said, "Well, he can see like a hawk, and can hear like a dog. For all we know he probably smells like a dog."

Now, remember; they've removed themselves to a distance they believe is out-of-ear-shot.

I interjected, "Well, as long as I don't smell like a GOAT!"

You should have seen the look on their faces! The third doctor's head was about to explode. My doctor had his mouth open and the ear doctor was snickering up his sleeve at the other two.

The third doctor said, "What did you say?!"

I said, "As long as I don't smell like a GOAT. It's bad enough smelling like a dog, but did you ever smell a goat?"

I seized the momentum.

I continued, "Goats really stink! My grandfather told me he once had a goat with no nose and it smelled terribly!"

The doctors appeared stunned, and the corpsmen were in tennis watching mode.

I kept it up. "So, since I can hear what you're saying in your huddle out of earshot; does that mean I pass the hearing test? Or, is that too subjective? I mean, do I have to be in the soundproof booth? By the way, did I tell you my dad's a watchmaker?"

They had a physical reaction to this.

"Yeah, he's a watchmaker. You might relate to this since you're in the navy. He says waterproof watches are not really waterproof; that's a marketing trick. Waterproof watches are actually water resistant."

"You know like the old joke, Is a frog waterproof? - No, he's differentially permeable."

I couldn't stop, "Let's talk about your sound proof booth. When I was in the soundproof booth with the door shut; I could not only hear the conversation between you and the corpsman and you and you", I said, pointing at the doctors in turn, "But I could hear him turn the switches on and off and manipulate the dials controlling the frequency and sound."

"The first time in the booth; I was focused on the test, so the sounds made by the corpsman manipulating the switches and dials were just incidental. By the second test I had determined the connection between the sounds made by the switches and dials and the sound coming out of the headphones. Your leaving the corpsman at the door looking from me to the sound operator facilitated this."

"By the third test I could anticipate the sound and know exactly when the corpsman initiated the sequences producing the sounds. So much for soundproof, huh?"

"So, by the time I took the third test I actually was cheating on the test, but being able to cheat on the test requires even better hearing than the test can test for, so does that mean I've passed? Maybe we should call Joseph Heller (Author of Catch-22) and ask him what he thinks."

By now the third doctor was thinking about becoming indignant. I could see it on his face, and I was ready. He saw the change in my face and re-thought himself.

Ok, so what do we do now? The two doctors called in a tie breaker and now the three of them can't come to an agreement.

Another huddle.

I shot them a look that said, "If, I can hear through the booth - I can certainly hear what you're saying over there!"

They immediately realized this was a bad idea and left the room. Now the corpsmen and I are looking at each other; they with a wide-eyed wonder and me with a smug grin.

About five minutes passed and the team of doctors came back into the room and announced, "We think your hearing is too sensitive to be in an aircraft. We think the noise from jets might damage your hearing."

I said, "Ok, Joseph Heller it is! If I score higher than you expect, but within the range your equipment can measure; I don't have enhanced hearing; I'm cheating, and I fail the test. If I prove I actually can hear not only what the equipment measures, but beyond its capability of measuring, then I have hearing too sensitive to be in jets, and I fail the test."

"If I have enhanced hearing; would not that make me an asset in the program? Especially combined with the enhanced eyesight, notwithstanding the fact - I smell like a dog?"

Frustrated, my doctor said, "We think the jet engines might damage your hearing."

I said, "Does it damage the hearing of the other pilots? I flew with one last week; his hearing seemed perfectly fine."

"He has normal hearing," said my doctor.

I said, "Well then the jets will damage my hearing only down to the level that it becomes normal hearing; qualifying me to fly. Unless you feel I can't fly, until my hearing is normal, but I can't get it to the normal level, unless I fly."

I threw up my hands and said, "We definitely need Joseph Heller for this!"

They hadn't yet caught on that I could hear across the room and held another huddle. Then the third doctor disappeared around the corner. He had just whispered one sentence during the huddle. "I'm getting Captain Adler."

Chapter 74

The Boss

Captain Adler was the flight surgeon in command of the medical unit. He was in charge of the entire medical program and staff - the highest person on the medical food chain, and as a medical doctor with fighter pilot wings, was at the top of the food chain among humans in general - up with the astronauts.

Captain Adler was, a 50ish, tall, athletic naval officer. He had the posture, bearing and swagger of a nineteenth century Prussian admiral and had only one rung to climb, before he was wearing stars on his shoulder boards.

When he walked in everyone stiffened. The enlisted personnel all sprang to their feet and any officers not directly involved backed up to the walls.

He was accompanied by the third doctor chatting away in his left ear. Even though the third doctor was six feet tall Captain Adler had to bend a little to align his ear to the third doctor's mouth.

I had programmed them to whisper.

Consider the irony.

The third doctor was telling Captain Adler; they had checked, double checked and triple checked my hearing. He said they validated the readout of the equipment and verified I can indeed hear in the ranges indicated by the test.

He added, "The results of the other tests are also above normal and have also been tested multiple times and validated."

I stashed the word higher for later, but I didn't need it.

Captain Adler said, "Where is the chart?"

Captain Adler flipped through the chart and looked over at me. He didn't have to ask who I was. I was the obvious odd man out in the room.

Captain Adler simply said, "Have you ever been in an airplane?"

I said, "Yes sir." (See, I'm not stupid.)

Captain Adler said, "Have you ever been around jets?"

I said, "Yes sir."

He said, "When?"

I said, "I worked at the Philadelphia International Airport during the year following high school. I was around jets and other aircraft all day long."

He said, "Did the sound bother you?"

I said, "No sir."

He turned to the other doctors, handed off the chart and said, "Our mission here is to identify potential candidates for the aviation program by administering the appropriate tests. He passed the test. Move him through the program."

Then he turned on his heels and left.

You could have heard a pin drop. You could, if your hearing was good enough, also hear me laughing inside.

After a minute or so, when they snapped out of it, the third doctor said, to my doctor, "You got this?"

He said, "Yes sir."

The third doctor walked off and the ear doctor, still snickering down his sleeve, walked away too.

My doctor looked at the chart one last time. Flipped through the pages and said, "I guess you can go."

"That's it?" I said. "Nothing else?"

He said, "Just check with the corpsman at the front desk, before you leave. Then you can go."

Chapter 75

Taps

There was a cute young female navy corpsman sitting at the desk, wearing a tired look of having been hit on by every clown who walked through the place, and this was a big place.

She looked up and said, "Are you Michael Cubbage?"

I said, "Yes I am."

She said, "Captain Adler wants to see you, before you leave. Please have a seat."

I said, "Ok."

I caught her sneak a peek at me out of the corner of her eyes. She had sky-blue eyes.

In two minutes, the corpsman said, "Captain Adler is ready to see you."

She jerked a blasé thumb over her right shoulder to a door which read, Captain A. Adler, Commanding Officer, Medical Unit.

The office had high ceilings with mahogany walls, floor to ceiling book cases, Ottomans on the floor and plenty of light coming from two floor to ceiling windows to the left of the Captain's desk.

The Captain was seated at his desk, a huge mahogany affair, twenty feet from the door. He stayed seated and said, "Sit down."

I sat in a large green leather-covered mahogany chair in front of his desk.

Captain Adler was wearing a crisp khaki uniform with his pilot's wings proudly displayed at the top of his chest over his other decorations. On his shoulders were the eagles defining his rank as a naval captain, equivalent to a full colonel in the army, air force, or Marines.

His hair was full and cut high and tight. He was in good shape, tall and slender.

When I sat down we studied each other for a few seconds and then he spoke.

He said, "So you want to be a pilot?"

I said, "Yes sir."

He said, "Why?"

I said I had been on an initiation flight and found it to be quite exciting. I added that the pilot who took me up said I was a natural.

Captain Adler said, "I see here; you were chemistry major at the Philadelphia College of Pharmacy & Science. That seems a little out of synch with Marine Corps Pilot."

I just looked at him. Was there a question here?

He asked, "Why chemistry?"

I said I had originally intended to go into medicine, but circumstances were not favorable to that.

Then he said, "Would you like to come back for some tests? I would like to set up some additional tests for you to take."

A cold sweat came over me! I had visions of being in a lab with wires attached to my head and a probe in my behind. Alarm bells were going off all inside my head. All of a sudden, I couldn't wait to get away from this place!

I said, "What would I have to do?"

He said, "Just check with the corpsman. Make sure she has your number and we'll set it up."

I said, "Ok."

I had dispensed with the sir. I got up to test him and he just looked at me.

I said, "Ok." Again, and headed for the door. I looked back to see what he was doing, but he was already looking at his desk, so I knew I was safe for the moment.

I made a beeline for my car and drove off the base. I may be a lot of things, but I'm not a lab rat. I just had an overall bad feeling. Maybe I'm wrong. Maybe he wanted to make me an astronaut.

I considered hanging it up at this point, but I had a chit for another initiation flight. That flight started the same as the other, but a nasty three-day Northeast mist rolled in and blanketed the area.

We took off, flew, and landed without ever seeing the ground.

This pilot, who was all business, said, "If you like this; you'll like flying because this is what 90% of it is like - flying blind with instruments."

Considering the party at the NCO Club, the physical and this non-adventure; I was done with the military. Aside from a quick run at ROTC, I stayed as far away from them as I could.

For the next six months I avoided the many phone calls and letters that came from the recruiter at the navy base. It wasn't until years later I would even entertain the idea of the military again, but even then briefly and not seriously.

Chapter 76

Sensitivity Vs. Difficulty With Social Interactions

A lot happened in that second physical. It is hard to break paradigms people hold, even with objective information.

When the objective testing showed superior hearing, the doctors saw cheating. When cheating was dismissed, they saw sensitive hearing. Since the ability to hear through the booth was not part of their testing program, they couldn't process including it in the evaluation.

Their absurd logic could not be budged despite three Joseph Heller infusions and simple linear logical refutation. My skills were improving from the incidents in high school, though.

I had just taken on three M.D.s and muddled them so badly that they had to call in their boss as a tie-breaker, the adult equivalent of calling for mommy. The interaction was one of many examples of what my mouth was like, unabridged!

Even though the end result was leaving the program, I could add a win for my side against a bureaucratic monster roaming everywhere. I could negotiate with the best of them using logic and knowledge.

My only regret was not having the social skills to get a phone number from the corpsman with the sky-blue eyes!

And since nothing happens in a vacuum, I soon found out the Marines and my girlfriend were a package deal. Shortly after I announced the Marines were now persona non grata in my life, she announced I was persona non grata in hers!

Which only intensified my regret of not having gotten the phone number!

Chapter 77

Pedestrian Jobs

The latest figures I've read say 60% of Aspies are unemployed, and 40% are employed in pedestrian jobs. I don't know about those figures, but I certainly worked my share of pedestrian jobs before I finally got my ass in gear.

I think of those today as valuable learning points and stepping stones. I got a much broader exposure to people of all shapes and colors. It opened my eyes to different cultures, dialects, preferences, paradigms, tastes, and dangers.

The Bank

I worked for about a year for a bank. The job I was hired for was teller, but I guess they watched me during training and felt the coin and currency department would be a better fit. It was in a cellar in the main branch, where I spent an entire summer recharging my pale - never seeing the sun.

This was the central repository for the storage and distribution of coins and bills to the other branches. It was also the place where all the night deposits were processed. I had that job.

I would open the locked bags businesses threw into the night deposit depository on the wall of the branches. I would count the money and validate the deposit slip. The cash went into the next room for storage, and the deposit slips to accounting.

About the only exciting thing that happened that year was the move off the gold and silver standard for currency. Paper currency became intrinsically useless, but for a time, you could cash the gold and silver certificates two to one. We were in the perfect spot for that.

And the price of silver went sky-high. Everyone was on the lookout for both the silver certificates and the 90% silver coins. They would replace them with their own money and at lunch time they would run to the federal reserve to cash them in.

It was also a habit of people at this time to have a large container in their homes, usually, a giant whisky bottle or water jug, into which they would put all their loose change at the end of the day.

I worked with a man later on who told me that during that time period, he cashed in enough silver to pay off his mortgage.

The Bowling Alley

This was an experience. I had dreams of bowling alleys for years after this.

I think it was the noise.

I don't know what the general paradigm about bowling alleys is, but there was a lot of activity in there. From what I can discern, there seems to be a paradigm that it is a gathering place for a certain narrow strata of society, but from my vantage point at the center of the room, the social mix was much more inclusive.

One of my favorite things has always been, in direct contradiction to the current stereotypical literature, *people-watching*.

A great place for people-watching is the central area of any big city. Broad and Locust Streets in Philly is good. First and First, or as Jerry Seinfeld calls it, *The nexus of the universe*, is another, as are Wall and Water, Soho in general, and anywhere along Broadway.

My favorite place for this was the Wildwood, New Jersey, boardwalk, but since this was restricted to the summer, the window I had in the center of the bowling alley was perfect. Along with the constant flow of people into the venue, there was a constant flow of traffic from one end to the other via the aisle in front of the counter.

Adding the lively social activity on, among, and between the lanes provided a great formula for observation.

Charles Darwin would have loved it.

Certain settings pop up as those patterns identifiable as smaller versions of life - microcosm - the bowling alley being a salient example. It served as a gathering place for unattended groups of teens, young couples, married couples, and semi-serious singles.

There were covalently bonded groups called *leagues* whose members were comprised of roofers, firefighters, nurses, neighborhood klatches, local businessmen, and extensions of existing organizations such as Lions, Rotary, and the Loyal Order of Moose.

Families bought their children. Grandchildren brought their grandparents. Parties were held to celebrate birthdays, confirmations, and engagements.

People considered bowling a hobby, a form of exercise, or just a way to blow off steam. Among those semi-serious singles could be found middle-class aspirants to the pros, as well as those who worked at maintaining a low profile.

For some, it was just a place to get away—a diversion from whatever existence required a dedicated time to focus, play, practice, or just relax.

My dad was an aspiring pro, so he was familiar with the venue. He brought me with him often as a boy, so I had a familiarity at least with the building. I mentioned I was looking for a part-time job to supplement the bank job, so he spoke to the manager.

I met with the manager and started the next weekend, working the busy times, Friday nights, and all-day Saturday and Sunday.

My duties included assigning bowling lanes, renting the special shoes required to walk on the polished oak lanes, monitoring the functioning of the pin-setting machines, and making change for the assorted vending and ball-cleaning machines.

Yes, there was a machine to clean your bowling ball. You see, although many folks utilized one of the hundreds of balls available for use on the racks behind the lanes, there were many folks who chose to bring their own.

Serious bowlers had their own special kit, which they brought to the lanes in a personal bowling bag.

Bowling bags told a story. They were personalized items, and quality ranged from basic vinyl to expensive leather. Some wore messages, indicating they were a gift from a loved one; some bore insignia or symbol of affiliation; many bore the owner's name or monogram, and some bore letters revealing Esq., PhD, or M.D.

Women and children were always in search of a lighter ball with the holes closer together for smaller hands. I could point them out from the desk as they contrasted the hundreds of black balls with their purple color or sparkled surface.

The most frequent request was for a 10-pound bowling ball.

Every so often, I would get a call at the front desk asking, "Do you have 10-pound balls?"

It was invariably from the pay phone halfway down the hall, where giggling teenage girls huddled to see my reaction. I would wag the phone at them, and they would break out in peals of laughter.

I wonder what they would have done, if I answered, "Yes."

As the atmosphere of the lanes was overwhelmingly upbeat and positive, the extreme social inundation had a less severe effect. Most of the social contact with the hundreds of people who flowed past the desk was with people having fun, pleasantly conversing, or requiring help to facilitate more fun.

The most challenging thing with these interactions was when someone's lane malfunctioned, which was usually quickly remedied, or someone displeased with their lane assignment, which was also easily remedied.

The most frequent interaction was with someone requesting change. This was usually one of the teenagers or a child with their parents. The children were fond of the vending machines which held treats, but required correct change. Most often, they would present a one-dollar bill saying, "Excuse me - Change please."

This request was so frequent that even years after I stopped working there, anytime someone said, "Excuse me," I would automatically hand them three quarters, two dimes, and a nickel!

The Security Company

At some point, the manager in the bowling alley decided it would be prudent to hire a security guard. I wasn't privy to the reasoning.

Our guard contingent consisted of a bear-like fellow and his decidedly stick-like partner.

Their job was to linger around the area between the desk and the front door to discourage mayhem. I don't remember any particular mayhem, but that notwithstanding, was their job.

I found by speaking to 'Bear' that he was employed by a company owned by a retired policeman and operated out of his house. Hearing his stories got me interested, so I applied. I was hired on the spot and provided uniforms.

The owner asked, "Do you have a gun?"

I replied, "Yes."

"Report to this address," he said to me.

He handed me a paper with my schedule and address. My instructions were, ***"They are building an auction site at this address. There have been thefts of material and equipment by armed burglars. Make sure you arrive armed. There's a telephone inside the site, if you need help."***

I showed up at midnight to relieve the 4 to 12 guard. I had a gun on my belt, a lunch in a bag, and a flashlight.

Before he left, the other guard showed me the phone, gave me a quick walk-through of the site, wished me luck, and before leaving, said, "These people have been showing up with shotguns. Be careful!"

The building was about 65% complete, but the entire exterior structure, including the roof, was in place. I checked the phone for dial tone, walked around to get a feel for the place, and then went out and sat in my '69 Chevy Impala.

Watching an empty building site for eight hours allows time for reflection.

I was visited during the night by a police car who had come to check the site and by a couple in a car looking for a make-out place. No one else ever came in there. After a few months, the place was sufficiently sealed up, and I was sent to another assignment.

Next was a meat processing plant supplying beef for restaurants up and down the East Coast. It was a one-story brick building in an industrial area of a Philly suburb.

I, of course, had the Midnight shift.

The plant operated 24-7. They would grind up beef arriving in refrigerator trucks and form it into hamburger patties. It was an extremely clean environment, and with each midnight shift, the crew would completely disassemble the stainless-steel processing plant into its components and steam-clean the entire operation.

By 8:00 AM, the plant was completely sanitized and reassembled. I would watch as the 2,000-pound tub of waste meat blasted from the innards of the grinders and patty-forming machines was rolled to the truck destined for the pig farm.

I was also supposed to stand at the door and watch everyone leave in the morning. I guess, so they didn't take a side of beef home with them.

During lulls and at lunchtime, I held literacy classes for the warehouse crew. There are few things as satisfying as watching someone discover reading. The goal of one of the operators was to get a GED. He would stop by my desk as often as he could get away from pallets, boxes, and supplies.

One of my main regrets associated with the inability to properly socially interact during this period was not keeping in touch with folks like this to see how he did on his GED project.

Chapter 78

Ralston House

My older sister was the Assistant Administratrix (sorry, that's what they called it) for a large retirement home in West Philly. She sold them on the idea of replacing the resident who was currently acting as a night watchman with a security detachment.

I became the first Head of Security. I guess this story also sheds some light on how flowery titles can be. One minute, there was a septuagenarian resident performing the duties of night watchman; the next, it was being performed by the new Head of Security, me.

This is not quite so bad as it sounds. The then-watchman had expressed the need for some relief and wanted to try to continue with weekend duties, but wanted relief during the week. I filled in during the weekdays, while he remained on weekend duty.

He did so, until he asked to be relieved altogether, and they hired a weekend man.

This was a good gig, because aside from fire watch, which involved hourly walk-throughs of the building, the job was largely sedentary. This was ideal, as I was still attending Temple University, so I could go to classes days and work from midnight to eight.

It should be noted: during the hourly fire watch the portrait of Sarah Ralston was to be checked. The portrait was painted by Gilbert Stuart, the artist who painted the portrait of George Washington, used to design and which still graces the U.S. one dollar bill. The Ralston portrait, worth millions, had to be checked hourly for insurance purposes.

This type of job was ideal for me, as I worked to accumulate the social data to understand the normal social intercourse. But, I knew I had to work to the next level and fast.

On the same campus as the Ralston House stood the Hinchman House. When this house was built, it was the only structure standing in that area of

Philadelphia and served as the residence for the Hinchman family and farmhouse for the then farmland - now the center of the U of P campus.

My job included a free apartment that occupied the entire second floor of Hinchman House, within which remained the 18th Century period furniture, random oak floors, and a brick balcony overlooking Chestnut St. opposite Smokey Joe's Café.

An apartment from the American Revolution in the middle of the U of P campus at age 21 was a house in a peach orchard!

In addition to the aforementioned duties, I was often called upon for other tasks. In the early morning hours before the arrival of the cooks; I would put the large pots of water on the stove for the preparation of five dozen boiled eggs and ten gallons of oatmeal.

I was often drafted for weekend duties, which included chauffeuring residents on various road trips. My favorite among these field trips was to the Administrator's home in Sea Isle City, N.J.

Chapter 79

Celebrity

Rosemont College was in a suburb near Villanova, and many considered it to be the sister school, because both were exclusively and respectively female and male and were in close proximity.

My girlfriend-drought after the PLC affair continued, and David, being the friend he is, suggested I come to an event being hosted by his girlfriend.

Rosemont was another one of those mind-blowing revelations set on a huge suburban campus with turn-of-the-century stone buildings connected by roads rolling under the canopies of hundred-year-old hardwoods.

I met David at the coffee house his girlfriend ran and immediately hit it off with one of her classmates.

After a few dates, she invited me to attend their Christmas performance, which she described as a recital-like event of Christmas songs. I expected Jingle Bells, Silent Night, and so on.

When she stepped on stage in an evening gown and sang two selections from Handle's Messiah, she not only blew me away, but ruined Handle's Messiah for me in the way Judy Garland ruined *Over the Rainbow.* No one has been able to sing it properly since.

Her circle of friends were artists among whom I felt welcomed and well tolerated (I almost wrote appreciated). The circle included singers, instrumentalists, painters, and sculptors. Her sister, who attended a music college in Philly, for example, played the viola, *her* boyfriend the bass.

Since I was the only one with a car, we would often roll up to take her sister and her boyfriend on double dates. This group was fascinating. My girlfriend, in addition to singing like an angel and swimming at the Olympic level, spoke five languages and could tell you not only what brand of liquor was in a mixed drink but the brand of mixer as well.

Her sister and friends were extraordinary players of *Drop the Needle*. Drop the Needle is a game played with a phonograph. One player would choose a recording and, secreting the title, put it on the turntable. They would then drop the needle on some random spot on the spinning plate, and the others had to guess the piece and artist.

They could tell you the name of the orchestra, who was conducting, and the venue.

On one occasion, we decided, actually they decided, to see *P.D.Q. Bach* at the Academy of Music.

They explained that among pretentious music aficionados, the Bach family of composers were differentiated by their initials: J.S. Bach, J.C. Bach, etc., providing a source of amusement for much of the musical community.

Peter Shickele, a professor at Julliard and musical satirist, created *P.D.Q. Bach* as a fictitious lost relative of the Bach family. He invented the person P.D.Q. and composed music, which he attributed to him.

His performance was hilarious, especially with this group to interpret and translate.

This evening, I picked up my date and drove to the music college, another collection of stately stone buildings with arches and courtyards. It was a hidden oasis in the middle of inner-Philly, with parlors elaborately decorated with thick Persian rugs, 19th-century period furniture, and walls adorned with tapestries and intricately carved wood trim. It appeared as if an old English walled estate had fallen from the sky and landed beside the cobblestoned streets of one of the densest areas of the inner city.

When we arrived, it was obvious that a special event was in progress. When my date saw this, she burst out, “Marian Anderson is here tonight!”

Her head was on a swivel, taking in the bright lights illuminating the walks and the limousines delivering people in tuxedos and evening gowns.

As we walked into the campus, she said, “Wouldn’t it be something to be able to meet her?!” And added, “They probably won’t let you in tonight. You’ll have to wait outside!”

Her usual cool demeanor and *received* British accent noticeably disaffected. The *wait outside* remark particularly uncharacteristic.

Now, in case you’re not familiar with Marian Anderson, she was born in Philadelphia in 1897 and was the most famous American contralto singer - ever.

She had in her lifetime accumulated numerous awards including the first Presidential Medal of Freedom, a Congressional Gold Medal, the National Medal of Arts, and a Grammy Lifetime Achievement Award.

She sang for sold-out audiences worldwide, including performances on TV and in movies, as well as at Dwight D. Eisenhower's inauguration. Eisenhower appointed her as a delegate to the United Nations Human Rights Committee.

She sang for JFK's inauguration and christened the USS George Washington Carver nuclear submarine.

She entertained troops on U.S. bases during WWII and the Korean War, and the Metropolitan Opera named her one of the few permanent members of the opera company. She was awarded 24 honorary doctoral degrees by Howard University, Temple University, Smith College, and others.

The event was a $2,000 per plate fundraiser, spotlighting her life as a musical treasure. That's equivalent to almost $25,000 a plate in today's money.

When we arrived at the main entrance, the dean was on the stairs greeting the arrivals. This was not a big school, so the dean was familiar with me and my date, and as she predicted, he told her to go in to get her sister, adding, "Michael will stay here with me."

When she left, he took me to a room off the main hall, which turned out to be an elaborately outfitted parlor/library with bookcases of leather-bound classics built around huge stone fireplaces opposite settees for reading and conversation.

With a mischievous smile, he said, "Wait here in the green room."

I chose a nice, comfortable couch facing the fireplace and sat down to wait for my friends.

About a minute later, there was some cheery chatter outside, and the door opened. The dean escorted a woman in and asked her to wait here a few minutes. He winked at me and shut the door behind her.

When she turned, I stood with my mouth open, thinking, "*This* can't be happening!"

She walked directly to where I was standing, and as I extended my hand, I smiled and said, "You're Marian Anderson!"

She said, "Yes! Yes I am!"

"You know we come from the same neighborhood!" I blurted out.

She asked me where I was from and acknowledged we did come from the same part of SW Philly.

We chatted on the couch for twenty minutes or so about SW Philly, her travels, my plans, and just had a nice conversation. The attraction for the $2,000/plate tickets was seated next to me in the green room. When the dean returned and told me my friends were waiting outside, it was hard to break away.

"It was nice meeting you!" I told her.

Marian Anderson said, "It was nice meeting you too!"

I shook her hand and left.

As I drove to the academy, the others shared their excitement about Marian Anderson being at the school. My date chatted animatedly over the front seat with her sister and her boyfriend.

After five minutes or so, when there was a pause for breath, Miss '*you'll have to wait outside!*' turned to me and repeated, "Wouldn't it be something to actually meet her?!"

I said, "Yes, I just had a nice conversation with her in the green room while I was waiting for the three of you to come down. She's quite lovely."

They turned to stone!

Then they got mad.

Then, they bombarded me with questions for the remainder of the trip! They couldn't believe that I, the only non-musical, non-artistic one in the bunch, was the one who got to meet her.

What are the chances of that - do you suppose?

Chapter 80

Run-up to the Police Academy

I was still taking classes at Temple and riding the trolly when I noticed a sign announcing a test for the Philadelphia Police Department. I began to think perhaps the police department would be a suitable vocation. It would fill the void left by the abandonment of the military idea, and as a paramilitary organization might allow me to *go to war* during the day and return home each evening.

The job in the bowling alley exposed me to many police officers, who were fond of bowling as a hobby slash relaxation medium. They would stop by the desk and exchange stories with one of my co-workers, Carl, who was a retired captain from the fire department.

There's a comradery between cops and firefighters as they frequently meet and interact at scenes of accidents, fires, and hospital cases.

When I saw the advertisement on the trolly; I recalled a conversation with Carl after a group of officers left the counter. I asked him what he thought of the idea of the Philadelphia police.

He said, "I'd rather go to Vietnam in gasoline-soaked underwear, than be a Philly cop!"

"What do you mean?" I asked.

He said, "Those guys go to war every day of their lives! I couldn't do that!"

The next day, on the way to Temple U, I took a detour. City Hall was at the end of the trolly line, so I got off there and presented myself at the personnel office. I started a process spanning two years with a cadence of the first half of a New Orleans funeral.

Everything in the process was meant to screen out the *less-than-enthusiastic.* The first part is the application. If you can survive that, you've passed the first hurdle.

From her arch in a glass partition, a delightful civil servant handed me an application while pointing to the opposite wall.

Her only instructions were, "Bring back the pen!"

On the wall hung a shelf serving as a writing surface lined with other *hopefuls* applying for all sorts of city jobs: office worker, sanitation worker, police officer, mayor.

I filled in the application and returned to my new friend.

The only thing that moved was her arm. She was sitting as I left her, leaning on the desk with her chin on her fist. She took the application with her free hand, moved it to a time clock, and crunched the time onto the form, which continued to move in the same direction to a basket.

On the rebound, her hand picked up a mimeographed paper, which she dropped on the counter in front of me, demonstrating masterful economy of motion.

The paper informed me further instructions would follow by mail.

Efficiencies snuck into the system at some point, because within a few days, an envelope arrived containing a study guide and a scheduled location for the exam. I noticed my exam location was in the Northeast part of the city; curious I thought, as I lived in the Southwest.

I learned later that folks from the Northeast were taking their test in Southwest - screening technique number two.

I got right into reading the book for the test, my first reaction being, "You must be kidding".

It was little vignettes with pictures. Basically, a grade school reading test mated with a comic book. I memorized the book and waited for test day.

On test day, I waited outside the testing facility for two and a half hours past the scheduled start time. As I watched the crowds dwindle, I recorded screening technique number three.

Twenty-five thousand applied, but only eighteen thousand actually hung around to take it.

The grading process took nine months. Veterans received ten extra points, but I was not a vet. When that was figured out, I ranked 1,334. I figured with a 90% rejection/attrition rate; I was closer to 133.

Several months passed before an interview, then several for a physical, and more for the psychological exam.

After almost two years, the background investigation began with neighbors getting a visit from the detectives, and teachers you thought were surely dead by now were being asked, "What kind of student was he?"

I happened to be home when they interviewed my parents. At least they said nice things about me. (I eavesdropped to make sure.)

Now, at this time, the world was still trying to figure out how to fix itself, unlike now when everything is wonderful, and I was introduced to a new phrase, *affirmative action*. I'm sure a lot of work went into this by the government, but what it meant to me was added waiting. Wait for a judge to decide; women can be police officers; wait while another judge decides what number of minorities should be put into each class and how many should speak Spanish.

My number finally came up and a letter arrived to report to be measured for uniforms at the police academy. A group of over 50 were lined up for measurements for the uniforms we would be issued upon graduation.

Since Monday was Independence Day, we would start the academy the coming Tuesday.

We were given written instructions for when and where to report, as well as what to wear. The academy uniform was a white shirt, black pants, black belt, and plain black shoes that we would provide. They made it a point to emphasize straight-leg black pants, no bell bottoms!

My excitement was off the charts!

When they finished measuring us, they announced yet another delay. Another judge was in the process of reviewing the *number* of girls in the class, so we should go home and await further instructions.

I expected another extended wait, so as it was the long weekend for the Fourth of July, it was off to the Jersey Shore to celebrate!

Luckily, I left a phone number, because mid-day Tuesday the call came that we would start the next day! I borrowed a station wagon and made a mad rush back to the city to try and find white shirts, black pants, belts, and black uniform shoes.

Bell bottoms were in vogue, and it was hard to find straight-leg black pants! I ran all over looking for them, finally finding them in Gimbel's Department store outside the city.

Ironically, my car was broken into while I was in the store getting the pants. I had hidden my stuff in the compartment under the third seat, so they only got the flashlight from the glove compartment.

I could see the crew in the parking lot who did it.

Ohhhh... just you wait!

Chapter 81

Door to the Academy

On Wednesday, July 6, 1977, while Son of Sam terrorized NYC and San Francisco searched in vain for the Zodiac Killer, I stood at the doors of the Philadelphia Police Academy for the first time as a cadet. Dressed in the uniform of a white dress shirt, plain black pants, and shiny black shoes.

I had great expectations – I would not be disappointed!

I walked through the doors past other Spartan uniforms, dubbed waiter's costume, casually chatting, or tentative of entering.

The expectation on my face clearly shone in the large mirror in the hall beyond the threshold. Bold lettering urged a check of haircut, uniform, equipment, and pride. I could feel the honest smile.

The initial assembly was held in a large hall, resembling, in some aspects, the roll call room of most police stations. The difference being its obvious size and a stage replacing the judges' pulpit.

Arranged in rows of those familiar cold beige folding chairs were 100 places for us, reminiscent of those 100 seats in first grade. But, these seats were occupied by adults who ranged in age from 20 to 35 and who, for various reasons, had *chosen* to be here.

They had endured the two-year wait and left other jobs and situations to attend.

At 8:00 AM, 100 upturned faces were greeted with a call to attention. With our right hands raised, we were sworn in as Philly's newest police officers.

Then, as what normal people would describe as *reality settling in*, hand-outs were distributed.

Apparently, when we swore in, we magically became non-civilians. The handout explained that as police officers, we could no longer gamble, drink in bars, cheat on our wives, engage in political activities, or vote in uniform.

There was to be no smoking in public while in uniform, no outside jobs without permission, and fifty other restrictions.

This was a major pivot point in my life. I was trading a society of haphazard chaos for one with clearly defined rules. And which, since I rarely drank, never smoked or gambled, and didn't have a wife, seemed perfectly in line with my thinking.

Amid the audible moans among the class, as they read the list, I became encouraged, and as reality set in for them, expectations rose for me.

An instructor in a police lieutenant's uniform took the stage and tapped the mike to quiet the murmur.

Flanked by instructors of various ranks, he addressed us with, "Ok, ladies and gentlemen, you'll all be here for the next four months. During that time, there will be no days off without permission, and permission requires a memo to the Commandant. No one is to carry a gun or get into any kind of trouble whatsoever, or you're gone."

This elicited moans, which quickly dissipated when glaring looks from the flanking instructors flashed from the dais.

He continued, "This class is special in the history of the department. You are the first class of raw scores from the test, that is, the first class who did not receive the 10 extra veteran's-preference points. This class is predominately non-veteran. Every class before this one was over 90% veteran, but in this class, there are only six."

"Another special thing about this class is; over 50% of the class have college degrees, also a first. Of the remaining, most have at least two years of college, and there are several with master's degrees, one PhD, and one cadet in the third year of law school. We expect great things from this class!"

Four months later, the lieutenant again spoke down from the dais, "This is the absolute worst class we've ever had in the academy. We've had more mischief and trouble from this class than any before!"

A familiar baritone among us sent back the reply, "That's what you get, when you start hiring smart people!"

The End

Opening to Book Two

Dinner in a high school cafeteria might not be your first choice when thinking of fine dining, but when it's on the set of *Rocky II* and includes lobster Newberg and the company of Hollywood Stars, it ain't bad. As the movie's scenes moved around Philly, the venues changed, but the food and company were consistently outstanding!

The extra attention I gave my uniform, which was often and flippantly ostracized by my fellow police officers, paid off when I was chosen to be Silvester Stallone's bodyguard for the duration of the Philadelphia scenes for the movie.

After making sure that Sly, as I like to call him, was seated and, as much as he could, was enjoying his meal, I finally sat down to have mine. You see, the film was written by, directed by, and starring Silvester Stallone, so he had a lot on his mind.

I no sooner got situated and reached for my napkin when a gentle voice caressed my ears with the question, "Is anyone sitting here?"

What happened next was mesmerizing. I looked up into the most beautiful face I had ever seen, and momentarily froze before responding, "No, please have a seat!"

The thoughts racing through my head ran from, "*Where had such an angelic creature as this come from?*" to "*How on earth did they make her look so dowdy for the movie*?!"

Talia Shire, Adrian to *Rocky* fans, had a face like a China Doll! It was like seeing the ballet for the first time - a visual feast. I was also transfixed by the fact her personality was absolutely charming. My paradigm was; big stars were cold and distant.

The paradigm was forever shattered when Burt Young appeared and asked if he could sit there too! This Pauly was nothing like the one you saw in the film. He was a soft-spoken, gentle, warm, and lovable person.

After brief introductions, we sat, ate, conversed, and had a nice dinner. Adrian and Pauly became my meal partners for the duration—never changing persona of nice, gentle folks.

Now, how does this happen, you wonder. How does the Aspie get to do this job? And, why did Adrian and Pauly remain my meal partners?

I think the idea of having someone *not* faun and fuss over you is sometimes refreshing to a big star. Treating them like normal folks gave them time to just sit, eat, and relax.

Had I jumped up like a normal person and asked for autographs and photos, I really believe they would have found a more peaceful place to have their meals.

This theme will show up frequently in the following stories. The Aspie way of not being caught up in fads, trends, or other normal behavior, or thinking of celebrities as anything other than just, people.

www.ingramcontent.com/pod-product-compliance
Lightning Source LLC
Chambersburg PA
CBHW030622310726
48979CB00003B/838

* 9 7 8 1 8 3 6 6 3 3 8 9 1 *